DEATH'S DOOR

Where Right and Glory Lead

A Science Fiction Novel by
William A. DeSouza

Cover Art:
MLC Designs4U

Publisher's Note:

This is a work of fiction. All names, characters,
places, and events are the work of the author's
imagination.

Any resemblance to real persons, places, or events is
coincidental.

Solstice Publishing - www.solsticepublishing.com

Copyright 2015

William A. DeSouza

My heartfelt thanks and gratitude goes out to Christine for her encouragement and support while writing this book.

Chapter One

"Captain to the bridge." The announcement repeated itself twice more in quick succession before Captain Mohamed Abijah found the comm panel in the dark.

The frantic call through the cabin intercom speakers had woken him from a deep sleep. At first, the veteran merchant marine captain wasn't even sure if what he heard was real of part of his dreams. He'd been traveling the shipping lanes for the better part of forty standard years and this trip was turning out to be the most problematic voyage yet, with one issue to deal with after another. He had hoped that when he turned in for the evening he would get a full sleep period.

Captain Abijah reached over his head and turned up the cabin lights by sliding his fingers along the lighting switch, but only to quarter illumination. *Even that's too bright,* he thought.

His eyes still closed, he sleepily responded, "Isaac, there better be a good reason for waking me up at—" He paused, carefully opened one eye, and looked at the chronometer on the wall above the door. "Oh-four-hundred."

"My apologies, sir, but there's a ship on a steep approach and they won't respond to hail," said the young third officer, on his first cruise since graduating from the merchant marine command school.

Second Lieutenant Abdul Bari had impressed the Captain so far, and Abijah never once had reservations about his abilities or competence since leaving port, so the panic in the man's voice was concerning to say the least.

"What's our status?"

"We're still dead-slow in this asteroid belt with another three point six million kilometers to go before we get back to clear space. We have no comms outside the belt and that ship is still coming in fast and on a direct trajectory to intercept. They'll overshoot us if they maintain velocity. If they start their turnover in the next twenty-two minutes they'll intercept in just over fifty minutes."

What was obviously left out of the report was the question of how any ship could transit at that speed through an asteroid belt without becoming another part of the debris field.

Abijah was pissed at being woken up and pissed at the delay in transit of their cargo. That was going to cost them a hefty penalty in fines. If they had to stop and talk to someone lost in this sector, it wouldn't improve his mood. This asteroid belt was not on their charts and had never been reported during the navigation briefing by the Shipping Guild.

I never would have taken this route if it were up to me, he thought with disgust. The route was selected by the Guild computer, which should have known about any navigation hazards.

Abijah had to drop his ship back into real space in a hurry when their long-range sensors located the threat. By then it was too late to calculate another route around the belt as they were in the thick of it.

"All right, I'll be up in a moment." He was about to switch off, then had a thought. "Bari, has the computer ID'd the ship's transponder codes? Can you tell the type?"

"No, sir. There is no transponder signal and the sensors can't pin down the type of ship. I couldn't tell you if it's a cargo, transport or military. Sorry, sir." There was a tinge of regret in Bari's voice, as if he may have screwed up somehow.

Abijah recognized the young officer's self-incriminations, "This isn't your fault, Bari. These aren't military grade electronics; there's only so much data you can pull from them at this range."

He lurched out of his bunk and slipped on the gray coveralls that almost all the crew wore. On board the cargo ship *Kestrel*, the only colour other than grey appeared in the food and personal decorations of the crew's quarters. Each crew member took great pains to ensure their personal space reflected their personality, religion, or family. Transporting goods from point A to point B was not a glamorous life by any stretch of the imagination. It could get very boring if you didn't have something to remind you of who you were—or your home and family, if you had one.

As Abijah half-walked, half-ran toward the lift, he tried to come up with reasons for the Guild computers to choose this route. For the life of him, he just could not understand the logic behind it. This should have been a normal run for the *Kestrel*; it wasn't like their first time on this run, although it was the first time this route was assigned. There were many routes a ship could take to get from one planet to the next. There was no indication of any other hazard on the regular shipping routes. It made no sense.

Damn sloppy work, he thought sourly.

His thoughts quickly moved to the present issue. *Why would there be another ship on an intercept course and what was the urgency in the middle of a navigation hazard like an asteroid belt? No captain would take that sort of chance.*

At the lift he pressed the entry code for priority access. The indicator lights flashed on the wall panel and the door opened.

The *Kestrel* was considered a mid-sized freighter, at just over nine hundred thousand metric tons with fifteen decks of human-accessible space. The captain's personal quarters were located five decks from the main bridge and Abijah counted each level as the slow lift ascended

As he watched the indicator during the ascent toward the bridge, the collision alarms went off and the alert lights flashed yellow. Abijah twisted his head up and stared at the flashing alert lights, his mouth opened in shock and confusion.

The lift doors opened onto the bridge of the cargo ship. Abijah caught site of a flurry of frantic, almost panicked activity. His third officer bent over the communication station with fear in his eyes, screaming into his headset. "Unidentified ship, stop firing! This is the unarmed civilian cargo vessel *Kestrel*—stop firing!"

"What the hell is going on?" Abijah shouted over the din, trying to maintain some semblance of calm.

"Captain, the other ship just fired on us!" The sound of panic and dread squeaked from the mouth of the young bridge officer. "A warning shot wide off the port beam. They made turnover just a few seconds ago—but how?"

Abijah joined Bari, leaning over the sensor board and staring at the plot with the eyes of an experienced spacer. "That's no damn murchie ship if they can make that kind of deceleration turn and burn. They'd have to have military dampeners for—"

"Sir!" interrupted Jeffery Davies, the comm officer on watch. "Incoming hail from the ship. They're ordering us to come to a full stop and prepare to be boarded."

"Prepare to *what*?!" Abijah sounded a bit more panicked than he'd have liked. "Nav, plot a course out of this mess and make it fast. I don't care which direction, just make it the fastest." He tried to reduce his own panicked voice. "Helm, increase speed to three thousand kay."

The helm officer turned, "Sir, we can't go that fast in this belt. We'll be smashed—"

"I don't give a rutlidge's ass about that. We'll be worse off if these nuts get to us first! Now get the engines up to three thousand and get us the hell out of here!" Abijah didn't want to get angry with his own crew. It wasn't their fault, and he could certainly understand that the helm officer was only stating the obvious. But at this time, there was a more pressing danger to the crew and ship than being smashed against an asteroid.

Abijah had read the reports before leaving port about pirate activity in a number of sectors. He'd even talked to other captains who had experienced acts of piracy firsthand. But this run was safe; he'd never heard so much of a peep from a pirate on this run. Mind you, he'd never been given this route on the run before. His normal route took them along a nice safe sector. His normal route did not include asteroid belts or pirates.

"They're firing again!" screamed the sensor tech.

Abijah was stunned for a moment. *This must be a bad dream,* he thought quickly, before being brought back to reality by a massive explosion that rocked the *Kestrel* and knocked him to the floor.

Damage alarms sounded right away and warning lights flashed all over the bridge as every control panel lit up.

"Comm, alert the crew, get everyone to stations and unlock the escape pods just in case. Engineering, what's our status?" Abijah picked himself up and made his way over to his command chair, strapping himself in.

After a moment, the engineering tech responded. "Main motors are down. Commander Bradley reports they were blown by a missile when—"

A second explosion rocked the cargo ship, cutting off the tech's damage report mid-sentence.

Along the length of the ship, overhead piping ripped from their fixtures and bulkheads failed as explosions cascaded along the ships tight crew spaces.

On the bridge, fires broke out as power surges blew panel after panel. Large chunks of composite material, piping, and sparks fell onto the crew as they tried hard to contain the damage with whatever emergency equipment they could grab.

Abijah heard a scream cut off mid-wail—he swung his head just in time to see an electrical panel fail and short out. He watched in stunned silence as the engineering tech slumped forward in his harness, blood leaking from his ears. Sparks flew from the same station as power conduits exploded, sending shrapnel into the chest and face of the dead tech.

The big ship seemed to lurch in space as it drifted out of control, its main drive motors shut down.

"Bradley to the bridge!" The frantic shout over the comm speaker repeated three more times.

"Bradley, this is Abijah, we're under attack and drifting. Can you get me any maneuvering power?"

"I can't even get lighting to work right now. We're on backup power and that's fading fast, with half the conduits blowing," Bradley sounded weary and his voice drawn. "I'll try to get you what I can for now, though. What the hell is going on?" Panic had started to grip the engineering officer.

Abijah ignored the question as he slammed his fist down on the chair arm, cursing under his breath. "At least get the chemical thrusters online to stabilize our drift." He cut the circuit. "Comm—ship to ship."

The comm officer turned back and nodded the channel was open.

"Attacking ship, this is the captain of the cargo ship *Kestrel*. Stop your attack. We are an unarmed vessel." He repeated the plea.

No immediate response. Time passed, each second an eternity to the bridge crew as they regarded the chronometer.

Then: "*Kestrel*, open your docking ports for boarding and have all your crew gather in the main mess. You will not be warned again. Any deviation from these orders or any crewmembers found unwilling to comply will result in your total destruction. Launching any escape pods will result in your total destruction. Sending any distress, or any signal, will result in your total destruction." The channel was abruptly cut without giving the captain time to respond or ask why.

Abijah, still seated in the command chair, leaned back in shock and disbelief as he and the bridge crew sat in stunned silence, not knowing what the next few minutes would bring.

***

The office of Naval Command was tucked away deep inside the defense department building. NavCom was only one of a dozen departments, but it commanded one of the largest pieces of real estate within the towering group of buildings that headquartered the Terrain Armed Forces.

The two guards standing on either side of the entrance to NavCom headquarters came to attention as the outer door slid opened. The guards, armed with pulse combat rifles and wearing full battle armour, served more than an ornamental function.

Visitors passing through the armoured entrance are reminded right away of the security around them at all times. Besides the well-armed guards, two more pulse cannons mounted to remote tripods lay on either side of the entrance, controlled by the security station, which lay behind more armed guards. Sensors, video pick-ups, X-ray screens, and chemical and explosive detectors screened each visitor to NavCom. Signs placed at each doorway and along the kilometers of corridors in NavCom reminded everyone of the constant scrutiny they were under each day.

Just inside the entrance, a man greeted Affleck. "Good morning, Admiral. It's nice to meet you. I am Major General Worley, the Air Chief Marshal's Adjutant. He's running a bit behind and asked me to escort you to his office. This way—please." He shook Affleck's hand, then with palm open, guided the Rear Admiral.

"Thank you, Major General," Affleck responded kindly as he followed Worley.

The ACM's office was not far along a corridor near the main entrance. Hung along the stark white walls were numerous unit and squadron crests in relief, as well as several holo-pictures of ships of the line, their names and service awards engraved in brass relief plaques below each picture. Affleck had visited NavCom on many occasions and met the ACM many times, but he'd never had the chance to wander along this particular passageway to visit in the ACM's office.

And even in this instance, he wasn't entirely certain why he was here.

Two more fully armoured guards stood on either side of the tall double doors at the end of the passage, a security desk was off to one side. One of the guards opened the large door. It was heavy-looking and solid, designed to look like wood.

Just inside the doors, an outer office held a small waiting area and two desks, one currently occupied by a young rating who came to attention as soon as the door opened. Just to the left of that desk was another set of double doors, also guarded by two more fully armed guards.

One of the guards keyed in a code on the door panel and it swung open.

"Come in and take a seat, Admiral. Can I offer you a coffee, or something stronger?" Worley asked as they were ushered into the inner chamber of the Air Chief Marshal's office.

Worley nodded to the guard and the door closed quietly. "We'll be joined shortly by the Air Chief Marshal and the command staff," he continued.

The inner chamber was richly appointed with both real and simulated woods, leather and an array of synthetic materials. A large desk with an equally large and comfortable looking chair sat in the centre of the room with a meeting table for ten in a joining anteroom.

To the left was another sitting area with a small table in the centre and six plush single chairs arranged around it, small arm tables beside each chair. Pictures on the wall depicted past Air Marshals and famous generals and admirals of Earth's past.

"Thank you, I'll have a coffee. Black, please," replied Affleck.

Worley poured the steaming beverage into a cup and handed it to the Admiral, who accepted it. Taking the first sip was ambrosia to the palate. Affleck always admired a well-brewed pot of java. The fact that he'd been up for the last twenty hours trying to get his flagship sorted out at the yards with the dock master only made it all the more welcoming.

He placed the cup on a side table and sat in one of the comfortable chairs. Equal in rank to Worley, he did not have a problem in voicing his concerns.

"I must admit that I was surprised to see the order to report after my battle group arrived in system," he said. "We haven't been home in several months and I was under the impression that we would be stood down for refit and rest." It was hardly a complaint, but it was unusual to have a refit interrupted without explanation.

Worley was about to answer when the door opened and a senior officer, who Affleck at first assumed was a Group Captain, announced, "Room!"

This brought Affleck and Worley to attention as the other flag officers entered.

First to enter the office was Air Chief Marshal Thomas Veale. "Stand easy, gentlemen. Let's not stand on ceremony here, shall we?" he said in a relaxed voice.

He reached out his hand and shook Affleck's, "Good to see you again, Walter. I know that you weren't expecting to be pulled off the refit of your sips as soon as you docked, but some…" He paused. "Events have conspired to force our hand."

Getting right to the introductions, he continued, "I think you know Admiral Francis Leyton, our new chief of naval operations, and Vice Admiral John Clifford, his Chief of Staff. This is Vice Admiral Cunningham, head of navy intelligence, and Brigadier General Vansant Sabato, Central Command. And you've already met Major General Worley."

"Admiral Leyton, good to see you again, sir," said Affleck, and was greeted with a warm smile from the Admiral. He stood to attention at each of the introductions, shaking hands with the assembled admirals and generals.

The officers followed Veale into the inner office and the door closed. Affleck noted that the lock on the door cycled, ensuring the group would not be disturbed. A red glow strip around the entire door came on, telling the occupants that anti-snooping devises were activated. Veale then invited everyone to sit.

Affleck was impressed with the gathered group and now even more curious why he was invited to attend this meeting. His mind raced through the possible alternatives. Fortunately, other than the time it took for a round of coffee and beverages to be served by an aide, he would not have to wait long to find out why Veale had called the meeting.

The aide placed the serving tray on a side table, turned and walked out the side door he arrived as quietly as he had entered. As soon as the door closed, the guard cycled the lock and the meeting began in earnest.

"Walter, the situation has become tenuous, and with the Shipping Guild pressing for action from the government, we find ourselves compelled to act," the ACM said. "You've faced rebel and pirate action— what's your assessment?"

"Well, sir, if the reports I have seen are correct, then I would say that there's more to these raids than meets the eye. You know from my records that I have clashed with pirate bandits, but those were one-offs. Small raiding ships that strike quickly, pinch cargo, and run for a quick sale on the black market. These latest reports suggest a more organized effort."

Cunningham interjected. "You're not far off with your assessment of an organized effort, Admiral. The official reports are only the tip of the iceberg. In the past twelve months, thirty-eight murchie ships have been taken. All of them have been on scheduled runs and all have been attacked by well-armed and organized crews. Intel suggests an escalation in brutality that is unprecedented—"

"Unprecedented is a damn polite way of putting it," Leyton interrupted, sounding frustrated. "What these bastards are doing goes way past simple piracy. This is fast becoming an act of war."

"Sirs, if I may ask," said Affleck. "We have been sending escorts out to watch the shipping lanes. What have they been coming up against?"

"Nothing," answered Veale. "Yes, we have three anti-piracy task forces operating on the more active runs. And, no, they have not encountered a single incident. We just don't have the resources as yet to cover every run, never mind having ships stationed along the entire run."

Affleck's eyes opened wide as a thought occurred to him. "What you are suggesting, if I am hearing you correctly, is that the pirates are being fed information that gives them a decisive advantage."

"I think he's got it," quipped Brigadier General Sabato as he reached for the coffee urn.

"Admiral, you seem to have grasped our dilemma, and yes, it is something that we are closely looking into," Veale said.

The group moved on to discuss Affleck's experience with unconventional warfare in space and on the ground and the readiness of his battle group. It was as if he was being interviewed for a position with some civilian firm, and he found the whole experience disconcerting. Affleck was keenly aware that if they wanted to know about his past experiences, they only had to look up his service history. Stranger still were the implications of the discussion. It was unthinkable that a pirate force was receiving information from inside the government or military.

Still, he made the effort to respond with some enthusiasm and answer each question with as much detail as operational security would allow. The military was, after all, much like a game. Play the game by the rules and all was right with the world.

Eventually, however, the political game could get frustrating. One particular question irked him.

"I'm sorry, but what could my involvement in the Pickering Clash have to do with my current readiness? That incident was almost twenty standard years ago and I was only a minor player in the settlement plan and subsequent conflict," he asked with some irritation.

Affleck's memories of the Pickering Clash was bittersweet. He had received a major promotion at the time with several commendations, but it did not replace the hundreds of men and women lost in the battle, following an ambush on planet Pickering by the very citizens he was sent to rescue and resettle.

Veale held up his hand. "Not to worry, Admiral. You're not in any hot water, and this isn't a test. Well, okay, it is a test—of a sort. We need to know who you are deep down, not just what's written on the reports and evaluations. That's just fluff for the most part. The mission we have in mind will take a certain...how can I put this delicately? Independence and ruthlessness mixed with some restraint."

"With all due respect, sir," Affleck said, "you're going to have to be more direct than that."

Veale smiled slightly and glanced over toward Vice Admiral Cunningham. "It's simple, really. We want you to do a job that will test your crews and ground troops on levels they have never seen. There is also some question about operational security. We suspect that the military or civilian government may have been compromised, as you have already surmised. Right now we are looking at the bureaucracy and—" He paused. "Certain 'assets' within our ranks that may also be suspect. We are not certain how high this goes and we are not taking any chances."

Affleck was taken aback by the extent of infiltration suggested by the ACM. Subversion to this magnitude was unprecedented today.

In the end, Affleck was offered the operation with a full flotilla: two battle groups, with two full regiments of ground troops and the opportunity to pay back the carnage that was expanding due to increasing pirate activity. The mission: put an end to the pirate attacks that were increasing at an alarming rate. If not stopped, they would have a devastating effect on the newly elected government of the New Confederation.

Chapter Two

On board the TAF navy ship *Athabaskan*, Trooper Heather Brassard stood by her locker as she and her fellow troopers suited up and gathered their kit. Her unit was the second squad, third platoon of Alpha Company of the Terrestrial Light Armoured Guards and they were in full motion as they geared up for a mission.

TAF units were made up of squads of fifteen to twenty-two people. There were five squads in each platoon: four combat and one command, which also included the support and heavy weapons detachment. Company units were made up of four to six platoons and a regiment was made up of four to six companies, one of which contained armour, and artillery support. In the Armoured Guards, the armoured company was one of the largest and included an armoured transport section. The third platoon had five squads at full complement, with newly graduated recruits or newbies filling out the ranks of veterans.

 The red glow of the blackout lights made dark shadows stretch from floor to ceiling, creating a surreal scene in the locker room.

This was Heather's eighth combat mission since graduating basic and specialized training and she was already considered a veteran. The men and women of the Terrain Armed Forces were the best: humanity's finest from Earth and a hundred other worlds. They were volunteers with a renewed pride in their mission to protect the aligned worlds of the New

Confederation. They protected humans from non-aligned or rogue states that might threaten the peace—and from time to time, protected them from themselves. Colony worlds with predatory native populations were harsh places to live, and even harsher places to die.

Heather was as lean and fit as one can get without genetic sculpting. Standing at 185 centimeters, she had short-cropped dirty blond hair, brown eyes and an oval face. At twenty-nine, she was considered young to be enrolled in the TAF—especially since the average human lifespan was one hundred and sixty. Genetic sculpting and nanotechnology, along with cell regeneration drugs, had been designed a century earlier to keep humans young and in good health. Most recruits signed up in their mid- to late thirties believing they had many years to dedicate to the service.

Heather was smart; she finished her education in record time, and many of her professors even went so far as to say gifted. "A natural learner with a keen eye for detail," they often said in their annual reviews.

She also knew what she wanted in life, and the TAF was what she wanted, more than anything. Her father had spent over sixty years there, and her mother had thirty-six active years and was still part of the reserves. Heather felt the same pride and sense of family in the Force as she did in her parents.

She picked up the upper body armour and pulled it over her head. The breastplate and back shield were easy to slip on and she already had her leg and arm guards secured and plugged in. TAF body armour was made out of a composite ceramic alloy called plaststeel—not only ten times lighter than the equivalent size of traditional steel sheets, but ten times stronger. Plaststeel was molded to the wearer and covered in an impact absorbent material. While it was designed to take a full-frontal hit with a ten-millimeter dart and survive, what happened to the human body inside the armour was another issue. Humans had always been the limiting factor in any weapon system.

Plaststeel body armour required the wearer to first put on an electronic telemetry one-piece underwear. This "wired long john" sent the user's vitals and location to squad leaders as well as command and information control—the CIC. The software could also administer medication used in pain control, including radiation and chemical nerve agents, for immediate treatment on the battlefield.

Small tubes running throughout the garment and plugged into the microcomputer carried a liquid that kept the wearer at a comfortable temperature range as collection bags stored the body's waste for recycled use. Sometimes you just didn't think about where your drinking water came from in the field.

Heather picked up her weapon, a seven-millimeter automatic caseless pulse rifle, and her combat helmet, then moved for the lift that would take her and her squad to the waiting drop ship aboard the *TAF—Navy Ship Athabaskan*. Sergeant Bruce Taylor, the squad sergeant, did one last inspection at the lift doors.

"Gear up, people" he barked, "Stow your trash, and I want final check out in thirty. Squad leaders, orders group in five; get your squads ready."

Taylor had spent the last twenty years in the TAF, working his way up the ranks and learning to stay alive in the process. The rank of sergeant can come quickly with a mortality rate as high as those in most frontline combat units.

His darkly tanned skin, bald head, and muscular frame of 183 centimeters, along with his deep baritone voice, made him stand out in a crowd. Still, he had a mild and gentle manner when it was called for that distinguished him among his troopers.

"Sergeant," called Corporal Christian Carmichael over the squad frequency. "Do we have the mission brief yet?" Carmichael was checking the man-portable missile pods and ensuring they were on stand-by. Eagerness sounded in his voice.

"Not yet, Carmichael. The lieutenant is on his way down now," said Taylor. "I can tell you that it changed from one squad to a full-platoon operation. The other squads are gearing up now and will be down in two."

Operations rotated between squads, platoons, and regiments, which gave everyone a break between missions. This was now the third platoon's operational mission and the troopers would find out soon enough what it was all about.

To a casual untrained observer, the drop ship bay would have looked like a disorganized and frenzied mess, but preparing a drop ship required an enormous amount of coordination. Stowing individual and crew served weapons, ammunition, power packs, food and personal gear took time and cooperation. Loading drop ship support weaponry took even more.

The large space in the lower half of the troop ship was immense. Drop ships, shuttles and transports lined the bay in two rows. Dozens of navy and ground troop support personnel readied the drop ships of third platoon Alpha Company in a coordinated effort that underscored the urgency in reading the ships for combat.

Missile launch ramps on the drop ships glided out to be mated with the high-velocity missiles, or HVM, that would bring death on the ground to anyone foolish enough to resist the TAF. Plasma guns were now charged and made safe by the gunners. Multi-barrel bolt launchers that fired twenty-millimeter darts at almost twenty times the speed of sound, guided by a magnetic containment field as they ripped down the tri-barrel guns, were loaded and locked down.

The lift doors opened and a hush came over the troopers as the platoon master sergeant and the lieutenant stepped onto a platform in the drop bay.

Lieutenant Gerald Fitzpatrick was of old Irish stock. His family name was well known in the TAF, and he was well on his way to distinguishing himself as a leader. At forty-eight he was the youngest lieutenant with two dozen combat missions under his belt. His deep blue eyes, dirty blond hair, and well-kept goatee gave him a look that seemed out of place in the military. People who did not know him and saw him out of uniform would think he looked more at home on a beach. Those who did know him, however, regarded him as a cunning and calculating man who not only showed compassion for his troopers, but commanded their respect. They would lay down their own lives for him as much as he would do the same for them.

On the platoon net he announced a stand-to for orders. "Squad NCOs, call parade. This is it, boys and girls." The troopers dropped what they were doing. Formal parades in the drop bay were not usually practical or advisable, but a cluster of one hundred and fourteen personnel around the speaker was manageable.

"It's a search and destroy mission," Fitzpatrick began. "Command has intelligence on pirate activity in this sector."

Fitzpatrick let that sink in for a moment. He knew everyone wanted a piece of the pirates.

As some colony worlds drifted and grew apart from the Confederation, they took to perpetrating raids on neighboring colonies and fringe worlds to survive. While there were other legitimate and long-term solutions to keep a colony afloat, it did not take long for some to see the immediate payback of pirating. They would form their own pirate raiders or hire outside help.

In time, the various pirate groups grew larger and more violent. No longer content with simply taking cargo, now they took the lives of all captured crew—no witness, no fuss, no muss. It was hard not to find someone unaffected by the sheer scope of the violence. The brutality seemed only to escalate with each attack.

Recent activity had been increasing in the main shipping lanes and there was an outcry from the Shipping Guilds along with their crews and families for the government and military to do something about it. By now, there were enough alarms and warnings to fill a database with several thousand briefs. The documents and "caution notices" the TAF and Confederation sent out informing shippers of pirate activity and shipping routes to avoid were ineffective, and though the TAF sent out escorts with merchant convoys on the fringe, there were never enough ships to cover all the routes or resources to investigate all reports of pirate activity.

Fitzpatrick turned over the briefing to the regimental spook who joined the group. Each regiment had someone from navy intelligence assigned to it, and the troopers often called them "spooks"—a holdover from the mid-twentieth century.

The spook, David Hoffman, stepped up on the small platform and nodded toward the lieutenant in thanks. "You all know the rumors about pirate activity in this sector." He eyed each trooper as he spoke, each word chosen with care.

Turning toward a briefing screen set up at the far end of the bay, Hoffman activated a sector map. "Fleet Intelligence intercepted several coded transmissions in and out of this area."

He highlighted a portion of the map. "This intel by itself would not normally warrant an S&D mission, but we also found this…"

Hoffman changed the image to show an old-style cargo ship. The image, taken by a survey probe, was not very clear, but tremendous blast damage near the stern section and damage to at least two of the four main drive engines could be seen. As the probe camera panned, more damage became apparent. The bridge, located on the superstructure to afford more cargo space, was gone—a gaping hole sixty meters across at least.

"This was the *Kestrel*," the regimental spook said. "It was discovered off the fifth moon of St. Andrew. Analysis of the blast damage and hyperwave residual readings, along with physical evidence left by the boarders and found by our search-and-rescue teams, point to our current location as the most probable jumping-off point for the raiders. The SAR techs found no survivors."

The image changed on the screen, showing telemetry data. "This data is currently three hours old. The probe was launched when we first entered this system. It shows previous but high ship activity around the planet IM-five zero two one six."

Hoffman changed the view once again to show IM50216, a planet not deemed important enough for a name. Even its star was insignificant: a K-type star with a surface temperature of less than five thousand Kelvin, and only point eight of Sol's mass.

The monitor split into two images: telemetry data on the right and a video image of the probe fly-over on the left.

"IM-five zero two one six is a rock with little cover. The probe found three small settlements or outposts of some kind along this track, including this launch site." He pointed them out, including a view of the launch site that showed two orbital shuttles, three combat support shuttles, and an older combat cruiser. The combat cruiser was twice the size of assault shuttles and carried a vast array of offensive weapons. A red trace line superimposed on the image linked all three settlements.

"Electromagnetic signatures confirm advanced weapons systems in place. We suspect they have ship-grade plasma cannons located here, here, and here. We believe the only combat-ready site is the launch area, but we'll keep an eye on the others."

Someone in the group whistled and other numerous expletives were also overheard throughout the gathered platoon. Pirates were not supposed to be this well-equipped. They usually hoarded the majority of their bounty—they didn't spend it on equipment. But the defensive weaponry and assault shuttles on the screen suggested otherwise.

Heather remained quiet; she was soaking in as many details as she needed. She was beginning to form her own opinion, however, and it mirrored the others in her platoon.

Clearing his throat, Hoffman continued. "No transports or other ships, including sensor ships or pickets, have been located in system or in orbit. This is unusual and we're not sure why, considering what we have seen to date, so we are keeping a close watch."

Bringing up a terrain map of the launch site and superimposing an aerial shot taken by the probe, Hoffman went on. "This is your main objective. Third platoon will drop and secure this site, take prisoners, and gather information. Try to keep the shuttles and cruiser in one piece. We would like to hack into their nav-comm and data logs. I'll give you back to your LT for the mission details if there are no questions."

No one spoke.

"Thank you and good luck." Hoffman picked up his data chips and, reader in hand, left the bay.

Fitzpatrick stepped forward. "Squads one and four will drop on the west side of the launch site and take out the control tower's communication building and secure the shuttles and cruiser. We believe that these pose the greatest risk, but we also want to neutralize the plasma cannons ASAP. We want to save data and take prisoners, but if they're not willing to listen to reason, use all force necessary to secure the area. Make them risk their lives, not yours."

Heather listened intently. The difference between life and death was a fine line and not knowing your role in a drop was only one of many ways to cross that line. She knew the squad sergeants would have more detailed info on the squad tasks. The lieutenant continued.

"Second squad will take out these two plasma cannons. You will have two troopers from the platoon weapons detachment with powered armour. That should persuade any holdouts to give up, but don't count on it."

Lovely, thought Heather. *It's only when they think we're about to get dropped in the shit that they break out the power armour.*

Fitzpatrick addressed the third squad's sergeant. "Sergeant Wong, you will take your squad and secure this." He highlighted what looked to be a likely barrack area.

The lieutenant now eyed the group as a whole, "Without any detailed intel, I'm going to assume that we may run into escape or access tunnels between buildings. The weapons detachment will be issued cave-rats, and they'll be available to any squad that needs assistance. They will also have the eighty-millimeter mortars in support, just in case. Any questions?"

He looked around and checked his reader. Again, no one had any direct questions—at least not right now. "You can check with your squad sergeants if any questions come to mind. All right, we launch in fifteen mikes. The first round is on me when we get back. Sergeants, carry on."

Fitzpatrick grabbed his helmet and put it on, leaving the securing strap loose. He picked up his rifle and headed for the platoon command drop ship, followed by the platoon master sergeant. Squad sergeants barked orders and last-minute preparations continued between troopers and naval personnel.

***

Heather boarded her squad drop ship from the rear ramp as soon as the command was given. *Eagle*

302 was a sleek, streamlined assault ship used by all branches of the TAF. It was not the newest model, but it was a tried and tested design that had proven itself in combat many times over. It had room for a pilot and gunner sitting in tandem in the tight but well laid-out cockpit. Winglets mid-fuselage and a double fined v-tail rear section made it look like an ungainly insect. Weapons bays were internal in the wings and underbelly, with the plasma cannon in the lower section of the nose along with the atmospheric probe.

The crew compartment sat in the lower rear with access doors on both sides. There was a retractable loading ramp directly aft with the upper half of the rear section dedicated to air defense missiles and their launch tubes. It was not as fast as a close support fighter, but it was maneuverable and designed to survive multiple hits from enemy rockets, plasma blasts, and other small arms.

Each trooper took their assigned spots and locked down personal and squad weapons.

***

Corporal Gerry Saskia of third squad in *Eagle 303* ensured his people and gear were stowed properly, then locked himself in. Saskia was a "lifer"; he'd been the TAF for almost forty-eight years, but still a corporal. He was good—one of the best, but striking your commander when drunk was not a way to get ahead in the TAF.

Five drop ships were readied for final count down. Each squad including the command section is assigned their own drop ship. The ability for a TAF combat unit to be as mobile and flexible as possible was crucial to successfully completing a mission. Drop ships would carry troops, weapons, powered armour, ammunition, medical supplies, and food. They could also be used for close air support once they discharged their load and when required, they also had the capacity to be used as medevac.

Athabaskan's navy personnel moved quickly but efficiently behind blast doors after all equipment was stowed and secured—the two-minute warning was sounded throughout the ship alerting everyone a drop was imminent.

***

Heather readied herself for the release. Her pulse quickened and she felt her heart beat faster as she anticipated the moment. She loved the rush a combat drop gave her as adrenaline pumped through her blood.

Below each drop ship, wide doors opened with the aid of huge hydraulic rams as swing arms securing each ship from above, lowered them into their initial position. At the same time red blackout lights switched on in the bay. With the yellow warning lights spinning like an insane ballerina, the bay was awash in the garish colour of blood.

The speakers came to life with a feminine but artificial voice. "Warning, drop ship launch sequence has begun. All personnel evacuate bay area."

The AI warning repeated itself two more times with the sound of the klaxon in the background.

***

Lieutenant Fitzpatrick locked himself in the shock frame and did a check on his troops. Men and women who volunteered to fight and die for an ideal that not even he could understand all the time were getting ready with determined precision. He took note of the adrenaline rush all his troopers were beginning to experience, including himself. He could see the effects on their bodies in his monitors as he checked his platoons' readiness.

"Master sergeant," he said. "Final count down in five on my mark. Mark"

Bulkhead doors lowered and were secured as the last of the navy personnel left the drop bay. Another warning klaxon sounded and a secondary door opened below each drop ship with a rush, as the remaining atmosphere in the bay escaped into space. The swing arms lowered the ships down the remainder of the way and then locked them into position, making no sound in the now present vacuum.

Master Sergeant Bell opened a channel on the platoon next to the drop ship pilots. "In five, four, three…"

At zero the sky fell in and the previous meal was almost served again that day for some of the troopers, especially the newbies. Each ship released at the same time, and after clearing the *Athabaskan,* started the steep dive that would take them on a trajectory to their intended target. At their rate of descent, a regular passenger shuttle would have burned up as it entered the planet's atmosphere, but combat drop shuttles were made to withstand enormous heat and pressures.

***

Warrant Officer Ellery Scott handled *Eagle 301* with the grace of a zen master. She was a veteran of over sixty drops and remembered each one in vivid detail. She banked her ship two degrees to port and lined up behind *Eagle 300,* the platoon command drop ship. Her instrument monitors reflected off her helmet visor as she eased the stick.

"Eagle three double oh to all Eagle threes," said Chief Warrant Officer Di Carlo, command pilot for the platoon command ship. "On my mark, begin your run."

Di Carlo opened the distance between each ship and checked her HUD. Blue triangles identified the drop ships in third platoon—all on their assigned glide path.

"Mark."

Each drop ship started its attack run. *Eagle 301* and *304* with first and fourth squads screamed toward the control tower and shuttles on the ground.

Streaks of fire lit up across the dark sky on IM50216 as drop ship gunners took their plasma cannons off standby as soon as they hit atmosphere and clean air. They opened the missile doors and began to lock in targets. First squad would take on the shuttle and fourth went for the control tower. *302* went for the plasma cannons and *303* dived toward the barracks area.

Di Carlo made her way to an open stretch of ground two-thirds of the way between the barracks and shuttles on the ground. "Death from above" was an old Earth military idiom, but right now it seemed appropriate. Life would be exchanged for death in a human conflict that never seemed to end. Who would pay the ultimate price with their life this time?

From Heather's perspective, it would not be her. She did not have that kind of bank account. She readied herself to help the pirates make their final withdrawal.

Chapter Three

Captain Spotswood sat in his office going over next week's duty roster. He could barely keep his eyes open. It was dark outside—but then again, it was always dark with not much in the way of illumination from the K-type star. IM50216 did not have a moon to reflect any light, and so at two-thirty in the morning, there no light other than what was provided by the artificial lights of the compound and buildings.

A bottle of amber-coloured alcohol sat on the desk, three-quarters empty, its label discoloured and peeling around its edges, while a small glass sloshed from side to side as if just filled. Data chips lay scattered about on the desk and side table. The overhead lights were off but a desk lamp cast long dark shadows, mixed with the glow from the desk reader.

There was not much in the way of furniture in the dingy office. Besides the desk and side table were three hefty-looking storage cabinets, each with a large bar across the top and bottom and bio-locks affixed to one side.

Spotswood was an adventure seeker and could never get enough time in space. Plying the space lanes for power and glory was what made him happiest—not sitting in some planet side office checking off lists. He knew he'd pissed off his former commander, Hyde Beaufort, when he plotted the wrong intercept course on a fat cargo hauler.

It wasn't his fault though. *If that navigator knew his job this would have never happened. One simple calculation out of place and I get screwed.*

Of course, Spotswood did not reflect that his one simple mistake cost the crew a month's worth of credits, or that it was his responsibility as the navigation officer to ensure the plot was correct.

That idiot navigator will never make that mistake again, he thought. *If he ever gets out of the hospital, he'll be lucky if he sees light and shadow.*

Spotswood's thoughts were interrupted when two of his men opened the outer door to his office.

"Hey, boss," said Andrew Wong. "We expecting a transport today?"

Wong had a scar across his right cheek. That, his dark and wind-burnt skin, and his scraggy black hair tied back made him look like a pirate of old Earth. Not too many people knew he had given himself the scar to achieve the desired effect.

"Not today. Why?" responded Spotswood with as much disdain as he could muster. He did not want to be disturbed and had turned off his comm link to avoid having to talk to anyone. He was in a foul mood and he knew it. *Probably why Wong brought a witness,* he mused.

"We got an inbound hit on an intercept course and it's reading steady," Wong responded. The loathing was equal in his tone. He didn't even bother to look directly at Spotswood, instead trying to see what was on the reader.

"Any transponder?" asked Spotswood. He quickly turned the screen over.

"Cargo ship *Athabaskan*, but nothing in our data about it. And before you ask: they haven't responded to hail since they dropped out of hyper." Wong hated being questioned. *Spotswood screwed the pooch, so he ends up here and now makes my life hell,* he thought. *No way that's going to happen.*

Spotswood tossed the portable reader and data chip on the desk and stood. He could see Wong's displeasure. He'd been riding Wong and the rest of the garrison hard since his arrival, but he didn't care. If he had to suffer the indignity of being sent to this rock, he'd make everyone share his misery.

"Don't get your knickers in a knot, Wong. Just because it's not in our data table doesn't mean anything. Remember that hauler three weeks ago?" He moved from behind the desk and stepped toward the window to look out.

Wong followed him with his eyes and nodded.

"Chances are this one got into a scrap with that same asteroid belt. Where did it come out of hyper?"

Wong checked his reader. "Just inside the system limit."

"See?" said Spotswood condescendingly. "If it was anything else they would have come out beyond the limit and come in under stealth. Now stop bothering me. Go get a team ready and warm up shuttle two."

Spotswood figured he might as well take advantage of the opportunity. If a fat hauler with a full belly of valuable cargo dropped in, who was he to argue?

He turned quickly toward the departing Wong, "And Wong, keep trying to hail them…in a friendly way." Spotswood smiled despite his foul mood. *Some extra prize money will be good for the soul,* he thought. "We wouldn't want to spook them, would we?" He laughed.

Wong nodded and left the office without another word.

Outside the office, he rolled his eyes at his companion. "You were a big help back there. You were going to back me up, remember? A ship coming here unannounced for any reason is a problem. What if we were discovered? The least we should be doing is a general alert, get everyone up and armed."

Zarko Samouk looked at his friend and shrugged. "What would, or could, I have said that would have changed his mind?" He was about ten centimeters shorter than Wong and had to almost run to keep up to Wong's gazelle-like steps. "That pompous git barely knows the difference between his ass and the business end of a plasma cannon. And look, he's probably right about this ship. They're not hiding and other than no communication so far, they haven't done anything out of the ordinary."

Samouk looked up toward the sky and the blackness of space around him, then over toward the shuttle pad as they walked.

"We'll gear up a boarding team and prep an assault shuttle like he said." He took out his communicator and started to get a boarding team equipped up and ready.

Wong glanced at his friend, "I hope you're right, Zarko. I really do. I'm getting sick of this shit. There's no profit in it."

That was Wong's last thought as he was cut in half by a salvo of twenty-millimeter darts from a drop ship that came out of nowhere.

Zarko flew back and landed on his back, his mouth open, a silent and a stunned look in his eyes. Blood and parts of his friend splattered his body and the ground around him.

***

Heather Brassard did a final check out of her equipment and powered up her systems. She put her combat helmet on and lowered the face shield. At once her heads-up display came alive and data lines showed her system status. Telltales turned from red to amber to green showing that all was right in her tiny section of the universe.

She looked around. Everyone else was doing the same system checks and going through their own pre-combat rituals. Some prayed, some chanted and meditated quietly, while others slept or read.

Sergeant Taylor came on the squad net and downloaded a terrain map, updated by CIC on the *Athabaskan,* to the squad members.

"Everyone keep your wits about you," he said. "CIC confirms that heat plumes are increasing from one of the assault shuttles and they note some activity around the barracks area. CIC also verifies EM emissions from the plasma cannons we're going after, but that could be normal venting and recharge. It doesn't look like they're powered up for combat. I've downloaded all current data to your readers. Read it on the drop."

"Newbies will stick to your trainers. You *will not* screw up!" he added with a snap.

He purposely used a harsh voice—a new trooper screwing up could end the party very quickly. Second squad had two newbies and although they were showing promise in training, combat would prove them—or kill them.

"When we disgorge, power armour will take point," Taylor continued. "We'll be coming in head first, so move like your ass is on fire. The drop ship will take off, heading into the cannons to get a strafing run in as they accelerate to orbit and re-group in case we need support or medevac."

Taking off toward the plasma cannon would allow the drop ship to cut the angle of attack for the enemy. If they wanted to take the shot they would have to traverse, leaving the weakest shielded section of the gun turret vulnerable to attack from the squad. The enemy would also be firing into the strongest section of the small ship.

The difficulty with this kind of an attack was a complete lack of cover. A two-meter boulder could afford some protection for ground troops, but a forty-kiloton drop ship was a bit harder to hide. Landing on top of the target was the only way to use the element of surprise and cut down on the enemy's response time. Assuming of course, the enemy *was* surprised.

Lead Trooper Marek Whitehead and Corporal Trevor Ritchie looked at each other, their face shield raised.

"Lovely time for a stroll, don't you think, Trev, old boy?" asked Marek with a mock British accent. A twinkle in his eye and an ear-to-ear grin on his face indicated his playful nature.

Marek and Trevor were the two troopers in power armour attached to second squad. Power armour was a bulky affair that the wearer put on in two pieces: first a bottom and then the top half that enclosed the user in 235 kilos of plaststeel, electronics, communication, weapons, and ammunition. Each joint was power assisted in a sealed environment that was airtight and lubricated, keeping the joints power-driven and hinged in such a way that allowed the user to walk and operate in battle conditions from zero to four Gs with ease.

But, of course, you had to know what you were doing. The armour was not easy to operate, but a skilled trooper could be equipped with a variety of weapons, including a flamethrower, darts, plasma cannons, grenade launchers, and anti-armour and anti-air configurations. A well-equipped trooper could put down a considerable amount of fire. While power armour would not take the place of a tank, it did allow small unit fire support at the front line level. That could mean the difference in a firefight. Unfortunately, it also meant power armour users were a prime target.

Trevor grinned and looked over at Taylor. "Anything else you'd like us to do, Sarge? Breakfast in bed, scrub and polish the drop ship perhaps?" he added with an increasingly mocking grin.

With the face shield now lowered, Taylor was not able to see the grin, but he only ignored the jibe.

"Lock and load people—CIC update confirms at least one assault shuttle prepping for take off. The plasma cannons are still not powered up but that will change in one minute. We're about to light up their world in forty-five seconds," said Taylor.

Activity in the drop ship went up several notches. Even Marek and Trevor became serious. The business of killing was about to commence. This was a vulnerable time for any assault—as the ships came in fast and steep, an alert gunner on the ground could take you out and you would never even know it.

Heather picked up her assault gun from the rack and inserted a magazine, then switched on its power. She took her body armour systems off standby and made her weapon safe. It just wouldn't do to make it to the ground and have a weapon go off when it shouldn't. Her heads-up display with her helmet systems lit up her face shield, and she was feeling pumped and ready for action.

Troopers Whitehead and Ritchie unstrapped and powered up their armour, taking their place at the head of the loading ramp, bracing themselves for landing. Each trooper knew their place in the squad and they would be ready.

Eagle 302's pilot throttled up and watched the altimeter count down. Three thousand…two thousand…one thousand. At nine hundred meters he hit the retro rockets and applied the air brakes. Grilled flaps popped open on the topside and upper wing section as well as under the carriage to catch the flow of air.

At the same time the four scramjet engines rotated almost 180 degrees to slow the drop ship to just under mach two, or six hundred and eighty meters per second. The small ship shuddered violently, as if it would crack open at any time. Wing and belly mounted missile launchers opened to the air and telltales in the cockpit went from standby to green.

At four hundred meters the drop ship started to level out and its gunner sited and plotted targets, coding them as primary and secondary. The violent rocking and vibration died down as the forward velocity was reduced and clean air opened up.

"Stand by!" commanded Taylor.

The first volley of missiles fired from the drop ships went screaming toward their targets. Heat and displacement waves marked trajectories on the small ship's tracking sensor. Heather took her weapon off safe.

The drop ship swooped low and began to kick up dust and other loose rubble from the parched ground. At ten meters, the rear ramp began to open and Heather could see the compound lights through the dim haze of dust and debris. Small rocks and dust swept back in a vortex pattern, kicked up by the engines as the drop ship settled lower and the engine pods rotated. She knew her targets would be toward the front of the ship, but that did not mean no one was behind them. She knew enough to scan for targets everywhere.

At five meters, she felt a deep thud followed by others and knew they were now getting small arms and squad weapons fire. *Steady, girl,* she told herself. One meter off the ground and the end of the loading ramp hit the dirt as the ship flared with its nose pointing up slightly.

"Go!" shouted Taylor as several more small arms rounds ricocheted off the hull.

Heather launched off the drop ship ramp and quickly moved out toward her assigned position to take up cover. The ground was rocky, from loose sand to fist-sized rocks, and the terrain had very little real cover.

A large *Whomp!* was more felt than heard not too far off to port as a grenade went off. The concussion kicked up more dust and rocks, adding to the already choking mix.

Whitehead and Ritchie moved out, followed by the rest of the squad. Troopers moved left and right out the rear, perpendicular to the ship, out to sixty meters of the ramp, and turned toward their target. Heather could see the flash of small arms fire coming from and around the plasma cannon turret base, but the turrets was not pointing toward them. As a matter of fact, it didn't look like they were powered up at all.

Thank the gods for small favors, she thought.

Through her night imaging built into her combat helmet she could see two troopers go down on her right. Wounded or dead?

"Medic," she called on the squad frequency. She knew Taylor would see their vitals on his helmet display but it was still standard practice to call for assistance just in case. She saw one of the two medics run toward her fallen comrades, but she could only hope for the best.

Heather chose her targets using her HUD's thermal imaging systems. Even in the darkest of night or the thickest of fog and smoke, the TAF's thermal systems could cut through and pinpoint a target.

Kneeling, she squeezed the trigger, then moved toward some low cover—not much more than scrub and small boulders, but it did provide some protection.

Ritchie took aim at more movement ahead and then moved off to his right to get a better angle.

The compound lights were barely visible through the haze of smoke, dust, and dirt. The drop ship was cycling up its engines to take off as the gunner hit the plasma cannons, burning a hole through one of the buildings and eliminating an unknown number of pirates. Their bodies could be seen in the blown-out section, twisted at awkward angles.

The roar of the four scramjet engines was deafening and a number of the pirates without ear protection winced in pain, dropping their weapons and putting their hands up to cover their ears as the ship lifted off. One was almost cut in half by a bolt of plasma fired from Ritchie in power armour. The pilot throttled up to full power. His gunner took aim with an HVM and fired on the first of the two turrets, alternating with several bursts from the twenty-millimeter multi-barrel cannon.

Sparks and shrapnel flew as the HVM detonated at the base of one of the turrets. One of the pirates with a rocket-propelled grenade was blown apart, and two others were lying prone and unmoving. Several others ran for what cover they could find.

As the heavier debris of rocks and body parts settled, a light dust continued to float in the air. In the confusion of battle, the squad moved forward. The drop ship rotated its engines and moved forward at the same time it rose higher and accelerated.

A second HVM flew from the underwing pylons while another burst of fire from the twenty-millimeter ripped through armour, metal, and flesh. A number of smaller buildings were burning, and the fire and smoke only added to the mayhem.

Sergeant Taylor came on the squad net and ordered a "fire and move"—one half of the squad would provide cover while the other half moved forward.

"Left section cover. Carmichael, move toward that shed with right section."

Carmichael looked toward the shed, a good-sized maintenance or storage building. He clicked twice in acknowledgement and on a section frequency gave the order to move.

Heather was assigned to left section when the 22-man squad split. She got up from a prone position and ran toward the shed. She moved with speed, keeping one eye on her step and the other on possible targets. She dove out of the way when a series of darts impacted in a line toward her. *Ranging rounds,* she thought. *Thank the makers for bad gunners.*

The right section with Taylor fired at the same time and kicked up more ground cover.

Taylor called for four grenades at thirty meters front. Four troopers in his right section loaded and fired the twenty-millimeter high-explosive grenades in succession. Each grenade landed and exploded, one after another. One pirate trying to escape from the first was killed by the second detonation.

"Left section in position, Sarge. On three, we have you covered." reported Carmichael as the sound of gunfire increased.

"Right, we're moving now," responded Taylor as he got his people up and moving under the cover of fire from the other section.

Two explosions went off to the front and left of Carmichael and he had to drop even lower.

Heather moved around what she determined must have been another maintenance shed and took aim at someone moving up a ladder on one of the plasma cannons. She fired a short burst and the target went down. Blood splattered from his left side as flesh and bone exploded where her rounds hit.

She noticed a hatch or access port on the base of one of the plasma cannons. She checked the corner of the shed and, not noticing anyone, ran for the plasma cannon.

Moving closer she found the opening. She removed three of her grenades, crouched, and set the timer to thirty seconds. She ran for the shed, reaching it in time to take cover as the grenades went off, blowing the door out of its track. She ran back and went inside, doing a quick sweep. She fired a quick burst at some movement and checked her arc. One pirate was slumped over a console. No one else was inside; it was a small power room with apparent damage to several panels.

She walked over to one and noticed that the damage was to the power regulator and charging boards. *That must have been the reason for not using the cannons on us*, she thought.

She called Sergeant Taylor on the squad net and informed him of the damage to the cannon and her plan to blow the turret. TAF troopers were trained to be flexible and use their judgment to exploit any situation. "Improvise, adapt, and overcome" was drilled into them from the beginning of training. Taylor acknowledged and began to move his section around the other side of the objective.

One trooper reported seeing movement off in the distance. Taylor sent two of his men to investigate. The amount of resistance was lessening and only a few holdouts seemed intent on finishing this with the ultimate sacrifice for their cause. The two troopers came across three pirates trying to leave the party, and quickly eliminated them.

Heather finished setting her grenades at key points and stepped through the door, leaning her back against the cool armour plating of the turret. She checked to ensure the immediate area was void of pirates.

"Fire in the hole," she called on the squad net and dashed across to the shed her section was now behind.

Another burst of automatic fire from a heavy section weapon wiped up dust just in front of her as darts slammed by. She felt a sting in her left leg but kept going with a quick jog to the right and then again left. The last five meters she dove for cover as another burst of fire missed—though not by much. She took a second to examine her leg, but only noted a scratch to her leg guards.

A rocket-propelled grenade went off nearby, and she heard a secondary explosion as Marek Whitehead's power armour went up. White-hot heat and flame shot back where he was. The rocket propelled grenade struck him dead center at less than forty meters. He had no chance to eject.

Ritchie saw what happened and also saw the pirate that took out his friend. A burst of plasma shot out and burned the pirate in half. Heather was in the line of fire, and had to duck behind the shed to avoid the heat wave from the plasma burst. She blinked twice to get rid of the spots in front of her eyes—her face shield had not dimmed in time to fully protect her vision.

Only sporadic fire remained when the five grenades Heather planted inside the turret went off.

She was thrown forward onto the ground as the concussion rocked the shed. Corporal Carmichael was picked up and tossed three meters up and six meters out, knocking the wind out of him. Other troopers not behind cover or lying prone went flying.

All firing from the pirates stopped and three of them dropped their weapons, stood slowly and interlocked their fingers behind their heads. A dejected and blank look on their faces showed their fight was over as troopers nearby led them away, under what cover they could find. They removed any electronics and weapons from the surrendering pirates but left any armour for protection, then bound their hands and legs with quick ties, making sure they were secured to each other.

Heather got to her feet and saw Carmichael raise himself slowly, using the butt of his weapon for support. The plasma cannon she set the changes in had a gaping hole in the side where the door was located. The turret was listing at an awkward angle and smoke poured out the plume chamber in the upper section.

One body hung out of a hole in the turret near the gun. Other bodies were strewn about the ground and a scorch mark was visible on the ground where

Whitehead's power armour stood just before the RPG hit.

Taylor announced that the other squads were reporting in and they too were starting to mop up. Two drop ships were on their way in with intelligence and weapons and electronic specialists to gather information. Though the battle was over, the site still had to be cleared and secured.

"Corporal Carmichael," called Taylor on the squad net. "Police up any weapons and stragglers. Set up a holding pen on the south east side of that turret." He pointed.

"Brassard, take two section and clear the two outer buildings," said Carmichael.

"Right, corporal," responded Heather. "Two section on me."

The wind was starting to pick up a bit as they moved quickly across the short distance to the buildings. It was enough to blow away some of the battle smoke but kicked up more sand and dust in its place, making it harder to see any detail without electronic aids.

The buildings looked like administration structures, maintenance shops, and more storage—no large access openings, some small windows, and three visible doors, one of them a double. *This looks like a good place to start,* she thought. She and her section loaded fresh magazines and power packs as they approached.

While Heather was engaged, Carmichael had one section stand the perimeter and detailed three troopers to pick up any ammo and kit from the dead and wounded. They also collected any documents and readers.

Four troopers were selected as guards for their prisoners. Several pirates had already been rounded up and taken to the holding area, blindfolded, with hands and feet bound.

Heather and her section reached the first building and spread out. "Williams and Bird, take the rear," she directed. "Ratte and Brown, the west door." She wanted the doors blocked so no one got out.

She took the rest of the section and hit the main entrance. She tried the door after checking for traps. Locked.

"Blow it," she ordered and backed out of the way.

The det-cord sparked and a split second later the charge exploded, splintering the locking mechanism and allowing the door to swing open. The power was off, no light, but she could still see in black-and-white using her thermal imaging. Hotter temperatures showed up as whiter shades.

Bending low and staying close to the wall, Heather moved ahead with the section spread out to avoid being ambushed.

The room was small with a table and loungers scattered about. Dust hung in the air and caked everything, including the floor. One door stood opposite her.

"We're in." she said on the section frequency. "No movement and no sign in first room, it's clear. Moving on to the next room."

Trooper Alfred Moodie moved up to the closed door and took a position across from Heather. The others split up on either side but not directly in front, in case of small arms fire when the door opened.

Silently, Moodie placed more det-cord and another charge around the hinged side of the door and plugged in a remote.

"Ready?" he asked. Everyone acknowledged with a thumbs-up.

"Fire in the hole!" He pressed the detonator.

The blast took the door off its hinges and threw it back and to the right. A scream could be heard on the other side but it was cut off in mid-yell. Heather took out a grenade and set the timer to two seconds. She tossed it in and took cover as small arms fire grazed the door opening kicking up splinters.

A bang sounded as the grenade went off. Shrapnel flew, as did pieces of wall, floor and ceiling. A small fire ignited when some window coverings caught a spark.

Heather took her section through the open door firing. Her targeting systems showed three warm bodies hiding behind overturned tables and a computer console. One of the troopers in Heather's section went down behind her, grabbing his knee as he fell. *He'll live*, she thought. She dived for cover and sited her target quickly. One quick three-round burst and the warm body was already getting cold.

Heather could hear the rumble of a drop ship coming in but did not let that distract her. The two remaining pirates in the room also heard the drop ship and decided that going on would get them killed.

"Stop! Hold your fire," shouted the one closest to Heather. "We yield."

Heather, using her helmet external speakers, said, "Throw out your weapons and stand with your arms above your head. If I can't see both your hands, we open fire." The sound of her voice echoed in the room.

The first thing to be thrown over the barricade was two assault rifles. Then two more, one pistol, two knives, a bandolier of grenades, and Heather could have sworn a sink was also tossed. She almost laughed. For a small base of ragtag pirates, there seemed to be an abundance of ordnance. Other than the plasma turrets and the defensive weapons, this offensive kit was not mentioned on the mission brief. She made a mental note to pass this information on to Sergeant Taylor.

Two pirates stood with hands very much visible. Heather directed two of her team to search and secure them.

"How many more in the building?" she asked one of the pirates.

He did not answer at first, turning his head and looking away.

She fired a short burst into the ground just in front of him. "I don't have time to fuck with you, so talk or—"

The pirate jumped back.

"No one. There's no one else."

She called Williams, Bird, Ratte, and Brown and ordered them to complete the search from the other end of the building as she sent four from this end. A ninth trooper removed the two pirates to the holding pen. As the pirate indicated, no others were found.

When Heather and her team emerged from the second building, the distant sun was just coming over the low hills on the horizon. It did not make the cold and wind-swept planet any more hospitable, however.

"Sergeant, we sent two to the holding pen and have one wounded," she reported. "Horton got hit in the knee but the medics are treating him now."

"Good work, Brassard. The tech team is down and starting their work. Carmichael has the rest of the squad forming up. Meet up with him and get ready for lift. We're heading to RV with the platoon.

A military police section came in with the techs for security."

"Roger that, Sergeant." Heather relayed the information to her section and they headed for the drop zone just outside the compound area.

Second squad did not survive unscathed: three dead and five wounded. It was hard for Heather to walk by the body bags at the DZ of men and women she had known, laughed and cried with, shared a drink and fought battles with. Seeing them like this was like a distant memory. Was it real? Memories without substance—*a week from now, will I remember their faces, their voice? I can't touch a memory like I could touch them,* Heather contemplated in sad silence.

Chapter Four

Heather tried to shake herself out of the funk she was in as she made her way to her ride. It never did any good to dwell on death too long. She was now boarding the drop ship so second squad could go to the platoon RV. As she climbed the ramp, she watched as a detachment of military police stood guard over the prisoners in a holding pen near the drop zone. They would be transporting the pirates to *Athabaskan* as soon as the transport shuttles arrived.

The intelligence team had already finished up in the area and had just left for the platoon RV in order to complete their work retrieving any data from any of the still-intact computer cores. The possibility of getting nav-comm information from the shuttles didn't look good, as they were badly damaged in the assault and the cruiser was completely destroyed.

Heather secured her weapon in its rack and locked herself in the shock frame. The drop ship lifted off as soon as everyone was secured and the ramp elevated.

It was gliding over the barren planet on its way to the RV when she heard Sergeant Taylor on the squad net. "Second squad, listen up. Change in orders. The mop up has gone ahead of schedule, so we're heading back to the *Athabaskan*."

That announcement was greeted with a round of cheers from the troopers. Heather looked forward to a shower and sleep. This op was not long by any standard, but adrenaline did strange things to a body. It could give you the strength to lift three hundred kilograms to save a life and the stamina to fight a pitched running battle for hours, but as soon as you stopped, even for a short time, your body gave out, completely drained.

It'll be nice to get showered and catch a nap, she thought. That would have to wait however because as soon as the platoon docked and the launch bay pressurized, there was still a lot of work to complete before being released to free time.

By the time the drop ships docked, some of the platoon had already begun to unload stores and kit.

"Weapons cleaning will be completed and inspected by zero-nine-thirty hours," announced Lieutenant Fitzpatrick, standing on an elevated level near his drop ship. "Personal kit and squad stores cleaned and stowed by ten-thirty. Platoon parade is at ten-thirty-one hours and the Regimental Quarter Master assures me that if we do not meet those times, he will have this platoon cleaning the exterior vent tubes on the ship."

This part of military life not even the highest-ranking flag officers could escape. Not one person in the launch bay thought the lieutenant was joking. The RQM did not have a sense of humor. Although a lieutenant—or for that matter, a colonel—outranked an RQM, you never messed with your Regimental Quarter Master Sergeant. The joke was that God himself asked permission from the RQM. Since the invention of the first military club or stick used by armies, RQM's believed they, and only they, owned all the equipment in a military unit. You only got to borrow it for a short time. And may the gods help you if you lose or break any of it.

Breakfast will just have to wait, thought Heather with resignation.

Fitzpatrick had another announcement before they got to work, however. "On a related but personal note, you all did a good job down there," he said, his voice soft and sincere. "The first round is on my tab. We'll drink to friends past and present." His voice almost cracked with emotion. But as an officer, and in front of his troops, he maintained composure. "Sergeants, carry on." He ducked back into his drop ship to retrieve his kit and start on his cleaning duties.

Junior officers had been hit hardest by the death of their troopers. They were new to the experience, and it was also their direct orders that had sent men and women to die. Fitzpatrick was not immune to those feelings. His parents had spent some time talking to him about that part of military life, but nothing could prepare him for it. After his initial combat mission, he'd sat down to write the letter to the family of a dead corporal, but broke down and had to see the regiment's counselor.

The shuttle carrying the dead had arrived and body bags were laid out in a corner of the bay in preparation for final disposition. Six dead and eight wounded in the platoon was a high price for any operation. Yet death was, as one trooper said, "part of the life you lived with in this line of work."

Heather turned in her unused ammunition, grenades and chargers, then began cleaning her weapon. After she turned in her rifle to the RQM, she helped others in her squad clean and stow kit.

At first, things were quiet in the bay—as they were after every mission. But as time moved forward, so did the conversations, emotions, and attitudes. While no one would come right out and say it, everyone felt the same way: sadness over losing a friend, anger toward the enemy, regret for family, friends, dreams, and hopes left behind, relief that they were safe, and guilt over that relief.

You can't win sometimes, thought Heather.

She looked up from locking down an access panel when she heard her name and saw Peter Talbot making his way over to where she stood. He may have been tired, but he still had a bounce in his step.

Peter was just a hair shorter than Heather, with a squared-off jaw, deep-set blue-green eyes, and a well-defined body. He was, by all accounts, good-looking. At least Heather thought so.

"What's up, Peter?" she said as he stepped closer.

Heather had had an on-again, off-again relationship with Peter since basic training—more off than on as their duties kept them apart more times than not. They both agreed when they began the relationship that it was strictly a physical union and nothing more. Once in a while, it felt good to wake up beside someone after an intense night of passion. But both of them now wondered secretly if it may have progressed into something more.

"I came over to see if you're up for company later," he whispered in a hushed tone. He was feeling drained but he still had that eager smile.

"Sure," Heather said. "How about twenty-one-thirty in the mess?"

Talbot smiled and nodded. "Sounds good. See ya then."

He turned, picking up a tool tray in order to finish a repair.

Heather watched him walk away and grinned, shaking her head. "He is cute," she said quietly to herself.

At 1031 hours the platoon did a final muster parade. The RQM approved the returned kit and the cleanup.

Heather only half listened, fatigue quickly overtaking her and the platoon. She wondered why the return of stores took so long and was so involved. Intellectually she saw the need for order and clean, functional equipment. Right now sleep was taking over the need for order and she just wanted to finish the cleaning and get to her quarters. The lieutenant stood on a storage container. "The platoon is stood down until zero-six-hundred tomorrow morning. Squad leaders, dismiss your troops."

Heather made her way to her small cabin. Only nine square meters, it was not much, but it was home and it was comfortable—as long as you didn't need to pace. The cabin had a single bed with personal storage underneath and above, a built-in desk with a chair, comm link and tabletop reader with computer access to one side, and nothing else.

Providing individual cabin space was a lesson learned a long time ago in the beginning of multi-crew space flight. Individual breathing space was crucial to the mental and physical wellbeing of the crew. Early space-going vessels had attempted to save mass by housing three to four crewmembers in one cabin. As two crewmembers were on shift, two would sleep. This was called hot-racking, as the bunks would still be warm when shift changes happened—a holdover from the wet navy days with deep-water submersibles.

But the loss of personal space and identity became problematic as colony planets spread out into the cosmos and travel time increased. A few high-profile murders helped speed up new designs. Along with new hyperdrive systems and artificial intelligence improvements to automation, ship sizes increased and personal space returned. Each person was now allowed to decorate their quarters to personal taste, within a weight limit.

Heather had put up a couple of antique posters from Earth's early twentieth century on the wall to add some colour. One was of the Cunard White Star shipping line, showing the old New York skyline in the background and two ships in the foreground. The second was an advertisement of Air Orient airlines. It had more colour and was her favorite. They were given to her by an old friend when she enlisted, so she was very fond of them.

Heather arrived at her cabin and after closing and locking her door, collapsed on her bunk. She was asleep before she hit the sheets.

***

After dismissing his platoon, Lieutenant Fitzpatrick turned and headed for the lift. He was on his way to a meeting with his company commander. Sleep would have to wait. Fitzpatrick was still required to give an after-action report on the mission—plus, he was curious about what intelligence had found.

"A quick coffee and stem patch should keep me going for another ten minutes," he said sarcastically to himself.

At the lift, he keyed in his access code. The doors opened. He moved out of the way to let a navy rating off, then stepped in and pressed the control panel for deck fourteen—Regimental Headquarters. The lifts were quick, but as he stared at the indicator count off each deck he found his eyes closing.

The doors opened. He decided he would make two stops before getting to sleep: RHQ with Company Captain Ian Thomas, then to update the duty roster and say hello to a friend he hadn't seen for a while. Keeping up with friends was important to him, especially those posted to headquarters—it always paid to have the inside track at HQ.

The *NS Athabaskan,* a eighteen thousand metric ton troop carrier, was dedicated to the provisions of one regiment—in this case the Terrestrial Light Armoured Guards of the Terrain Armed Forces. The TLAG was allotted several decks on the ship.

Drop ships, armour, and transport shuttles were housed on deck thirty. Weapons, stores and technical sections on deck twenty through twenty-eight. TLAG troopers were housed on decks fifteen to nineteen along with officers, while Headquarters occupied deck fourteen. The navy, with CIC, ship defense, weapons and missile storage, crew quarters, engine and hyper drive filled the rest of the ship interior. The command bridge was located at the heart of the superstructure with the auxiliary bridge ten decks lower and toward the stern. This was a design element incorporated into all newer TAF ships to reduce the chance of damage to the command deck and command structure in battle.

Elements of the TAF had gone through many changes in the past three hundred years, but one constant throughout that time was the navy. They paid a heavy price for that unwavering dedication to tradition, for ship design had not progressed much during those early years.

The old design concepts held over from the wet-navy days on Earth and Europa often proved dangerous in deep space. Housing the superstructure on the forward topside of the hull made too tempting a target, and after public outcry over the resulting loss of life and equipment, it was moved deep into the hull. More changes to the status quo happened due to the perceptions and reactions of the general populace than anything else, Fitzgerald realized. *Something to keep in mind,* he thought.

The company staff sergeant met him just outside the company administrative area.

"Welcome home, lieutenant. Captain Thomas is waiting, Just go on in." Fitzpatrick nodded. He did not salute—on board ship was considered barracks. Coming to attention was, however, customary, and the staff sergeant became ramrod straight.

"Thank you, sergeant," Fitzgerald said.

They walked the short distance to the main company office where Fitzpatrick stopped at the door to Captain Thomas's office. He paused and knocked twice before going inside.

"You did very well dirt-side, Gerald," greeted Captain Thomas as he rose from behind his desk. Holding out his hand he shook Fitzpatrick's with a firm grip. "Take a seat," he offered, pointing to one of three armchairs. "Coffee?"

"Please," said Fitzpatrick as he sat, grateful for the offer.

Thomas poured a cup from an urn on the side table. Steam rose from the black liquid.

"You take it black, don't you?"

Fitzpatrick nodded as Thomas handed it to him, then sat down in one of the chairs beside him.

"Hoffman and his staff managed to recover some data on pirate activity in this sector," he began. "So far, it looks like this is the bunch that took out the *Kestrel.*"

Thomas's voice had a hard edge. He despised the tactics used by the pirates and had difficulty keeping the anger and frustration from showing. He could understand why some colonies went into the pirate business and at first even sympathized with them. But when the killings started, then got worse, that changed everything.

He checked his reader. "Their commander, a fellow named Spotswood—what did you make of him?"

"Not much, other than he didn't want to be taken. When we hit the dirt I think we were more than a surprise to him and his people," Fitzpatrick answered. "One shuttle was hot with what must have been a full combat crew on board but it didn't seem like we were the target." He winced as he remembered the scorched bodies in the shuttle wreckage still on the pad. It was one of the first targets taken out by the drop ship gunner on approach, and there were no survivors.

"We made our way to the tower, pad, and support buildings at the same time. One and four sections didn't have as difficult a time of it after the shuttle was destroyed—at least until they hit this Spotswood's office in what must have been the command building. He had several others barricaded with him and lots of weapons and ammo, and put up a good firefight. He was the only survivor of that contact. By the way, sir, every section reported an unusually large weapons cache."

"I know. Hoffman's preliminary report also mentioned that, and it's disturbing to say the least. Why such a large stockpile, and here of all places? I've sent off word to the Co that this may be part of a larger problem," said Thomas.

The captain must be worried for him to send this up to the Old Man now and not wait for the final reports, thought Fitzpatrick. "I take it Spotswood does not like our hospitality and is not being completely cooperative?" he asked aloud.

Spotswood and the other prisoners were on the first shuttle back to the *NS Athabaskan* right after the wounded, and were immediately led away to interrogation.

"Mr. Spotswood did not have anything flattering to say, no," said Thomas. "But I may have an explanation for why they may have seemed surprised by your little visit. Spotswood had the distinct impression the *NS Athabaskan* was a tramp hauler. He seemed quite upset at our deception and kept demanding compensation for it. Quite frankly, I think the man is a bit of a loon."

Fitzpatrick wasn't surprised. He knew the *Athabaskan*'s captain had fixed the transponder codes to mask the type of ship. That ruse didn't always work, however. All a good sensor tech had to do was look at the drive signature of a suspected ship. Freight and passenger transports did not have as powerful inertial compensators as military ships—too much space and power required. As such, they couldn't pull the same acceleration and so their hyper signatures had a distinctly smaller footprint.

Fitzpatrick nodded. "That would explain part of why. I agree that he is also not the most brilliant commander or tactician around."

Thomas stood, signaling the end of the meeting. "I want to thank you and your platoon again for a job well done. I look forward to reading your complete after-action report tomorrow. Now go get some sleep, lieutenant. I'll see to it that a copy of Hoffman's findings makes it to your inbox."

Fitzpatrick rose and the two men shook hands. Fitzpatrick came to attention. "Thank you, captain. I can use a little shuteye."

He turned and headed out the door, exhaustion showing on his face. He was still planning to see his old friend in headquarters group and finish his duty roster. He couldn't wait for a hot shower and sleep, however—and   not   in   that   order.

Chapter Five

Captain Thomas sat back down behind his desk; letting himself fall into the seat. He saw a little of himself in Fitzpatrick when he commanded a platoon: young, eager, and more concerned about the troopers under his command than about himself. They were qualities that he admired.

Far too long ago, and many friends away, he thought. *How many people do we lose each year to greed? Earth sends out colony after colony without the support they need to survive, and then we're surprised when they turn to piracy for survival.*

The comm link "all hands" announcement chime sounded, breaking Thomas away from his thoughts.

"Attention all hands, this is the captain. The battle group has just entered the system and will be in orbit in two hours. All crew stand by for re-supply operations." The announcement echoed slightly.

The *Athabaskan* had been conducting operations away from the battle group. It was much easier to sneak in one disguised ship as opposed to a whole battle group, but now it was time to bring all the ships together.

The announcement terminated and Thomas stood, straightened his uniform tunic, and picked up his reader. He turned toward the comm link and keyed the channel.

"Staff sergeant, I'll be back as soon as I can. I'm meeting with Regimental Command, but I'm going to see David Hoffman first," he said. "Did we hear back from his team on the interrogations?"

"Not yet, sir," responded the sergeant.

Thomas knew in the back of his mind that there wouldn't be any news yet, although it would have been convenient if there was some word. He would soon find out.

As Thomas walked along the corridor past members of his company, regiment, and ship's crew, he reflected on the people he had known in his life. Close friends and comrades, neighbors and acquaintances. How many of them were still alive? *Far fewer than I would like,* he thought.

***

Heather tentatively opened her eyes, her muscles tensed for action. She listened. Not hearing explosions or weapons fire, she looked around in the dark, relaxed, and breathed in slowly.

The only light was coming from her comm link standby screen and a portable reader on the desk. The only sound was the low rumble of the deck—the normal background noise of the ship's systems and the air from the ventilation ducts. Her mind was slowly catching up to her senses. She was home on the *Athabaskan,* in her quarters and she was safe.

Heather turned to her left and looked at the chronometer—2045 hours. Peter was going to meet her at 2130 in the mess.

She reached up above her bed and slid her hand up the light panel till it was around fifty percent. She still felt fatigued, as though her body was in need of about thirty more hours of sleep.

She swung her legs over the edge of her bunk and dipped her head down into her cradled hands, closing her eyes again. Peter was meeting her in forty-five minutes.

Just enough time to be sick, she thought darkly.

She stood and took two tentative steps to the door as she braced herself against the wall. She picked up her shower kit and headed to the platoon showers to freshen up. Each platoon had their own toilet and shower area, with men and women using the same facilities. Perceived modesty between the sexes had died off in the late twenty-first century when humanity began its exodus from Earth. The first ships, "slow movers" and "generation" ships, had limited space, so it was only natural that men and women shared the common space.

She walked down the corridor passing fellow troopers, stopping at times to say hello. Reaching the showers, she found an empty stall, disrobed, and lay down her towel on a bench. It was a quiet night; only four other troopers were there. She greeted them and then turned to hit the switch for the ultrasound shower.

Invisible waves of sound washed over her body. The waves made her skin tingle, and the sensation felt good. Many people enjoyed this feeling, though it was more imagined than real—at least according to the developers of the reverberation shower.

Heather let the feeling linger. Real or imagined, it felt good. With fresh water at a premium, showers were a mix of light ultrasound waves and a kind of dry-cleaning chemical. She slowly turned the dial for the chemical bath engineered to feel like water. The compounds cleansed the pores and washed away the dirt, oil, and grime loosened by the ultrasound shower.

After a few minutes, Heather looked around and noticed only one other trooper still left in the shower area. It didn't matter. She was starting to relax. She let the liquid wash over her body. Closing her eyes, she tilted her head back and ran her fingers through her short-cropped hair. The cool liquid spilled down her neck, washing over her breasts and thighs. *After all the killing, a little sleep and a shower can make life that much more bearable,* she thought as her spirits perked up.

***

Thomas rounded the corner and stopped at a hatch with "Navy Intelligence" inscribed on the nameplate. He entered his access number and the door slid open. The first thing that greeted him was a very large and beefy MP with side arm holstered and rifle across his chest in a port arms position.

"Can I help you, sir?" the MP said in a deep, clear, emotionless voice.

"I'm meeting Lieutenant-Commander Hoffman."

The MP took the ID chip Thomas handed him and passed it to another not-so-friendly and equally large guard behind a security desk.

The guard inserted the chip into a reader. "Please step forward for scan confirmation, captain."

Thomas stepped up to the desk and, placing both hands on a flat screen, looked into a retinal scanner. "Captain Ian Thomas, eight-two-nine-one-one-three-one-whisky-alpha, Terrestrial Light Armoured Guards," he recited

The computers AI confirmed Thomas's identity after only a second and the MP guard behind the desk returned his ID chip.

"Lieutenant-Commander Hoffman will meet you in interrogation room one. Leave any weapons, ammo, or charge packs on that tray and step through the detector." The MP pointed to a shelf with trays and bins and a rifle rack on the floor beside the shelf.

"I don't have any of that on me" he said before stepping through the detector in front of the hatch. The detectors warning lights and alarm did not go off, so he was cleared for entry.

Thomas looked over at the first MP and saw him return his weapon to a relaxed rest position at the same time returning the weapons selector switch to safe. It was somewhat disconcerting to know these guys would not hesitate to pull the trigger at the first sign of trouble.

Thomas thanked the guards, retrieved his ID chip and moved to the door. It slid open without a sound and he walked through and down a short passage to interrogation room number one. Just as he was about to sound the admittance chime, the door slid back and Hoffman came forward to welcome him.

"Ian, thanks for coming. You saved me a trip," said Hoffman.

Hoffman had a firm grip and a warm friendly smile. Thomas knew Hoffman from the academy days on Mars Training Station. They had formed a long-lasting friendship since then and even the vast distances of space and time could not keep them from communicating via message packet, exchanging stories and adventures. It was only in the past two years that they had ended up serving on the same ship.

"Thanks for seeing me, David. I know you've been busy with the cleanup from our op. I have an audience with the old man and the rest of Regimental command, and I have to update them."

"No need to apologize, Ian. I'm never too busy for an old friend" said Hoffman. He had spent time in a combat command before joining the intelligence community and knew the pressure Thomas was under to bring something to the table at the after action briefings.

"How is the old man, anyway?"

The "old man" was the Regimental Commanding Officer, Colonel Tarik Marouf. He'd come up through the ranks and was a tough, no-nonsense individual and not one to mince his words. Many joked that he had spent more time in uniform than in civilian dress. With over a hundred combat drops into active and hot zones, Marouf was revered by officers and soldiers alike.

"He's fine—not happy with the situation, of course, but then, who is?"

Hoffman led Thomas to a bare metal table and offered a chair, then sat in one opposite.

"Sorry for the sparse furnishings. I haven't had much of an opportunity to redecorate since getting this assignment," Hoffman joked as he sat down.

"I'll send you my decorator—he could do wonders for this place." Both men chuckled, but it was restrained.

"Seriously, though, Ian, no one is happy, and what I have for you will not make it any better."

Thomas looked at his friend. "You're just full of sunshine this evening, aren't you? I gather you were able to find out why Spotswood and his pirate friends were in this sector with enough arms, ammunition, and power packs to arm a small army as well as raiding our ships?"

"If you are asking did the interrogation go well? Then I would have to say yes."

So called 'truth drugs' have come a long way since the mid and late twentieth century. But still no drugs were better than 90 percent effective. However, administered directly into the vein at the

68

neck leading to the brain; they acted quickly. And with a good interrogator, the ninety percent could be improved to nearly ninety nine percent.

"We did get him to talk and the answers will either make perfect sense or no sense whatsoever. Either way, good people are going to die."

Chapter Six

The bridge of an *Iroquois Class* troop transport was not large by current standards, but it was efficiently laid out. The U-shaped layout had two levels of stations, with the captain on a raised platform in the middle rear of it all. Tactical and engineering stations took up the forward section while navigation and weapons occupied the port side and communication, along with other ships systems like damage control, was laid out starboard.

Captain Sophie Lahaie sat in her command chair at the centre of the bridge. Around her, men and women worked quietly but with purpose and speed. Petty Officer second class Chris Altman was on watch at the tactical station. Without taking his eyes off his station monitor, he called out to the officer on watch. "Sir, the battle group is now in standard orbit."

Master Seaman MacDonnell, sitting at the Communication console, spoke up. "Sir, Commander Battle Group sends his compliments and trusts that all is well."

Lieutenant Vickers, the officer on watch, repeated both messages to the captain. Captain Lahaie was right there, but all commands and reports from the bridge officers were repeated on the bridge as standard operating procedure to avoid confusion in a crisis. The watch officer also acted as a filter during combat to avoid information overload.

"Thank you, lieutenant" replied the Captain. "Comm, reply to Commander Battle Group: 'Welcome, we have some news and it cannot wait.'"

"Yes, sir," responded MacDonnell quickly. It was common to drop the feminine address with respect to rank and only use the masculine.

"Message sent and acknowledged, sir."

Captain Lahaie already knew what Hoffman's team had found and what it meant. She had read a preliminary report. All indications were that it was the beginning of something big and she was worried about the future of the Confederation.

She looked at her plot in distraction. She wanted—no, *needed* a diversion. The green icons of the battle group glowed bright in orbit around IM50216. They danced in space and time, interacting with each other, complementing and supporting each other on so many levels. The names and class of each ship were indicated beside its icon. For many, seeing the large plot for the first time could be hypnotic, but right now she had other concerns that would not allow her to become entranced.

Of all these ships, how many good people will we lose? she thought. This was not proving to be the distraction she was looking for.

***

"Hey!"

Heather, still standing in the shower looked up, her hair dripping, and saw Peter entering.

He was grinning like a five-year-old with a secret. Leaning against the half wall that separated the shower stalls from the locker area, he tossed a small sack on the closest bench.

Heather glanced around quickly to see if there was anyone else in the room before answering. "Hey right back at ya."

71

Trying to look tired and disinterested, she closed her eyes, yawned, and stretched.

Peter wasn't buying it. "Who are you trying to kid?" he asked. "Are you trying to skip out on me?"

He was wearing his workout clothes, a T-shirt and shorts. He had already removed his sneakers, tossing them under the bench with his bag. Perspiration glistened on his forehead in the overhead lights and Heather let her eyes and imagination drift down his body, fantasizing that she was a water drop sliding over his well-defined muscles.

He took his shirt off. She watched as a shiver ran down her spine and her thigh muscles tightened. *Son of a bitch, I have it bad,* she mused, a smile licking the corners of her lips.

Peter removed his shorts and stepped into the shower beside Heather. She reached out with both arms and grabbed him, pulling him in close.

She whispered softly in his ear, "I would never try and skip out on you. I thought we were going to meet in the mess."

Her voice trailed off and she kissed him. It was deep, passionate, and longing. Their bodies pressed so close they became one.

Heather felt that for this one moment, this brief instant, no one else existed in the universe. She knew this relationship wasn't supposed to last; it was simply a fulfillment of mutual need. Both Peter and Heather knew this and accepted it as a part of the life they lived—life on the edge, life lived to its fullest.

Right now, nothing mattered as their bodies joined in passion. After a time, they went back to Peter's cabin and made love again, just like it was the first time.

***

Heather woke but did not open her eyes. Her mind was clear, void of thought, but she was aware of the space she occupied and the passing of time. Then faint images of colour drifted past, becoming clearer, more in focus. The fuzzy images slowly coalesced into things familiar: pictures of home, family, friends, and of course, of Peter. Her lips curled into a thin smile.

She slowly opened her eyes one at a time, letting her senses regain consciousness. Her body and mind began to feel relaxed and clear but awake. It was a wonderful feeling after an evening of passion and sleep. No dreams or nightmares, at least none that she remembered.

She focused on Peter lying beside her on the floor. Single beds were not conducive to a restful sleep—or, for that matter, any other activity for two. She watched him breathe, his chest rising and falling in a gentle rhythm that, if she continued staring, would drive her wild again.

"I know you're staring. That's impolite in some circles" he said, his eyes still closed.

"So now I'm impolite?" she responded, jabbing him in the side.

"Okay, I give. You're not impolite—you're a fantastic person with a great bedside manner." He chuckled and gave her a light slap on the butt.

"Hey! And you're a bully."

She rolled to one side and sat up, lightly caressing the offended cheek, her back against the bulkhead.

"What time is it, anyway?" he asked as he sat up against his bunk to look at her.

She fumbled under her clothes and picked up her watch. "It's time for you to get a wall chrono—and time for me to hit the shower again, thanks to you."

She tried to look serious and bitter as she dressed but it came out as a playful smirk. Not the effect she was trying to achieve. Peter picked up on the attempt and feigned a hurtful dejected lover.

She threw a pillow at him as she left the compartment pulling her shirt over her head. "I'm hungry. Meet me in the mess," she said as she left and headed down the hall toward the showers.

***

Captain Thomas stared at Hoffman for some time before realizing what he was doing. He wasn't sure how much emotion he was showing.

"Telling me that good people are going to die is not news, David. What worries me more is the way you said it. What exactly are we talking about here?"

Hoffman did not react to the distress in Thomas's voice. He knew it was his job to ensure people on the *Athabaskan* had the intelligence they needed to complete a mission. That thought would have amused him at another time, but now it was his friend sitting across from him. The information he was about to pass on could get his old friend killed.

"Look, Ian, I wish I wasn't the one to pass this on to you, and this info is still classified, but as a friend."

Thomas knew the implications of his friend's statement.

"The pirates seem to be coordinating their efforts and massing for a major all-out push against the heart of the Confederation. The large number of weapons, ammo and charge packs your people found

74

only confirm what others have also been thinking. We've suspected it since the first cache the Mars Militia found two years ago. We never had confirmation with a live body, however, till—"

"Till my people went in and did such a wonderful job," interrupted Thomas.

Hoffman could only nod.

"You said the Mars Militia found a cache two *years* ago? Why didn't we hear about that till now?" The frustration and anger rising in Thomas's voice was clear.

"It was on a need-to-know basis—" Hoffman started to say but was cut off again.

"I need to know, David! My people need to know!" He paused, taking a cleansing breath, controlling his emotions. Captains were not supposed to get emotional. He knew about the need-to-know policy, something governments, militaries and intelligence agencies had used for centuries to control the flow of information, the flow of secrets.

"I'm sorry, David. I shouldn't take my frustration out on you. I know you would have told me if you could."

"Ian, I'm also sorry. I only wish I could have mentioned it to you. As it stands, we know now what we're up against in greater detail than we could have ever hoped for."

"What *are* we up against?" Thomas asked with some trepidation.

Hoffman reached over and passed his friend a memory chip. Thomas took it and inserted it into a reader taken from his pocket.

Hoffman continued. "Spotswood was a minor player who had delusions of grandeur. He had access to a lot of information during his time onboard a pirate dreadnought. Lucky for us, he kept a good chunk of it—no doubt for the wrong reasons. From what we've been able to decode so far, and with the other data we have possession of, they've been trying to expand their hold on fringe systems for some time. Although they did manage to turn several, it was only a small straw in a very large haystack."

He paused. Thomas was scanning the material.

Hoffman went on. "The pirates came up with some grand idea to expand into other star systems in a systematic way, joining forces as they stretched out their operational bases. That would have worked, but there was a lack of armaments and other supplies. They solved that problem and then they hit on this current scheme. A massive, all-out, coordinated assault on the core systems in the hopes that we would be in such disarray that they could just walk in and take control of the Confederation."

Thomas looked up from the reader, almost laughing. "That's insane! They don't have the logistics for an operation of this magnitude. And where would they get the manpower and arms for that large an op even if they wanted to?"

Hoffman stood, stretched, and took several steps before saying, "Have you ever been to the New Gloucester system?"

Thomas paused to consider before answering, "Only once, and it was long ago. I was there after our cadet training. I was required to see how some of our armaments were produced as part of my officer orientation program. It was touted to be a model mining operation, but that's all I remember. Why?"

New Gloucester was a Terrestrial class planet, close to Mars in size but with a climate very similar to Earth's temperate areas. It orbited a sun younger than Earth's, in a system that had only three developed core planets and three gas giants at the outer edge. Considered a "rim" planet on the outer edge of a lonely spiral arm, it didn't get many tourists. The one thing it did have when it was settled a hundred years ago was an abundant supply of fresh water and plant and basic animal life. It also helped that its solar system was littered with asteroids and planetoids rich in raw materials. Much of that material was used in the production of heavy grade electronics and weapon systems.

Based on the preliminary survey data alone, the decision was made to settle the planet as quickly as a ship could be readied and launched. In fact, the first settlers were sent there to mine the area and develop an infrastructure that could support a weapons industry hungry for more raw materials.

The plan for New Gloucester was flawless in design, if not in execution. The pre-fabricated factory ships sent there orbited the planet and processed the raw ore harvested from the two distinct asteroid belts at three and seven AU distance. Then low-orbit cargo shuttles transported the refined material to the surface of the planet and one of its moons for further refinement and manufacture. The miners and engineers and their families got very rich very fast with the corporation that set the whole operation up, Metcalfe Enterprises.

Thirty-eight years after mining began, however, the bubble burst and the bottom fell out of the arms industry. With the improvements in hyper drives and the inertial compensators that prevented a crew from becoming a mass of wet jell on the far bulkhead, faster travel times to other richer systems were now available.

The mining companies expanded their personal holdings and cut production costs. Metcalfe Enterprises could not afford to continue to mine the

New Gloucester system, with newer more abundant claims opening up much closer to the regular trade routes. Weapons development on the planet tapered off and then closed outright. The next thing to go was the manufacturing capabilities of the planet. Then the ore processing facilities were mothballed and the miners and their families forgotten, except for the twice-yearly supply transport. The speed at which operations closed had caught the settlers off guard.

"So you don't know about the mothballing of the New Gloucester production plants and ore refiners in the past sixty-odd years?" Hoffman asked Thomas.

"I had heard about some problems with mining companies closing some of their facilities but never paid much attention to it," said Thomas. "Nor did I ever think that they would just abandon their people. I suppose that shows my narrow-mindedness with things outside the military."

"Not everything is dependent on the military to function," Hoffman said, not quite keeping his distaste for that kind of attitude out of his voice. "Look, I don't want to come across as an ass, and this in no way reflects on you, but as a society, we humans tend to forget our past. We've been colonizing islands on Earth and then whole worlds since we learned how to sail on water. In all that time, we have only learned one thing: that money and profit is what really matters to the people and corporations that bankroll the colonization programs. The military has been important, don't get me wrong. But the mistake we make in forgetting our sordid past is that we keep repeating it. In this case, when the manufacturing and processing facility closed down, the mining company, Metcalfe Enterprises, stopped sending supply ships to the planet. They figured the Confederation would continue any supply run. They considered the people to be settlers and not employees. Some idiot in Colony Administration then figured the military would take care of the problem, the thought being that this was a corporate world and not a 'real' colony. In the end though, the ones that took care of the problem were the pirates. The military stayed away from the problem and allowed the bureaucracy to sort things out."

Thomas could not believe what he was hearing. He had hoped that humans had overcome the stupidity that almost brought them to the brink. *We polluted our planet, killed off over half the life on Earth in wars and other disasters. Our greed, ignorance, and arrogance caused so much suffering—and still we haven't learned anything. How far have we come?*

"How did the pirates take care of the problem?"

"They saw an opportunity and took over. The information we've pulled from the computers dirt-side and from Spotswood, plus previous intel operations, shows that only a few months after the supply ships stopped, a pirate—and by all accounts a businessman—named General Joseph Lebakie sent in a small battle group. Anyone still walking was pressed into his service. From all reports, it was a slaughter. Those who did not join the general were spaced out his air lock. Spotswood revealed that about forty percent of the remaining settlers joined. This Lebakie restarted up the processing plants in orbit, and once he had enough refined material, rebuilt the design and production facilities. He has all he needs to fulfill his delusions of grandeur. Let's face it—when the Confederation dropped the colony and left the settles at the mercy of Lebakie, what other option did they have?"

Thomas could only agree. "What about the—"
He was cut off mid-sentence when the ship's battle
stations alarm sounded. He stood up and looked over
at Hoffman, who also stood with an equally shocked
expression.

The next announcement came a few seconds
later as both men left the interrogation room quickly.

"General quarters, all hands to battle stations!
This is not a drill! This is not a drill!"

Chapter Seven

"**W**here are they now?" asked Captain Lahaie. Her plot not yet updated with the new data. *Damn it, where did the bastards come from?* she asked herself. "Power up my engines and get me online, people," she ordered, a tinge of frustration beginning to show.

"Tactical now online, captain," said Petty Officer Altman. "I'm sending the feed to your plot now, sir. New targets—one point eight million kilometers and closing."

Three ships of unknown type had somehow snuck in the back door and surprised the battle group. Lahaie sat staring at the red icons on the screen. She was not a happy camper and she needed to know how and why this happened. She did not want to be the one at the receiving end of the battle group commander's wrath for dropping the ball. *Someone was asleep at the switch*, she thought.

"Sound general quarters," she commanded. "Tie me into the command net."

"General quarters, aye," repeated Sub-Lieutenant Carl Vachon, the deck officer on watch.

"We're being painted—missile launch! Impact in ten minutes!" came the startled and excited report from Altman.

"Take evasive measures. Helm, engine status?"

"Engines at eighty percent—enough for maneuvering, Captain," responded the helm officer, Christine Falardeau.

Lahaie stayed calm while she checked her plot and the nav-comm display briefly. *It just wouldn't do*

to show the crew the mess I just made in my pants,
she thought sarcastically.

"Ahead full, on my mark, change course to one twenty-nine point four by three sixty-five point five. Thirty-five degrees positive angle. Mark."

Lahaie turned to the deck officer. "All hands, collision alert. Missile impact in nine minutes."

"All hands, collision alert, missile impact in nine minutes, aye," said a very anxious Vachon, the sound of the klaxon blaring in the background. Modern ships were capable of moving quickly, but from what was essentially an orbital standing start, it took time to power up and accelerate.

Lahaie glanced at the other ships in the battle group. *Summerside, Whitehorse,* and *Nanaimo* were moving to intercept the oncoming barrage of missiles aimed at her and her fellow ships. The smaller Kingston Class cruisers were used for missile defense and close-in support for the battle group.

"All missile defense stations manned and report active tracking on all inbound targets," came the report from tactical.

"CIC reports target ships are older Crusader Class. No other targets in sector. The *Invincible* has launched an answering broadside."

Small thanks for little comforts, thought Lahaie.

She watched on the plot as the *Invincible*'s missiles shot out from their launch tubes at eight times the speed of sound. At a thousand meters, they acquired their targets, taking over from CIC and shipboard tracking. The AI that took control had no feelings of guilt, only a determination to seek out its target and detonate its payload.

A smaller version of the ship's hyper engine kicked in and the missiles hurled themselves at near light speed toward the three pirate cruisers approaching. Even at that speed, at this distance it would take almost six minutes for them to reach their targets.

"Captain," called Master Seaman MacDonnell, "The admiral is moving the transports to the rear. Nav-comm is receiving updated coordinates now."

"Time to missile impact?" asked Lahaie.

"Five minutes. CIC reports that two missile targets are still on our track. *Whitehorse* is launching their intercept missiles."

"Course change. One fifteen point eight by two sixty point oh. Eighty-degree negative angle. Let's not keep the admiral waiting."

Intercept missiles were small and fast. Their seeker warheads were multi-purpose: they would lock onto their targets using either a heat plume signature on atmospheric missiles or a hard sensor lock, or by sensing the displacement in a gravity field.

Lahaie could see from her plot that the antimissile interceptors were doing their job. Of the original load fired at the battle group, only three made it through the defensive screen, and caused only minimal damage on the outer shields of two cruisers, the *Matlan* and the *Horton*.

As the battle group reformed, the broadsides fired by the *Invincible* reached their targets. A second load fired by the destroyer *Aurora* was also about to rain destruction and death. The first missile group exploded, fifteen missiles traveling at near light speeds releasing the power of a small sun in a blink of an eye. The lead cruiser flickered once as the magnetic containment field surrounding her fuel cells released, and then she was gone.

The other two ships started to change course but it was too late. The second group of missiles targeting the far pirate vessel struck home amidships. Air was bleeding from its side like a wounded animal fleeing the hunt. The *Aurora*'s missiles found the last ship as it completed its turn and was about to make the jump to hyper.

A stern shot was the one a ship's captain looked for but rarely received. The weakest part of a ship was left open, and it meant very little armaments to return fire. The results were almost always the same: a nicely worded comm to the family of crewmembers lost. And this case was no different. Someone was going to have to write a lot of condolence letters for this crew.

The battle was over quickly. Lahaie stood and walked over to the communications station, "Stand down from alert stations, secure from general quarters."

She had no emotion in her voice. Two ships destroyed and one crippled. *What was so important to them that was worth giving up their lives? What was on those ships?*

The voice of the communications officer intruded on her. "Captain, Commander battle group is on line for you."

"I'll take it in my ready room," said Lahaie as she walked toward the door.

* * *

Heather was just about to enter the shower when the alert signal sounded. She stopped and looked at the speaker grill nearest her with confused dismay.

"What the hell is going on now?" she asked.

Peter stepped out into the corridor and looked at Heather, still in sight.

"You ever get the feeling we've pissed off someone?" he asked as they started running toward the boat bay.

"So much for that shower," she said as they double-timed it.

Ground combat troops on a navy ship in a space battle have very little to do. The safest place for them is geared up in zero-atmosphere suits and sitting in their drop ships and shuttles in the event of a hull breach. At least they have a chance of survival that way.

Heather and Peter reached the squad room at the same time the collision alert sounded. Troopers filed into the room in various stages of confusion and dress.

"I thought this sector was ours," one trooper said as he snapped closed the seal on his helmet.

Each trooper checked their status lights and their buddies. At the weapons rack brought out by the quartermaster, they picked up the remainder of their kit and made their way to shuttles and drop ships, secure in the knowledge that should the *Athabaskan* disintegrate around them, some of the Regiment may survive.

***

Thomas moved quickly to the lift with Hoffman. "You gotta love this shit. What happened to advance warnings?"

"You tell me. I'll meet you later and we'll ask the admiral. I'm sure he'll be happy to answer that one."

"Ya know, David, sarcasm does not become you."

The lift door opened and Thomas entered while Hoffman continued down the corridor toward his emergency station. Thomas entered the command for the lift to take him to the boat bays, then comm'd the company sergeant and got a status update.

It didn't take long for the lift to reach the lower deck and boat bays. The doors opened and he ran toward his storage locker. Arriving there, he took note of the company readiness.

His portable reader chirped, announcing an incoming message. He opened it and checked the troop list his sergeant had just uploaded. *All personnel present and loading ships*, it said.

Thomas hated this part of combat. Space battles gave him the willies because he was powerless to affect the outcome. He and his people were only along for the ride—and what a ride it could be.

He recalled the last time he'd gone along for this ride on the *Sherwood* in one of his first combat missions. It was an older Highland Class troop transport. The first indication of a problem was when the first of two missiles struck the ship just forward of the stern. The enemy in that case was a rebel colony bent on separating the ruling system government from their heads. It was only supposed to be a small band of unorganized separatists, but it was far from unorganized—and they were well equipped after some government forces defected to their side.

He remembered when the *Sherwood* was rocked by an explosion, and he had felt the vibrations through the deck plates of his drop ship. The abandon ship's call went out and the drop ship hold clamps released. The small drop ship banked violently as secondary explosions went off near by and two troopers were thrown about when their restraints failed. One of the troopers had been impaled on the weapons rack hold-back bar and the other knocked unconscious. Thomas remembered the almost perfect spheres of blood floating around the small compartment in zero-G and the blank stare on the dead trooper's face.

Thomas shook himself back to reality and comm'd his platoon and squad leaders. "Check your people and ensure they're secure. I do not want any free floaters."

He looked at the chronometer above the rear hatch. He had noted the time when he boarded the drop ship, and with a second glance, realized that only two minutes had elapsed. *Time in your mind always takes longer than reality*, he mused.

His thoughts drifted to all those times in combat when a heated battle ended and the mind had a moment to rest. The battle always seemed to go on for hours, yet in reality it had only been a very short time. No more than half the time that the brain perceived. Thomas always marveled at how the human mind processed the passing of time and events, especially under stress.

***

Heather secured her weapon in the bracket and locked herself into the shock frame while the rest of her squad did the same. Sergeant Taylor performed a double-check.

It was rare for Heather to feel vulnerable and exposed, but in this instance, she did. This was different from a combat drop. *At least on a drop we know what to expect,* she thought. *With this, you never knew what was going to happen or when.*

The internal speakers on her helmet came to life, disturbing Heather's thoughts. "All hands brace for impact!"

Heather glanced up and looked at the other troopers. That was the other thing that distinguished this from a combat drop: silence. No one said a word or made a sound. On any other drop there would be the normal background noise of troopers talking or laughing away their nerves. Not now. Each trooper contemplated life and death in their own way. Not much time left for casual conversation.

Her hand started to cramp up and she noticed for the first time how tightly she was holding onto the shock frame. She slowly released her grip and relaxed, letting her body slump back against the restraints.

"Okay, Heather, you're not a rookie and you've done this far too often to let it unsettle you," she said to herself. With the visor on her helmet down, no one could hear her. She glanced down to make sure her comm was not set to transmit.

"All hands stand down. Secure from general quarters," came the announcement everyone wanted to hear.

Slowly, life on the *Athabaskan* went back to a relatively normal state. Kit was returned and stowed, and regular duties resumed.

***

The battle group sorted itself out while recovery operations were carried out. Search and Rescue shuttles from the carrier *Bonaventure* scoured the debris field for survival pods from the two destroyed pirate ships while a combined arms boarding party from the carrier *Bonaventure* and troop carrier

Iroquois boarded the sole surviving combatant. Fighter cover and long range reconnaissance was provided by the Voodoo wing off the *Bonaventure*.

"Voodoo Control, this is Voodoo one five. I've completed my sweep and the backyard is clean. Moving to next waypoint," said Flight Lieutenant Saunders.

She entered the new course and the small fighters AI responded by aiming her in a new direction. Saunders had started out in the armoured corps but only attained the rank of sergeant before getting bored. She had transferred to the air wing and never looked back. She checked her wingman and, after ensuring he was still with her, hit the thruster for maximum burn to the updated coordinates. Other pilots reported a clear sector, but no one let down their guard for a second. This was still a dangerous time for the battle group.

***

On the *Athabaskan,* senior officers from the battle groups, ground forces, and navy began to meet to review the new material and formulate a comprehensive plan for the next stage in the operation. Shuttles were being accommodated in the main cargo hangar and a rotating squad of the *Athabaskan*'s junior officers was tasked to provide escorts for the arriving officers.

On this occasion, Lahaie, the CO of the Terrestrial Light Armoured Guards Colonel Tarik Marouf, and senior officers from the Guard's unit, along with *Athabaskan*'s company, turned out to welcome the battle group commander, Rear-Admiral Walter Affleck.

The admiral's shuttle was on final approach so the greeting party had a few minutes to sort themselves out. The other shuttles were already secured and this would be the last arrival.

At any other time, an arrival of a rear admiral would warrant an honor guard at the very least. This was not a time for ceremony, however, and the grim nature of the task ahead did not put the attendees in good spirits.

Finally the computer AI's voice sounded. "Stand by to secure shuttle."

Lahaie felt the vibrations of the shuttle docking with the recovery arms. It was faint, almost lost amongst the background clutter, but she knew.

She turned to the party of officers. "He's here."

She knew it obvious, but a heads-up to the junior officers was always a good idea.

The amber warning lights on the shuttle bays capture arm triggered, informing all present that the bay doors were about to open. A quick rush of air was all anyone felt as the bay pressure equalized and the main doors lifted, giving everyone access to the shuttle.

The top of a dark gray shuttle became visible as it began rising slowly. The markings of the battle group flagship *York* was just coming into view. A black shield with a stylized lion standing guard over Earth with wings on either side was emblazoned on the upper aft section of the shuttles tail. Vents could be seen purging on the opposite starboard side.

As the movement of the shuttle ceased, Lahaie walked to the rear hatch and waited just off to one side, standing at parade rest. The inner door closed beneath the shuttle and the bay indicators showed the outer safety door closing. Everyone eyed the shuttle hatch lock as it cycled and the rear hatch began to open.

Marouf leaned toward his aide. "Is Hoffman ready to present?" he whispered.

"Yes, sir. I spoke with him just before the admiral's shuttle docked."

Lahaie looked toward Marouf, whose quick nod told her that the briefing was ready. There was nothing more she could do and not much more she could add to improve either their odds in battle or the reaction of the senior command staff to the information they were about to receive. She suspected, however, that Affleck already had a good idea what would be divulged.

The shuttle's hatch warning chime stopped after it was fully opened. Admiral Walter Affleck was not a tall man, but he was imposing. He had spent part of his long career in the ground forces before transferring to the navy. He spent many of his off hours in the gym building his body and the rest of the time building his mind.

Senior officers don't need to be told to show their commander respect. Everyone came to attention with the snap of a whip. The admiral returned the salute and continued down the shuttle's rear hatch.

On either side, two bodyguards from the Joint Task Force flanked him. The JTF were the elite of the TAF and its members were experts in their field. They provided security, recon, extraction forces, and special operation missions. Extra security had been mandatory for all admirals since the *Eridan* mutiny thirty-two years earlier.

"Welcome aboard, admiral," said Lahaie. "I wish we could have rolled out the red carpet for you."

"Nonsense, Sophie. It's always good to see you and the *Athabaskan*. A red carpet would only get in the way." Affleck reached out and shook Lahaie's offered hand. He turned to Marouf and, after a parade ground salute, shook his hand and offered a warm smile. "Tarik, how've you been? Still chasing women and blowing up buildings?"

"Admiral, if I were still chasing women you'd be right beside me and if I was blowing things up you would help me wire it."

"We have to have that drink we keep putting off and show these young bucks how to have a good time," said the admiral. "But before any of that, let's see if we can't put some bad guys away."

"Sounds good to me, sir."

Lahaie and Marouf introduced the assembled staff. Many Affleck knew on sight, and he remembered the details of their service records that even they had forgotten. Others were so new to their rank or posts that he had not had time to make their acquaintance. He made a mental note to review those files as soon as possible.

"This way, admiral," said Lahaie as she ushered the group to the lift that would take them to the conference room.

The admiral put both hands behind his back as they walked. "This business is a pain in the ass. We need to perform an enema on these bastards, and soon. Trade is down forty-five percent overall in the past month alone, and in zones where incidents have occurred, it's reduced by over seventy percent. The shipping guilds are demanding action and frankly, I'm out of options. The admiralty has placed this on the top of their list for good reason."

No one disagreed. He continued. "The Confederation leadership is calling for blood and, quite frankly, do not give a rat's ass one way or another whose blood they get. I would just as soon it not be mine, thank you, or anyone else I know."

He smiled. The others laughed quietly. Death was never funny, but in times of stress you tended to find humor in many places.

The lift slowed gently to a halt and the doors slid open. Lahaie was the first out, with the admiral following. At the large conference room. Two JTF troopers were already posted on either side of the outer door and two on the inside, all with loaded sidearm and automatic bead rifles at the ready.

The conference room was full, every seat occupied by senior officers from each ship in the battle group, both ground and navy. Their relaxed battle dress meant the room was a bland mix of navy black, army green, and tan. There were almost as many conversations as there were officers and the array of topics being discussed ranged from the current mission, personnel, sports, entertainment events and more.

Lahaie entered the conference room in front of the Admiral and called for attention. "Room!"

Everyone stood to attention, and the background conversation and noise suddenly hushed. The admiral and his party entered, and the JTF corporal closed the door, locking everyone inside.

Affleck proceeded to the head of the conference table. "Thank you, please be seated," he said.

Everyone sat and eyed the admiral expectantly.

"You have all seen the preliminary briefing, so I won't go into that aspect of the report, other than to say this: we have a situation that is rapidly getting out of control. This battle group has been tasked with the mission of bringing things back under control. I have been pleased with our initial success. However, now comes the hard part. We can not afford to relax and let our guard down."

He scanned the room for effect. He knew that what he just said was both necessary and unnecessary. This group did not have to be reminded of the obvious. Sometimes, however, a reminder provided emphasis.

"I'll turn the meeting over to Lieutenant-Commander Hoffman."

"Thank you, sir," Hoffman responded. He stood and nodded to his assistant, who activated the holo projector at the center of the conference table. The overhead lights dimmed, leaving only the rim pocket lamps and a holo image of a star system.

"This is the New Gloucester system."

Hoffman highlighted the planetary system and increased the magnification to show the system's sun and first four planets with the asteroid belt on the outside edge.

"What we know is this: the planet we now orbit, IM50216, was being used as an arms storage and launch point for the pirates—until we interfered with their plan." A few snickers were heard in the audience.

"The three ships that entered the system were bringing in two commodities, more weapons, and fresh combat troops to be housed and trained dirt side. They did not expect to find our little party here, which suggests the planetary base commander did not have time to send a distress call. We also know from an examination of the surviving ships' comm logs that they also did not get a chance to warn their superiors of our presence. The estimated loss of personnel on the three enemy cruisers we engaged is counted roughly at five thousand. The bulk of the ground troops were in the two destroyed ships."

The significant loss of life did not sit well with anyone at the table. While pirates were considered the scum of humanity, they were still humanity.

Hoffman continued. "As you are aware from the prelim briefing material I transmitted to your readers earlier, New Gloucester was an arms manufacturing and storage depot until it was closed by Metcalfe Enterprises."

Ian Thomas sat back in his chair. He had heard this part already and did not care to listen to it again. It only emphasized some of the worst aspects of humanity, not to mention the reason he was wearing a uniform.. It did renew his appreciation of his friend's talents, however. Intelligence was not an exact science, but Hoffman had an affinity for accurate interpretation. *That's really what it is: an interpretation of facts not yet in evidence,* Thomas mused. Hoffman was able to use available data—in this case, information gathered from Fitzpatrick's raid, the interrogation of Spotswood, intelligence already gathered from previous missions, and data files downloaded from the surviving pirate cruiser—and put together a picture that was remarkably true to life. The fact the three ships showed up when they did was just sheer luck. No one could have predicted the three ships entering the system at the same time as the battle group.

Hoffman spoke clearly. "It looks as if the pirate leadership is almost ready to launch operations against the heart of the Confederation and our government. This is the only conclusion that can be gleaned from the wealth of evidence gathered."

That last bit of news rousted Thomas from his thoughts. "Our proposed plan is to shut down the factory on New Gloucester and destroy any trace of pirate activity as well as cripple their ability to fabricate replacements," Hoffman went on. "We have an idea of their main base of operations and it is hoped that information still being processed and gathered from the New Gloucester navigation and comm logs of the surviving cruiser will confirm this."

Skeptical murmurs were heard around the room. Hoffman's assistant changed the view on the holo projection and red and yellow icons appeared.

"We have also confirmed the following information using stealth probe fly-in plus data from the current mission," Hoffman said. "The pirates have eight dreadnought class ships of the line. They are stationed in a parking orbit around the second moon and the planet itself. They also have one replenishment freighter here."

He pointed out an elliptical orbit with a light pen. "Ten battleships here—and cruiser and corvette size ships that are currently being used to ring the system as pickets. We also know they have old ore freighters that they've converted into troop carriers, but we do not have estimated numbers on them at this time. They are indicated in yellow."

"Is that all? Well, and here I thought they had a large force," said Captain Bonspiel of the dreadnought *Prince Rupert* in his best sarcastic tone.

"No one said this would be a cake walk, captain," the admiral responded as he stood, interrupting Hoffman's response. Rebuked, Bonspiel sank back into his chair.

"Before I ask the lieutenant-commander to continue, I want to point out some 'truths' that some of us have forgotten or may not have been aware of," Affleck said. "First, this violence ends now. The Confederation bureaucracy has tied the local system administrator's hands with tape of every colour imaginable. This has created a situation where pirate law has rained supreme. Local governors were not empowered nor provided with resources to stem the systematic abandonment of fringe worlds which became a haven and lucrative breeding ground for the pirates."

Affleck's tone was harsh and biting—as he intended. "Second, the ability for the TAF to respond to the threat has been weakened over the past two decades. Many of you have seen friends and colleagues go on half pay because of cuts to our operating budgets. Ships and other resources have been mothballed and new line ships under construction in the yard have been halted. This next bit is going to come as a shock to all of you: I have been authorized to inform you that as of now, these setbacks have come to an end. The bureaucracy within the Confederation government has been informed of some changes effective immediately. There has been a shakeup and the newly elected leadership has, so far, shown some backbone and fired or arrested those in the public service who could not accept the reality of the situation. In essence, we are seeing a purging of the bilges."

This news had the effect of making some around the table very nervous. Not all officers earned their rank through ability. Family connections and bribery worked just as well sometimes.

"The corruption and graft, along with the old boys' network, is now at an end," the admiral finished. He leveled a gaze at each person in the room.

Lieutenant-Commander Hoffman took the lead from the admiral and proceeded with the briefing.

"You are all under the impression that military intelligence sometimes is a contradiction in terms, and I would agree with that statement. I did not start out in, or some will say with, intelligence."

That at least put a smile back on some of their faces, he thought.

"That being said, I am confident of the following—the commander of the planetary garrison did not send a message or warning of any kind to his leadership. Also, the three ships, as mentioned previously, did not get a mayday out and according to the surviving ship logs and interrogations, will not be considered overdue for another two weeks. This presents us with an opportunity that my colleague's and I believe this battle group should exploit."

Hoffman finished and returned to his chair. He was not totally surprised with the reaction of some of the officers present. While the vast majority wanted to ram their main batteries down the throats of every pirate, some would rather play it safe and keep the status quo. These tended to be the very officers the admiral had warned about a few moments ago. *Who wants to play it safe?* he thought. *Where's the fun and adventure in that?*

The meeting proceeded. In the middle of planning for the upcoming battle, a messenger interrupted and presented the admiral with a data chip. This in itself was highly unusual. If the message was important enough to interrupt the briefing, the admiral could have been comm'd from the bridge.

The admiral did not look surprised, however— more as if he was expecting the intrusion. He inserted the chip into a reader and reviewed the contents. Then, to everyone's shock, he ordered the two JTF troopers standing guard outside to come inside.

One does not normally expect to have two armed troopers dressed in full combat gear invited into a high-level battle group meeting. When they leveled their bead rifles and took the safety off, well, that got everyone's pulse racing.

Affleck announced the contents of the chip: warrants had been sworn out by the TAF Command and signed by the civilian Minister for Defense and Prime Minister for the immediate arrest of two senior ship's captains on charges of corruption, bribery, theft, acceptance of stolen material, conspiracy to commit theft, and conduct to the prejudice of good order and discipline. The warrant also included several lower ranked officers.

No one was more surprised than the two captains in question. Dunn and Delroy were led away in irons by the JTF troopers. The admiral gave field promotions to their first officers after the disgraced captains were removed.

The warrant also included several lower ranked officers. Those present were taken into custody while others would soon come to learn their fate.

Chapter Eight

Field General Mackenzie King walked down the sparsely appointed hallway with a reader in his left hand. His uniform was pressed and the seam on his pants was crisp and straight. The general was early for his next meeting and so took his time as he walked. It was the first time he had ever noticed how empty the hall and corridors really were.

Guards were posted at every entrance and exit, as well as at each fire station along the long corridor. All were well armed with weapons at the ready, some wearing power armour. The walls, a light gray-blue, and the dark gray low pile carpeting did not improve the cold, stark look and feel of the place.

"We really do need someone to come in and brighten up the place," the general said quietly to himself as he walked. He smiled inwardly but on the outside, his face was as cold as the walls around him.

Near the end of the corridor, his pace slowed even more. Directly ahead was a security desk with one guard seated at a console, while five others stood at parade rest with side arms holstered and bead rifles at the ready. Each guard wore a full combat load with the helmet visor down so the general could not see faces or their expressions.

I doubt very much they even have human emotions and expressions, he thought. *It's astounding what some will do for credits every month.*

He stopped at the desk, and as he did, the guards all came to attention. *At least they know their place in this universe*, he reflected with wicked satisfaction.

The seated guard looked up at the visitor and without preamble, reached out. The general handed over his chip. Encoded upon the fire-, blast- and water-resistant chip was the complete medical history, DNA, retinal and fingerprint scan of its owner. And this was only one part of the process.

The general placed both hands on a scanner and looked into a desktop viewer for the retinal scan. The guard looked at his reader and back at the general. Satisfied, he removed the chip from the reader access port and handed it back. "Please remove your side arm, general. The storage bin is on that table."

The guard pointed to the opposite side of the corridor and waved the general through. King unholstered his personal weapon, checked the safety, and removed the power pack and clip, placing it into one of the bins.

In spite of the security, the general could imagine several ways that any determined group or individual could cause massive damage and casualties. This current level of security, though he'd admit it to no one but himself, was to protect those inside from rogue elements of their own people.

He passed through a sensor gate that scanned for weapons, chemicals, drugs, and anything that could be used as a weapon. *I'm glad bad news can't be scanned,* he thought.

He walked past three more guards. At the end of the corridor, two guards in power armour stood on either side of French doors. Just in front of the doors was a desk with a desktop reader and a pile of data chips along with a portable reader storage rack. Sitting on the other side of the desk was a diminutive sergeant who looked more intimidated about the pile of work in front of him than the approaching general. The sergeant looked up, then stood and saluted. The two guards in power armour also came to attention. Returning the salute, the General was waved in.

King opened the right door and walked into a large but almost empty office that matched the hallway in its starkness. He had of course visited here many times before, and each time would fantasize about how he would redecorate. The aimless thought was simply way to relieve the stress and pressures of the day. It did not help that, although he was consistently under strain, he seemed to be under the most pressure when he visited here.

He closed the door as he entered. Off to his right sat a long conference table that could seat up to twenty people. A large desk sat near the rear of the office, in front of two floor-to-ceiling rectangles— monitor screens built to create the illusion of windows. The image of tranquil scenes could be changed depending on mood or time of day. The deception also served to hide armoured exterior walls. Other than some small chairs and the desk, the room was void of any other furnishings. The walls, minus the "windows," were bare.

Sitting in what looked liked a very uncomfortable desk chair was the man King was here to see. The general always thought the office was in stark contrast to its owner. *He's the most colourful human I have ever met,* he mused. The man was short, lean and well-built, starting to lose some of his jet-black hair. He stood with a wide but genuine smile that showed a set of white teeth that could almost illuminate the room. The two men embraced each other and shook hands from the elbow down.

Taking a step back, Joseph Lebakie said, "Mackenzie, you are always a pleasant distraction to an otherwise dull and lifeless day."

He pointed to one of the couches. Both men were about to sit when a knock was heard at a side door.

"Come in, Gary," answered Lebakie.

"You can see through walls now?" King joked. "You really are doing well for yourself."

"Years of practice. I called Gary right after the guard passed you in. I thought some real coffee would go over well with bad news."

Just as King cocked an eyebrow, Corporal Gary Clark opened the door and wheeled in a serving tray with a carafe of fresh coffee, water, a tray of quarter-cut sandwiches, and a small plate of what looked like chocolate mint wafers. The corporal wheeled the tray next to the couch and after coming to attention, left without a word.

King retrieved a cup and a sandwich. "I was about to ask you why you think this is about bad news."

He poured coffee for Lebakie and handed it to him, then picked up a second cup, poured some for himself and sat back down after adding sweetener.

Taking a sip, Lebakie shook his head. "How long have we known each other?" he asked. "Outside of the odd casual event and gatherings, you've never met me here unless it was business, and that's often an indication of bad news for someone. What did you call this place once—a cross between nothing and nowhere? Listen," Lebakie said as he smiled, "I'm not as insulated as you and my staff tries to keep me. I do get out once and a while."

"I'll be sure your staff knows that," said King as he passed the reader in his hand to his friend. "It's

103

not a problem yet, but I am concerned. The supply ships sent out to IM50216 have not reported back and they're overdue by three hours. Also, that idiot Spotswood has not comm'd and this is his second missed scheduled check-in; it was due five and a half hours ago, local time. I don't like this feeling I'm getting."

Lebakie snorted. "I should have spaced that fool when I had a chance."

"But you didn't—why?"

"Why waste a live body, that's why. Look, that shit-for-brains was a useless navigation officer. He was a less than useless second officer. But he *is* a competent administrator. He kept that planet running and did manage to expand its operational base."

He took a mouthful of his coffee before continuing. "I assume you've confirmed the data and timings?"

King nodded.

"Have you checked with the rim outposts to see if it's a localized communication problem? No, don't answer that. I can see by the look on your face you've already done that."

King was concerned but not overly panicked at this point. Losing communication with a planet was almost as common as there are planets. Sunspots from nearby stars, plasma storms, even a heavy concentration of dust particles, could knock out a secure transmission site from a distant planet. While good shielding could diminish the problem, it could not completely prevent it.

King stood, walked over to the coffee urn, and poured himself another cup. "Do you want a refill?"

Lebakie did not answer right away; he was looking into his cup without really seeing it. King repeated his offer and cleared his throat.

"What? Oh, sorry. Yes, I think a refill would be good right now. I was just thinking—if the Confederation *did* take Spotswood and the supply ships out, they might have intel on New Gloucester."

King looked like he'd swallowed the coffee and the cup at the same time. "Now I never said that New Gloucester has been compromised. Even thinking the worst, Spotswood did not have much data on our operations, and data on the three ships would have been wiped automatically on capture or destruction. At the most, it would only come across as a navigation waypoint."

"A waypoint to where? No, I agree, it's too soon to hit the panic bells," Lebakie said quickly.

He reached over to a small side table and picked up a remote unit. After entering his code, he brought up a holo map of the sector on a screen.

"New Gloucester is out in the middle of nowhere. My concern is that *any* reference to it will raise suspicion." He narrowed the field of view on the holo map.

"The Confederation has gotten too big and has never supported its colony worlds. New Gloucester is only one of many. Since the isolated worlds are out of the normal trade routes, any increase in activity will alert the authorities."

King stirred. "You don't have to sell me on the cause, Joe. We go back a long way and I trust your judgment. That said, this organization has also gotten too big too fast, and the cracks are starting to show. How many captured ships have had their crews spaced? How many deaths are we responsible for?"

Ah! It comes out now, thought Lebakie. *This is what's been bothering you, my friend. But does that mean that you're a liability to me now? Are you getting too soft to make the tough decision?*

"We are not responsible for any deaths, General King. We were not the ones to start down this road. The blasted Confederation and their ill-conceived expansion policy started this," Lebakie said, raising his voice but not quite shouting. The words were bitter and heated and he regretted saying them even as he spoke them.

King sat motionless, unblinking but thoughtful. His emotions were clouded and confused. Lebakie, his oldest and dearest friend, was now disappointed in him, and that could be very unhealthy. *I'm not so thrilled about the situation either,* he thought. *But I at least know where and when to draw the line.*

Finally King spoke. "In my humble opinion, sir" —he let the emphasis on 'sir' drag like nails on a chalkboard— "we, this organization, have crossed a fine line between fighting for justice and becoming thugs out for cold-blooded revenge and profit."

Lebakie cut in. "I don't think you and I are so far apart on this, Mackenzie. I'm sorry for the harsh tone just now. While I do not take back what I said, I could have said it much better. I know you, and many others, are very displeased with what some of our people are doing, and I don't like it either. But for what it's worth, the random attacks are having the desired effect of keeping people away from this and other important sectors. They also keep the project quiet by sending the TAF searching in other directions. No meddlesome neighbors to contend with, no authorities to bribe, and no questions to answer."

Pausing to collect his thoughts, Lebakie continued. "Look, I hate what's happened just as much as you do, but I am confident it will end very soon. You know we planned to get rid of any 'hired'

106

liabilities after the operation. But doing it too soon could jeopardize all that we've worked so hard for."

King stood and walked over to the coffee service. After placing his cup on the cart, he spoke quietly and with little emotion without looking directly at Lebakie. "I agree with most of what you just said. However, I will never see the spacing of crew as justified."

Lebakie was about to jump in, but King continued. "Let me finish, Joe, please. I know you don't approve either, but you do condone it by not stopping it. You have your reasons, and from your perspective, they are valid. The two of us go back a long time and have been through too much together to let this disagreement come between us. And so I want to assure you that I am still, as I have always been, behind you and the ideals of this mission one hundred percent."

King finished and waited for a response. *He can respect the difference of opinion between us or kill me on the spot*, he thought. *I've said my piece and I can't do or say anything else, but it had to be done.*

Lebakie did not wait to speak. "I want to make this clear: I have never doubted you or your commitment to this operation, or to me, my friend. We are still friends and I value your opinion, your open and frank honesty, and your friendship. I need someone at my side I can depend on and trust and I have that someone here."

"Thank you for that," said King, relieved. "I felt that things were getting out of control and I would have been remiss if I kept silent. I have a meeting with department heads soon. I should be going. Any suggestions on the current situation?"

"Let's hold off on any action that would alert the Confederation, assuming they have not been tipped off. If we don't hear from Spotswood or the transports by tomorrow at this time, we'll assume something went wrong and put our contingency plan in place."

"Thanks, Joe. I hoped you would understand. And I meant what I said—I'm on the team one hundred percent," said King as the men shook hands.

As King left the office, Lebakie walked over to his desk, sat down and entered the access code of someone in another part of the building. *I know you too well, my friend,* he thought. *You are with us, but for how long? Can I take the chance that you might bail on the project?*

Lebakie's thoughts were interrupted as the screen came alive and someone said, "Yes, sir?"

"I have a job for you…"

Chapter Nine

Admiral Affleck stood straight, his hands clasped behind him, as he looked at the holo map of the New Gloucester system. It was a cliché posture worthier of a holo novel with characters out of the early twenty-first century, but he did not care. Around him, the men and women on watch in the combat control centre worked in near silence and efficient pride.

And they should be proud of themselves, he thought. *They have served the TAF and the Confederation well.*

An inner glow came over him as he looked at each person in the CIC. *Much has been lost to get this far, and more good people will be lost before the final destination is reached. But we have come a long way. Although we still have a lot to learn and a long journey ahead of us as a species, we are headed in the right direction. At least I hope to the gods that it's the right direction.*

His thoughts were interrupted when an Ensign handed him a reader. "Sir, *Rainbow Warrior* reports departure point is clear."

"Thank you," said the admiral. "Petty-Officer St. Kitts, my compliments to the flag bridge, bring the battle group on line, recall all pickets and sentry ships. When ready, make for departure point Alpha Two One Seven and prep for hyper jump. Set course for the Scotia system, best possible speed. We have

109

to pick up something there before our final destination to New Gloucester, please also let them know I'm on my way."

"Aye sir, departure point Alpha Two One Seven and prep for hyper jump. Course is for Scotia at best possible speed. Aye," repeated Petty-Officer St. Kitts as he comm'd the flag bridge two decks below.

The flagship *York* was an older Resolution Class super-dreadnought, refitted with updated weapons as well as bays and launchers. The ship had also been updated with new sensor arrays and a communication suite suitable for a flagship.

The Resolution Class had a long history that its crew was proud of. The *Fort Resolution*, the original ship of the class, was destroyed in a battle that saved the Fisher Strait colony worlds in an attack by a still unknown alien species. The heroic work of the captain and crew of the *Fort Resolution* in saving the colony was the TAF's first major skirmish in deep space and marked the foundation for real expansion of the Confederation. Prior to this, the Confederation could not guarantee the safety of the new colonies, but the *Fort Resolution* proved the viability of a deep space navy fleet capable of defending the borders, interest, and citizens of the Confederation.

Affleck exited the lift and walked down the short corridor to the flag bridge. He received a salute from the JTF guard at the door and his escorts fell into their assigned posts, one inside and one outside the entryway of the flag bridge.

"Admiral on the bridge," said one of the admiral's staff.

"What's the status of my battle group, ladies and gentlemen?" said the admiral as he sat down in his command chair.

The command chair sat at the centre rear of the flag bridge. Around him were four flat plasma screens that he could configure independently as he required. Currently he had one configured with an overlay of the battle group showing ship location, name, type, and status. A second screen showed a mirror image of the navigation station. Beside that was the tactical screen, split to show weapons status broken down by ship in the battle group along side of a tactical plot of the target based on intel from previous drone missions. It was old data, but it provided a base to begin. His fourth screen was blank and would not be active until it was absolutely necessary.

After reviewing the data for a few seconds he switched the screen off. Affleck always felt overwhelmed at the beginning of every mission. Information overload was always a possibility. Would he start to second-guess his own orders with too much conflicting information at his disposal? He signaled to his steward for coffee, which did not take long to arrive.

Captain Kugong, the chief of staff, answered the admiral. Kugong had been with the admiral for the past three years as his chief of staff. Prior to that, Kugong was on the flag's staff as the communications officer; his last post before becoming the chief of staff had been as senior tactical officer.

"All ships report ready for jump, sir. Lead ships are as per order of march: *Victoria*, *Muncton*, *Huron*, *Whitehorse* and *Corner Brook*. Supply replenishment ship *Provider* has made its rounds and all ships report stores and deliverables have been topped up."

Kugong continued his report after a brief pause, "Group-Captain Hammer reports all fighter squadrons are geared up and standing by for action. Those are his words, sir."

Both men smiled at that. Group-Captain Hammer was a top-notch fighter pilot and his rise through the ranks was not only exemplary, but colourful as well. Before joining the battle group, Hammer had been knocked down in rank a number of times for conduct not becoming an officer. He was a rare breed, though, and felt that the most important thing in life was life itself, not the accumulation of wealth or rank.

Being in the fighter wing, every day could very well be his last day as the average life span for a fighter pilot in action was less than ten minutes. Newbies who lasted more than two minutes in their first dogfight were considered fully qualified veterans. Hammer had over two hundred hours in combat and his survival was nothing short of a miracle. Some called him the Hammer of God, a title he never liked. He was always Affleck's first choice for the Air Boss position in the battle group and the admiral had to pull many strings to get him assigned.

"All squadrons report full compliment of combat fighters but we have three recon fighters down for maintenance. They should be operational by the last waypoint. We also received a message packet just before departure and Rear-Admiral Leslie Martin sends her compliments. She will RV with us in the Scotia system per your request. Fleet Command also responded to your assessment and signed off on your action plan."

Kugong finished his report and passed the reader to the admiral, who took it and scanned it quietly in silence. He knew the report was complete, but he wanted to think for a moment, finally saying,

"Convene a command staff meeting four hours after RV with Admiral Martin's force. Thank you."

Affleck deliberated the pros and cons of the plan of battle in his mind. Having a second battle group was going to make for a more straightforward mission, but it still would not be effortless or uncomplicated. Much could change the outcome, and any plan had to have flexibility built into it. *Am I missing anything in the current strategy?* he thought. The pirates had amassed a formidable fleet in New Gloucester and their determination would present great challenges. Weighing tactics good and bad helped him to focus and relax—something he had learned to do years earlier at the academy.

A reader was handed to Kugong, and after reading its contents, he said, "All fighter cover recovered and system pickets have laid a full sensor package. New course plotted and laid in, ready for your orders, sir."

"Thank you, Flint. Sound general quarters and let's get it on," commanded Affleck.

***

On board the *Athabaskan*, Heather and her squad were checking their equipment for the upcoming mission. She wasn't sure what that mission would entail at this point, but from all the preparation and all the ammunition and power packs being distributed, it had to be a big one.

Looks like we may get to take the battle to the pirates for a change, she thought. Peter was in one corner of the drop bay receiving power armour. He would replace Trooper Marek Whitehead, whose memorial had been held the day before.

Peter felt uncomfortable filling his spot on the roster, but he would do the job and do it well. Ritchie was checking Peter out on the armour. So far, all Peter had managed to do was destroy one packing crate of lubricant, which of course caused the launch bay decking to require major steaming and resurfacing.

"Come on, Peter, locking the sensor track isn't that hard," came Ritchie's strained voice over the comm as he ran over the target sensor lock process again.

"Not that hard for you, maybe, but the standard training period for power armour is two months. I'm cramming this in, what, two weeks?" Peter sounded winded, but not ready to pack it in just yet.

"Quit complaining, you wimp. I could override your left leg servo like this and watch you dance, just for fun." A wicked smile crept over Ritchie's face. He used the trainer remote link and took over the left leg servo on Peter's power armour raising it high. Alternating between legs, arms, and torso, Ritchie manipulated the controls to turn Peter into a life-size marionette. The worst for Peter was when one leg went left and the other right. Quite frankly, no one could ever remember seeing power armour doing the splits like that!

Other troopers in the launch bay stopped what they were doing and sat back to watch Peter yell and complain. Everyone was howling with laughter. Even Heather even had to laugh until tears came to her eyes. It felt good to laugh so much—not a little chuckle, but a good old-fashioned belly laugh. Laughing was therapeutic for everyone.

Much of Heather's platoon had gone to see the ship's analyst, including Heather herself. It was not unusual for TAF personnel to see the analyst after a mission. It helped them to cope with the stresses of combat and life. At one time in human history, a soldier would never admit to fatigue, stress, and post traumatic disorders. It would be seen as cowardice or laziness, and neither would it do your career any good. Now it had become second nature. The old saying "a healthy body, a healthy mind" held true, especially considering the consequences of neglecting the mind.

Sergeant Taylor entered the bay just in time to see Peter do an Irish jig in power armour.

"Now that's something I doubt I will ever see again," he said to himself as he removed his soft cap and scratched his head. Still, while Peter's gyrations were quite entertaining, he knew he had to put an end to it.

"What the hell is going on here?" he barked.

As soon as Heather heard Taylor's yell, she closed the case of power packs, loaded them on the pallet, and made herself scarce. Others did likewise in a flurry of activity to finish up and escape.

Ritchie was not so fortunate.

"What do you think you are doing, trooper?"

Dropping the remote, Ritchie stood and faced the sergeant at attention, "Sergeant, just having some fun at Trooper Talbot's expense. Ah, don't you mean 'corporal,' sergeant?"

"Keep this up, Ritchie, and I will mean 'trooper.' Just get him checked out and store the gear. Then go get some R and R," said Taylor. He walked off as Peter stood panting and out of breath. Taylor only shook his head, a pleased smile crossing his lips. It was good to see some of the strain and anxiety wear off.

There was always some nervous tension in the troops before any mission but there was no hiding the fact that this one was going to be on a scale the majority of troopers had never seen. Most of the regiment's troops had eight combat drops or less, and although considered seasoned, they had never gone into such a large operation. The largest drop many would have been involved in was a company size.

Fitzpatrick entered the bay at the same time and met Taylor at the lift doors. "How goes the battle, sergeant?"

"The squad is almost finished checking out their kit. Ritchie is terrorizing Talbot to the amusement of the squad and all is right with the universe."

Taylor motioned over his shoulder at Ritchie and the suit of power armour still hanging at a most unusual angle. A disembodied voice was coming from within, yelling something about the sexual habits of someone's mother. Fitzpatrick chuckled.

"Any word on the mission brief?" asked Taylor.

"I'll let you know as soon as I find out myself. Carry on" said Fitzpatrick.

As he left the bay he began to laugh out loud.

***

Heather entered her cabin and flopped on her bed. She reached down, undid her combat boots, and kicked them off. Closing her eyes, she began to feel relaxed, almost to the point of drifting off. She didn't want to sleep yet, however. Going on a mission as big as this only made her think of her family.

Originally from the Mars colony, Heather's family moved to New Kanpur, over thirty-eight light years from Sol, to find a better life. They did find it, though it was difficult in the beginning. Survivors from the original Indo-Pakistan-China conflict on earth originally settled the New Kanpur colony to get

116

away from the wasteland that was once their home. In the beginning, they did not welcome anyone coming from other parts of Earth. Heather's family was one of the first "outside" groups to join that colony and, although two generations removed from Earth, they were still seen as outsiders. It took some time, but the various groups eventually started working together to improve their living conditions.

Heather wanted to send a message to her parents who still lived on New Kanpur. She knew the message would not get to them for some time but the fact that she had sent one would make her feel much better and put her mind at rest should anything happen.

She rarely thought of the possibility of injury or death, but she was pragmatic about it. She did not believe in a god and felt that you had better make your time in the universe count for something—not for the benefit of an afterlife, but for her own piece of sanity and satisfaction here and now.

She drew all of her energy together and sat up. Sleep was very tempting, but this had to be done now if she wanted to get it out on the next message packet.

Sliding down to the end of the bed beside the small table with the comm unit, she entered her access code, started a new file, and began dictating the letter.

"Hi, Mom and Dad, it's been too long since we last spoke. I wish I could have been there for your birthday, Dad, but you know how it is in the TAF. 'Busy' is an understatement. I miss you guys so much and I'm looking forward to coming home on leave—which will be in two months, seventeen days, six hours, and thirty-seven minutes. Not that I'm counting or anything." She smiled at her own attempt at humor before continuing.

"I'm doing fine, so don't worry—although I'm sure you're doing enough for the whole family, Mom," she said in mock admonishment. "I just wanted to update you on my life, and you can return the favor on your next message out to me. My last mission went well. The LT gave me a commendation, along with the rest of the platoon, of course, but I can't talk about it in this message, I'll tell you when I get home. It felt good to be recognized for the effort, but credits would have been good too. The local shipboard pub doesn't take paper scroll commendations and it is nice to get out once and a while. Mom, before you go off thinking the worse, I'm being careful—I would never get inebriated shipboard. It just wouldn't be ladylike.

"You'll like this one, Mom: I'm seeing someone. Yes, it's the same person I mentioned in my last letter to you. I know the last time I said it was just casual and that we needed each other's company, but I've been thinking of him a lot these days. I'm not sure if it's a good thing or not. We do enjoy each other's company and we seem to have similar interests. Peter and I can have the odd scrap once and a while, but not often and not too close together. So that must be a good thing. I can just see Dad in the background shaking his head and saying 'Don't get too close, you know you're combat troops and that life can be fleeting.' You are saying that, aren't you, Dad—or at least thinking it?"

Heather lay back against the bulkhead smiling. "I've thought about it myself several dozen times over and I know Peter has too. Yes, Mom, we've spoken about it. At first, we decided to keep it as a close friendship. We could spend time with each other when we both needed, without any strings or baggage. Now I'm starting to believe it's moved to another level."

Heather did not have any apprehension about talking to her parents about this subject. Secrets were not tolerated, as her family believed they led to disharmony and mistrust. Her parents raised her to be open and honest, but with tact and discretion.

As she continued her letter, she paused and thought about her feelings for Peter, life, death, her parents, her friends, and her job.

"I'll have to explore this other level I think we're on in more detail. I guess I'm not sure if it's love, lust, or something else." She paused again. "It'll be fun trying to find out, though!" she said, almost laughing out loud.

A bout of loneliness threatened to overtake her emotions before she was able to wrestle it back down. She would never change who or what she was and what she did for a living, but she missed the conversations she had with her parents.

"I just wanted to let you know how I am and that I love you guys and miss you both a lot. I'll get out there on leave as I said I would and look forward to the rest. The last couple of missions have been rough and this next one will be even tougher, but I'm only telling you that so you know that I understand the reality. Don't worry too much about me and I love you both. I'll send another letter after the mission, but I don't know when that will be at this point. Take care, both of you, and kiss Aunt Sissy when you see her. I trust she's still on that vacation cruise. Love you."

She ended the letter, closed the file with the destination address, and pressed the send key. She immediately felt better, and sleep came quickly as she slid back to the centre of her bunk and put her head on the pillow.

***

Fitzpatrick was not likely to sleep much, especially when the ship was in hyperspace. Some people felt queasy in hyper and he was one of them.

Some time in the gym, a shower, and a trank will do me fine, he thought. *I'll sleep okay then.*

He reached the gym, changed, and started stretching before working on his upper body with the weight machine. Every member of the TAF, ground, and naval forces was in peak condition, spending several hours a week in the gym. Each platoon had access to their own small but fully equipped gym with a larger space reserved for the regiment. Navy personnel had their own areas for working out.

This gym had low and heavy gravity exercise rooms that allowed for many options. Fitzpatrick was using a heavy grav weight unit that tested his stamina, strength, and determination. He had set the level on six and was happy with that intensity.

After just a few minutes, Fitzpatrick noticed Sergeant Wong, the third squad's sergeant, enter the gym and make his way to the machine next to him.

"Evening, sir. Getting rid of the hyper blues?"

"I don't think I'll ever be rid of it, sergeant. More a case of putting it to bed for the night. What about you? Can't sleep either?" Fitzpatrick did another quick set and rested, toweling his face and hands off.

"Oh, I can sleep fine, but you know the paper trail never ends. Now that I'm caught up, I need to get from behind the desk and stretch out some of the kinks."

"I know the feeling," groaned Fitzpatrick as he pushed up on the bar, beginning his last rep.

Wong was working on a similar weight appliance set to level nine. He was born on a heavy gravity planet in the Aurora sector. Port Louis was less than one AU, or one hundred and twenty-seven million kilometers, from the primary. With a diameter of ten thousand kilometers, it was smaller than Earth, but it had a dense core and a rotation that created an eighteen-hour day. It was one of the most extreme gravity planets at two point four times that of Earth.

Like most harsh planets, the reason for colonization was not due to a pleasant climate and wonderful vista, but credits. Port Louis was rich in many raw materials that were now in short supply on Earth and some of the other colonies.

Sergeant Wong was in his early seventies and was in top shape. He was focusing on his legs when Fitzpatrick finished his strength workout and headed for the treadmill for his cardiovascular training.

"Later, sir."

"Don't hurt yourself, Wong. You still can't get out of the paperwork with a medical chit—and I know where you live," Fitzpatrick said, grinning.

He reached the treadmill in an adjoining area and set the speed and incline rate, then stepped on and started the machine. After several minutes, he began to think about the upcoming mission, running over scenarios and options for his people. It was not likely any of his speculations would come to fruition, but the mental exercise helped him to both relax and tone his mind.

***

The ability to travel faster than light, or FTL, was considered by many to be the single most important development in human history. Dr. Jonathan Manley had first discovered the rift that opens the door or portal between one reality and another. Like many discoveries in human history, this one was unintentional, a fluke accident that some considered good fortune. At the time, however, his crew had considered it extreme bad luck.

On his research ship, a runaway overload in the ship's fuel cell had caused the magnetic containment field that surrounded the plasma cell to expand into a bubble around the ship. As it did, the ship slid from this space into an alternate but parallel space.

Following the event, Manley had calculated the exact point of entry. When he and his crew reverse-engineered their initial accident and jumped back into real space, he realized the distance traveled was on the order of light years—but what was more remarkable was the time it took to travel that distance. It had only taken five weeks, as opposed to the two years normal travel would have taken.

It took fifty more years and the loss of twenty-five experimental ships and more than two hundred and fifty crew to perfect the jump drive, including charting the rifts and getting the data required for accurate, safe, navigation. Over the years, ships and drives improved, but humans still found the transition between this space and rift space so uncomfortable it was dubbed the "doorway to hell."

As disturbing as the transition could be, and as uncomfortable as it felt while in rift space for some, deck crews and anyone with off time would often stop work to look into the mesmerizing expanse of the rift through the magnetic field on the boat decks. Their human eyes were seeing colours and patterns the likes of which they had never seen. For many, the first time through was too confusing and mind-blowing to describe. Electromagnetic discharges would bounce between the hull and the charged shields, making for an incredible light show, a feast for the eyes and all the senses of the human brain.

The nature of rift space was such that the time and space you occupied kept you isolated. Only one ship could be in the same time and space; even if a whole armada entered the rift at the same time, each ship would have time and space to themselves—until they exited back into their own reality.

***

Captain Lahaie was just finishing the daily briefing with Colonel Marouf, his command officers and *Athabaskan*'s senior officers in the ready room off the main bridge.

The majority of the meeting was routine: duty rosters and their inevitable changes, department head reports and requests, and of course, mission updates.

"We exit the rift in approximately sixteen hours," Lahaie was saying. "The battle group will re-form with new elements from Admiral Martin's group, with a command staff meeting four hours after that." She looked at each officer to ensure comprehension.

Marouf indicated he had marked it in his schedule. Others were now doing the same.

"If there is nothing further, then, we should adjourn."

Marouf raised his hand. He was the same rank as Lahaie, but as the captain of *Athabaskan,* she reigned supreme on her ship.

"Sorry, captain. I just want to verify drop ship and shuttle availability. I have two reports that conflict as to readiness."

Lahaie turned to face Commander Underhill, four places to her right. Underhill commanded the air wing on the *Athabaskan* and would be equipped to respond.

Underhill checked her reader, then said, "I see what you mean about the confusion, colonel. Use the earlier status as current. The last check failed to confirm readiness on all birds. We have found three drop ship and seven transport shuttles non-serviceable. Mostly minor N/S issues, but enough to ground them. I can assure you that outside of one DS, all will be greenlit by the time we reach Scotia." She sounded confident.

"Thanks, commander," responded Marouf. "I just want to be clear."

"Right, let's adjourn then," said Lahaie as she stood.

Everyone rose and began to file out using the corridor hatch. Lahaie, after ensuring no one had anything to say in private, entered her bridge. While it didn't happen at every meeting, there were occasions when somebody wanted to have a word in confidence. She'd felt like the ship's counselor, or a priest in a confessional, more times than she could imagine. Thankfully, this was one of those rare occasions where everyone was clear on their tasks. No issues or problems for a ship's captain to solve.

The bridge was not far and it only took a moment to walk the short distance.

"Captain on the bridge!" announced Lieutenant Provost, the officer-on-watch.

"As you were. Status report," said the captain as she sat down. Lahaie listened to the report from

Provost and read the personnel report. More than two dozen of her people were listed as disabled in sickbay or confined to quarters with the typical symptoms associated with the rift. Nausea, diarrhea, listlessness—all temporary, but it took good people away from their duties nonetheless. None of it was too serious, but it was inconvenient.

The situation with the affected personnel would improve once they slid back into normal space, but until then, there was not much she could do. The ship was doing better than most, with no major problems reported and not many other concerns to deal with.

"Thank you, everyone." All eyes turned toward the captain. "In fifteen hours we slide into normal space and I want everyone rested and ready for action. Mr. Provost, please make changes to the duty roster to give everyone time to restore their energy. Have the watch on full strength one shift prior to slide."

"Aye, sir. I'll see to the changes and inform Lieutenant Vickers. He comes on watch in two hours."

Lahaie rose and walked off the bridge knowing it, and by extension her ship, was in good hands. She trusted her people and their skill and dedication. Once she was off the bridge everyone went back to work preparing for the slide to normal space and for any possible action that may take place.

***

Heather opened her eyes and sat upright with a start. With the lights and desk reader off, it was pitch-black, and the only sound was the constant hum of the ship and the air circulating through the vents on the floor and wall. She was sweating and her heart was pounding as she tried to focus her eyes to a point off in the distance.

She slowly looked around and realized that she'd only had a bad dream. Not quite a nightmare, but enough to seem all too real. It took a few seconds but she made the connection with reality and lay back in her bed.

I hate waking up like that, she thought. She glanced at the chronometer and noticed that she had only been asleep for an hour. *It feels like I've been sleeping for a dozen hours.*

Heather was not adversely affected while in the rift, but she did notice that she slept longer and had less energy. The bizarre dreams also seemed to increase. Since they were essentially alone while in the rift, there was no chance of coming across an enemy ship. So why should she feel that way? The question was always there. She knew that her mind and body used the opportunity to rest, but she could do without the weird dreams. While in action, you never knew when you would get any sleep and so catching up and getting ahead of the fatigue now was not a bad idea. Ship and unit duties were light during flight in the rift for those not affected by illness.

***

Hoffman sat alone in the mess, picking at his meal. He held a reader in one hand and a fork in the other as he stared at the screen. He did not read, or even see, the screen, however—his gaze went through the bulkheads and into deep space. His fork never touched the food. His thoughts were on the current mission, and in particular on the last probe data. Something did not seem right—something was out of place, but he could not put his finger on it. Too many pirate ships to account for, and the number did not fit with the timeline. If the pirates had started their buildup after they'd gotten hold of New Gloucester, they shouldn't have that many ships at their disposal. *So how?*

He could not answer his own question at this time but something did seem out of place. He always trusted his hunch and this time his hunches told him to be careful.

He started to put the reader down and noticed that he had a fork in his other hand, a piece of cold stew dangling on the end of it. He gazed at the dangling food with interest and turned it over on the fork. It was a way to distract his mind from the intense thoughts and doubts he was having. Give the mind something mundane to calculate or contemplate, and the headaches would likely become easer to manage. He was working himself up to a whopper of a headache right now, so any small distraction was welcomed.

He knew that on every mission, small or large, he would do his best to provide the required intelligence and then have doubts about his best. His misgivings were as regular as clockwork, and as certain as the day was long.

I just have to live with it, he finally realized, weighing everything a second and third time over. He knew that he would get over it. He remembered someone telling him once that having doubts is what makes us better at who we are, because humans strive to try harder to do better and erase the doubts. Analyzing his thoughts and doubts actually helped him to feel better, if only for a short time.

***

Fitzpatrick was exhausted as he walked into his cabin. He tore off his sweats, grabbed a towel and his shaving kit, and headed toward the showers. He had spent more time in the gym than he wanted to but it gave him a chance to work off some pre-mission frustration.

Fitzpatrick always found it harder to wait for a mission than actually going on it. He glanced at the chronometer as he left and noticed that there were ten hours left before they slid back to normal space.

I can get six hours' sleep and have enough time to get ready, he thought. It was a pleasing thought as he felt his body and mind giving way to exhaustion.

He reached the shower, disrobed, then stepped into a stall.

"Good evening, lieutenant. Just getting up or going to sleep?" asked Sergeant Bell, the platoon master sergeant.

Fitzpatrick had not seen Bell. *I must be more tired than I thought.*

"About to go down, sergeant. I'm going to knock myself out for a few hours. What about you? You look rested—did you get any sleep?"

"Not yet, sir. While I may seem bright-eyed and bushy-tailed, I'm about to hit the sack myself." Bell was just toweling off. He reached for his shorts, slipped into them, and then put on a shirt. "I'll see you in a few hours—we'll both be well rested and raring to go." He smiled as he left the showers.

***

Life onboard ship, while in the rift, was routine. You either slept or performed maintenance on systems and equipment. For the ground forces, there were also drills in the simulator and time on the small arms range. "Zipper heads," those troops assigned to the armoured units, spent most of their time in simulators blowing up simulated enemies with photonic ammunition. Prepping the tanks also took up time. Artillery and infantry spent their training hours on the range, honing their marksmanship and maintaining squad and platoon weapons. Aircrew, shuttle, drop ship, and fighter pilots also spent time on simulator runs to stay sharp.

The navy had much more to do in the rift and did not have any problem staying busy. Maintaining systems, engines, life support, and weapons on a regular daily basis helped time flow.

***

"All hands general quarters. All hands general quarters. Stand by to slide," the announcement from the bridge boomed throughout the ship.

Lieutenant Vickers was officer on watch as Captain Lahaie entered the bridge. "Captain on the bridge! All departments report ready for slide into Scotia system, captain."

"Thank you, Mr. Vickers. Time to slide?"

"Slide is in thirty minutes."

Lahaie checked the plot and ran through the status board, though she trusted her crew. Every department did indeed show green on the status board. Now it was time to take their operational status to the next level.

"Bring all hands to battle status and charge all weapons."

Vickers nodded and repeated the order. "All hands to battle stations and charge all weapons, aye."

Sliding from real space into the rift did not pose a danger outside of the normal engineering

129

challenges. Since you were essentially alone in the rift, you did not have to worry about a waiting enemy. Sliding in the other direction, however, was very dangerous. This was the most vulnerable time for a ship. There was always some disorientation to the crew. Those who were most susceptible to rift sickness were not on duty during the slide in order to minimize the downtime right after sliding. The ship could slide into an armada that might not be so friendly, and a bad day could turn into something worse if you did not have your head and wits about you and your finger on the trigger.

In time of conflict or uncharted space, TAF navy ships made it standard practice to slide into normal space loaded for bear. All missile tubes were loaded and placed on standby. Both main and auxiliary bridges were staffed with crew dressed in light pressure suits in case of a hull breach. The LPS were not armoured, but would at least provide some chance of survival if internal atmosphere were lost.

Damage control, medical, engineering, life support, sensors, communication, tactical—all stations reported ready for slide. All ground troops were loaded in drop ships and shuttles, locked down with weapons on safe. Heavy equipment, tanks, support weapons, and other ground vehicles were secured on transports.

***

On the carriers, long-range drones were made ready for launch. Programmed on automatic, their AIs would launch the probes at the instant of the slide back into real space, unaffected by any human weaknesses. They would race for the outer limits of the battle group sensor range, ready to relay data that may give advance warning of an ambush.

Fighter pilots suited up while their ground crews readied the sleek fighters for launch. Their mission was to provide an early defensive screen. Point defense missiles and turret guns on each ship were charged, armed, and positioned on standby, to be initially controlled by the ship's AI.

***

On the flag bridge of the *York,* Admiral Affleck sat ready, reviewing ship and battle group status. This may be a scheduled rendezvous with a friendly force, but nothing was ever taken for granted.

"Time to slide?"

"Five minutes, sixteen seconds," replied the battle group navigator, never taking his eyes off the screen.

The mood on the flag bridge was relaxed but professional. Affleck only glanced at the flagship's bridge monitor. He knew instinctively that throughout his force—and it was *his* force—every person would be ready for whatever came their way.

The admiral never noticed that his grip tightened on his armrest. He could hear everything around him, but focused on the elapsed time as it counted down the time to slide.

It did not take long—an almost unnoticed moment of time. But in that moment, the ship slid from the doorway of hell to real space. Hell never wanted to let go, so the ride back to reality was rough. The ship bounced and vibrated while instruments and computer systems compensated.

Humans were not computers, however, and they took a little longer to recover.

Flight Lieutenant Saunders did not suffer the full-blown disorienting effects of sliding that a few others in her wing experienced. Because of this, she was moved up the rotation and was on the flight line ready to launch. Her AI would perform the actual launch the nanosecond her carrier finished sliding.

She braced herself when the timer reached ten. Saunders felt her harness take up the slack as her pressure suit inflated around her legs to help keep the blood in her upper body. She would lose consciousness if the blood rushed to her legs and her brain was deprived for any period of time under the G-stress of launch. Once her fighter passed the threshold between the artificial gravity of the ship and the emptiness of space, she would relax and settle into her routine, taking over flight controls from the AI.

At launch minus five seconds, the final status check was completed—a visual by the pilot as well as an internal by the AI. This was the go/no-go moment. If any major system went down before minus five seconds, the launch of her Voodoo fighter would be scrubbed.

Saunders closed her eyes at minus two and an instant later felt the change as the carrier slid. Her harness tightened and the launch sled propelled her fighter out of the bay and into space.

"Voodoo control, this is Voodoo one five, all systems show green. Voodoo flight headed for station." Saunders signaled to her wingman and the rest of her flight. She released the AI from its flight command tasks and took manual control as she validated her plot and made sure she had a data link with the rest of the flight. Then, in a preset formation and flight plan, she headed away from the battle group to provide advanced air defense.

***

"Incoming transmission, sir. It's the *Montebello*, Rear-Admiral Martin's flagship."

The flag communications officer transferred the signal to Affleck's console. "Thank you," he said.

Entering his secure ID, Affleck brought up Admiral Martin's smiling face on the screen.

"Welcome to Scotia, admiral. I trust you had a good trip?" Admiral Martin was not a tall woman, but she was slender with long legs, which gave her the illusion of being taller than she was. She was in her mid-nineties, with cropped dirty-blond hair. The style had been fashionable ten years ago, but she was never one to follow current fashion trends. Martin was not a senior admiral, but not junior, either. She was well respected in the navy as an excellent tactician and commander. If it weren't for the fact that she'd left the navy at the age of fifty for twelve years to start a family, she would have been a full fleet admiral by this time.

"The voyage was uneventful and relaxing, but I'm here now," Affleck answered. "I hope we haven't kept you waiting, Leslie. How've you been?"

"I've never felt better, and I'm anxious to get started. Your place or mine?" Martin did not mince her words. She was matter-of-fact and to the point, something that had endeared her to Affleck many years prior to her marriage to one of her history professors at the Academy.

She had been seeing Affleck for about seven years at the time, and both of them had hoped

133

something long-term would be in the offering. Duty called, however, and the Morane Territory wars kept them apart. Afterward, they realized that, though being apart had not killed the relationship, both of them being in the service had. Both could die at any time, and while they accepted the risk, it would be too much to ask of any children they might have. The decision to split was mutual, and they'd broken up with their respect for one other intact. Martin had met her partner three years later and neither looked back.

"Mine," Affleck replied. "I've called for a command staff meeting in four hours. I want to make sure that we have our order of march set and that all ships have a full shakedown drill prior to the meeting. Do you have any concerns that we should resolve now?"

"We're all set at this end," Martin replied. "All ships have full payloads and we're battle ready. My executive office, Commander Decosta, will liaise with your team on the marching order for the regrouped flotilla. I'll shuttle over in two hours so we can meet in preparation for the command conference."

Affleck checked his chronometer in acknowledgment. "I'll see you in two hours then."

He signed off and set things in motion to shake down the flotilla, now consisting of two full battle groups. The forty-six ships of the line consisted of seven super-dreadnoughts; six Dunquerkue class dreadnoughts; fifteen Vanguard class and eight Type 50 battleships; eight Oscar and two Indefatigable lass battle cruisers.

Included were four troop transports, each with one complete ground force regiment, two Galaxy One class carriers, and twenty-two destroyers and frigates, of which fifteen were the newer Kingston class types—seventy-four ships in total, not counting fighters, drop ships, and shuttles.

The reformed flotilla was a formidable force.

Chapter Ten

Heather picked up her weapon and walked quickly to the hatchway, following closely behind the trooper in front.

The klaxon was still ringing in her ears as she rounded the corner and turned toward the waiting drop ship. This was the third drill in the past hour and it was no longer fun. She knew they were drilling with such intensity to prepare for combat, but she also knew that it was her duty as a soldier to complain about it.

She noticed Peter several troopers behind her in his power armour. He was making his way into the drop ship bay. She was happy that he'd finally got a handle on operating the armour. He had sent one unsuspecting trooper and three navy ratings to the infirmary before he was able to pass his operators test on the armour.

She ducked as she passed through the drop ship hatch and moved toward her assigned seat. Securing her weapon, she sat down and pulled the restraining bar down on the shock frame, securing herself in place.

Sergeant Taylor was the last trooper in the squad to pass through the hatch. He closed and secured it, making sure everyone else was restrained, then sat in the jump seat just right of the closed hatch.

There was a short countdown and then a noticeable vibration as the feeling of weightlessness announced itself in Heather's stomach. It wasn't called a drop ship for nothing, as the small craft sped quickly away from the transports underside.

"Drill terminated. Drill terminated. All drop ships return to docking arm—all troops stand down." The comm channel sounded in everyone's helmet over the squad net.

I hope this is the last drill, thought Heather. She wanted to get together with Peter as they had originally planned before the training schedule was posted.

***

"Voodoo control, Voodoo flight ready for launch." Saunders leaned back as the shock harness took up the strain. The telltales turned from standby yellow to go green.

The launch controller came back on the comm.. "Launching now."

The launch sled shot the sleek fighter out of the carrier. Saunders and her flight formed up at one thousand meters and took manual control of their fighters. Checking the plot and nav-comm, they raced outward to set up a defensive perimeter.

Other wings from the *Bonaventure* were launched. They, too, had their assigned positions around the periphery of the battle group. The carrier *Onslaught* was also taking part in the shakeout.

The exercise was designed to get the flotilla working in unison. It had been some time since the two battle groups operated together, but in the past hour, reaction time had been improving.

Saunders knew, at least intellectually, that this was an exercise, but the adrenaline pumped through her blood, her focus and concentration increased, and her reflexes quickened. Exercise or not, the dangers were the same as in combat—minus the destructive darts, lasers, and missiles being fired in your direction.

Space was vast, and as someone once said, it was a great big empty. With over seventy ships lying in a volume of space equal to the distance between Mars and Jupiter, she could only see her carrier.

After five minutes her flight passed ten thousand meters from the belly of the cruiser *James Bay* as it moved past to settle in its parking orbit, lining up in the order of march. Everything else around her was black but for the pinpricks of light shining in the distance of time and space. The only colour came from her instruments. The only sound was from her cockpit ventilation and the crackle from her radio as someone spoke.

Her heads-up display showed the green icons of the flotilla spread against the background of the cosmos. Eight blue icons represented the sensor drones launched by the battle group as it slid into real space. Thankfully, her HUD did not indicate any red dots.

Reality began to intrude on her solitude, however, as a warning light flashed and its accompanying alarm sounded.

She clicked her mike. "Voodoo control, this is Voodoo flight, final waypoint reached, exercise objective completed. We're headed back home."

She switched on the flight frequency and signaled her wingman to reform and the rest of the flight to return to the carrier.

***

The screen indicator showing a secure connection glowed green as Hoffman downloaded data to his reader from his secure database. He was getting ready for the upcoming briefing with the command staff on the *York*. It would not be a repeat of his last one, but an overview and update of recent probe data received as the reformed flotilla was shaking itself out.

Hoffman put the reader in his hip pocket and shut down the comm on his desk. The doubts he had earlier as he ate were all but gone. Something still nagged at him. *But that will pass*, he told himself. There were always unknowns, but that was part of life and war.

Reviewing his data helped him ensure he hadn't missed an important detail. He had ploughed through reams of intelligence reports by both civilian and military agencies and then compared that to the fly-by information from probes.

I was wrong. I didn't miss anything, and the data did in fact add up to explain the buildup of pirate ships. The timeline did fit my understanding of what was happening in the New Gloucester system. At least, that's what he told himself.

He was also getting over the headache that he gave himself in his internal deliberations. A quick visit with a medic at the infirmary had helped.

The door opened and he made his way out into a hall filled with navy ratings. Everyone was pulling double duty, getting ready for combat.

Knowing where and when you would go into action was not the norm. One might have a plan, but plans have a habit of changing and everyone knew this all too well. The job now was to plan for both the expected and the unexpected.

It seemed almost absurd to think that someone could plan for the unexpected. *How can anyone be prepared for something they know very little, if anything, about—never mind trying to anticipate the impact such an event could have on your plans?* Hoffman smiled at the thought. He remembered his old history professor telling him that human resilience was the answer. It was about the human will to push on wherever one was, no matter what the circumstance. But you had to want it more than the other guy, because he wanted it too.

Ian Thomas rushed up to Hoffman. "David, I'm glad I caught up with you. You're a hard man to ferret out. Stay in one spot for more than five minutes sometime. You may have mail trying to find you."

"What? And let the credit collectors know where I am? Never, sir—that would put a major crimp in my social life."

"You have no social life," Thomas retorted. "And that, my friend, is why I'm looking for you now—to invite you for a drink after the briefing. I think we'll both need one by then."

Hoffman looked skeptical, "*I* have no social life? And you're asking me to drink with you because, what, your calendar is full and you're slumming?"

He laughed, and Thomas joined in.

"Okay, so I'm in the same dreary socially deprived state as you. So? Are we on?"

"You bet. I'll comm you when I get back."

Hoffman continued toward the lift and the waiting shuttle that would ferry him to the flotilla-wide briefing, feeling a little less stressed. Friends are not hard to come by in the TAF, but having one around, alive, for as long as he and Ian Thomas had known each other was rare.

The ride over to the *York* was uneventful and quiet. The shuttle was filled with all the senior officers, but conversation was scarce. After the shuttle docked, Hoffman headed straight for the lifts, pressing the control pad and entered his secure ID.

The flag briefing room was located on a secure level that required special access. He did not have long to wait, but he did have to move off one side as two navy ratings glided an anti-grav cart full of what looked like medical supplies past him.

Hoffman entered and confirmed his destination on the control pad.

Chapter Eleven

Joseph Lebakie sat in his chair, reading reports from his commanders in the field.

It would be—he looked up at the wall chronometer, then at the unfinished list—forty-five more minutes at the very least before he finished. He hated the tedious, repetitive nature of every report, but it was a job that only he could or would trust himself to complete. He may have been a rogue and pirate, but he was an *organized* rogue and pirate. Running an operation this size required the skills and resources of a major corporation.

Off to one side of his desk was a lone reader, handed to him a few minutes prior. It contained a security report about a tragic accident that had occurred the previous night outside the home of his friend, General Mackenzie King.

King's shuttle had lost power on its way back from an inspection of the system defenses. At six hundred meters off the ground, the shuttle pilot radioed a distress call: they were losing power rapidly and could not maintain pitch or altitude. The pilot did manage to glide the stricken shuttle past crew and officer quarters, but according to witness accounts, there was an explosion in or near the engine pod, then dark smoke. A few seconds later a second explosion ripped through the shuttle skin, as the small fragile craft crashed fifteen hundred meters from King's front door. The cause was ruled a combination of mechanical and maintenance error.

Lebakie did not have to read the official report to know its contents. He had already received a private account of events—from the agent that caused the accident with a carefully placed micro-explosive.

Lebakie felt ill as he listened to the agent's account of the events, but did not stop or delay the speaker. This was not the first time such a report was presented to him by the agent, and it would not likely be the last. It was, however, the first time it was about a close, personal friend—someone he had known all his life.

It hurt deeply to have ordered his death.

"I never wanted this, but so be it. It's done and we have to move on," he said to no one.

The comm chimed. He keyed his access code and the face of the first sergeant guarding the outer door appeared.

"Yes?" he said.

"Sir, my apologies. Commander Walter Hobbin is here to see you. He's not on your list for today, however," said the sergeant.

That depends on what list you're talking about, thought Lebakie.

"Send him in, sergeant. He's a last-minute addition to the schedule." Lebakie terminated the connection and closed the privacy screen on his desk comm. He picked up the reader with the late General King's accident report, placing it into his pocket.

A knock on the door brought his head up. "Come!"

Commander Hobbin, formally of the pirate dreadnought *Foreboding*, opened the door with purpose and entered the office. He wore the black jumpsuit issued to shipboard personnel working for Lebakie.

Hobbin walked up to the desk. Standing at attention, he removed his cap, "Commander Walter Hobbin, reporting as ordered, sir."

143

Standing and walking around his desk, Lebakie watched his visitor, sizing him up.

""Thank you for coming on such short notice, Commander. Stand easy, please." The two men shook hands, and Lebakie gestured to two chairs. "I hope you don't mind, but we'll skip the small talk and get right to the point."

"Thank you, sir. I am curious as to why you wanted to see me," Hobbin said as they sat.

In reality, Hobbin was more than curious about the reason and timing of the meeting. He had just come off bridge watch when he saw the message indicator light on his comm. A short text message with an authentication code used to verify the identity of the sender confirmed that Lebakie himself sent it. The orders were to report without informing anyone about the meeting.

"As I'm sure you have heard by now, a tragic accident has befallen Field General Mackenzie King. Our organization has lost a great leader, and I have lost a good friend." Pausing, Lebakie rose and walked to a lone side table and poured himself a drink. "Can I offer you one, commander?"

"No, thank you, sir. I may have to interrupt this meeting if I take in any more liquids." Both men laughed lightly. Hobbin tried to size up Lebakie and what he was saying. He sounded hollow and saddened by the loss of King, but something did not *feel* right. *What's he up to?*

"Fair enough." Lebakie sat back down. "Because of our untimely loss and the near completion of our pre-operation phase, I have to scramble to replace General King," he went on.

Hobbin felt a pang of nervousness slip into his normally calm state of mind. To cover the movement he stood and walked to the drink service to pour himself a glass.

"Sorry, sir, I'll take that drink after all."

Lebakie smiled. "Now, don't worry. I'm not considering you for the job." Another joke, more light laughter. "That being said, I have heard some very positive and remarkable things about you. I have also read your personnel file and your fitness reports. Your superiors have nothing but high regard for you as a commander, and as a person. I am also impressed by your restraint. Many of my junior—and for that matter, some of my senior—people have forgotten or chose to ignore that virtue. I know that in my last conversation with General King he brought up that disturbing point."

Lebakie took a sip from the red liquor in his glass before continuing. "This unfortunate behavior is something that I am sensitive to, and to see an officer such as you not get drawn into the brutality that has become such a sore point in my organization is refreshing."

Hobbin heard the words, and while he appreciated the compliment, he did not hear sincerity in Lebakie's voice or see it in his body language. It was too automatic, like he was reading from a script or a book.

Lebakie shifted in his seat and leaned forward. "I need someone of your skills and character to take over the standing fleet in New Gloucester."

That's torn it, thought Hobbin. *He needs a fall guy in case it falls to pot, and I just got nominated. Great, wonderful, fantastic, shit!*

The wall screens showed a sun low on the horizon. Lebakie had paused, but Hobbin did not notice. His mind and thoughts were full of misgivings and validation at the same time.

In a way, though he knew it would make him vulnerable, he was pleased with the opportunity. He had worked hard to rise through the ranks, starting off as an ordinary seaman in a merchant fleet in the Terrain system. He had joined the TAF navy in order to fulfill two dreams: go into deep space and be part of something bigger than himself. After rising to the rank of captain and getting his own ship, a series of incidents involving gambling credits and drugs broke him. Disgraced and discharged from the TAF, he found a place in Lebakie's private company of pirates. He never blamed anyone else for his disgrace and always knew he ran a risk.

That thought and knowledge did not stop him from feeling sorry for himself. It was human nature, after all.

Lebakie cleared his throat and brought Hobbin back to the here and now. "Sorry, sir, I was just thinking."

"Really? I could hardly tell," Lebakie said, grinning. "What about, if you don't mind me asking?"

Collecting his thoughts, Hobbin answered, "Why choose me for the job? Please don't take this the wrong way, sir—I am extremely flattered by the offer. Can I speak freely?"

Lebakie nodded and raised his glass in an invitation for Hobbin to continue.

Hobbin put his cup down on a table, "I can only feel there is something you are not telling me. There are at least a dozen senior officers more qualified than myself. Promoting me over them, and given the number of levels you're bumping me up, leads me to conclude that you are looking for a sacrificial lamb if the shit hits the fan. Shit normally rolls downhill, but you're placing the bag squarely on top of my head. It only has one way to flow when the bag breaks."

Lebakie did not need to think about an answer. He hoped, and expected, Hobbin would ask.

"I'm jumping you to the head of the class for three main reasons. One, I need someone I can trust to take the standing fleet and get it ready for our final op. You have the experience in the TAF that no one else at your level has. This is, of course, an important commodity, considering we're going up against those very people. Two, you're not one of the 'in' crowd. As I mentioned, all of your commanding officers have praise and respect for you, but all of them add in their evaluation that you keep to yourself. You do not get involved in the politics of rank. To me, that means you have a fresh slate to start from. You haven't pissed off any one group within the organization to the point of causing distrust. Three, you're right in saying that shit rolls downhill. You're also correct in the supposition that you will take the heat if anything goes wrong. I've been around long enough to know that nothing will go exactly as planned. The gods of Murphy are alive and well, and I will not take chances with my plans. I've worked too long and too hard to build up my assets, and I will do anything to ensure that I keep them."

Lebakie looked straight into Hobbin's eyes. "I will not put anyone in place that could screw this up. I will back up my field commanders at all times. Earning my wrath does not come from a defeat. It comes from me not trusting you—from not following my orders. One of my assets is that I will trust everyone—once. It is seldom that anyone asks me to trust them a second time."

Hobbin was still unsure of the hidden reasons behind the stated ones. But he decided to give it a go—putting certain personal safeguards in place just in case that proverbial bag of excrement came crashing down around him.

Not wanting to put a curse on things and send the Murphy gods his way, he chose to think positive that everything would turn out for the best.

Lebakie paused, giving Hobbin a chance to ask, "What rank are we talking about, and what authority would I have?"

"I want to bring you up to the rank of admiral, with a corresponding jump in compensation and benefits. That goes without saying."

Hobbin started. A jump in rank would mean a jump in status, pay, and more of a share in prize money. It would also mean more responsibility—something he truly desired. Having served for as long as he had, earning the rank of captain in the TAF, and then only serving as a commander in this pirate fleet did not sit well with him. If Hobbin had a weak spot, a desire for responsibility, power, and control was it.

Trying not to seem too eager, Hobbin paused. "I would be honored to accept your generous offer," he said at last. "It represents an opportunity I cannot turn away. Thank you, sir. You will not regret this."

"I know I won't regret it, and I can depend on you to get the job done. You will leave immediately. The sergeant has a copy of your orders at the desk on your way out. Now, I think this calls for a drink."

The two men stood and shook hands. Lebakie poured two glasses of thick red liquor and handed a glass to Hobbin, who took it gratefully. Both men toasted and drank, each with a satisfied smile, and each with a own vastly different agenda.

Chapter Twelve

Ships of the reformed flotilla, now designated TAFNF25, glowed green in the holo-plot located in the large briefing room in the bowels of the flagship.

The room was a theatre in many respects, with tiered seating and a podium off to one side. It was mainly used when the flotilla was assembled, and with so many officers present, it came in handy. Around the perimeter on the upper section of the walls were video monitors with feeds from ships around the flotilla that were unable to send representatives. But the majority of ships' captains and their officers were now present, making introductions and exchanging stories.

Exactly three hours and fifty-nine minutes after arriving in sector, all conversation in the room ended abruptly. Affleck's staff stood at the door at attention as his executive officer called, "Room!"

Everyone stood to attention, including those attending via video link. Affleck entered and proceeded to the seats reserved for him and his staff. "Please sit easy," he said as he sat.

Following closely behind were two JTF guards in full combat dress, body armour and weapons. They closed and locked the door then stood at ease, guarding against intrusion and interruption.

All eyes were on the JTF troopers, Affleck noticed. Yet this was not going to be a repeat of the previous meeting. No need for any arrests here. Three additional captains from Admiral Martin's battle group and a number of junior officers and enlisted personnel from both battle groups had quietly been arrested in the past four hours, charged with corruption, bribery, and conduct to the prejudice of good order and discipline *Internal clean-up is complete, and now it's time to clean up the galaxy,* Affleck thought.

He put both hands on his knees and stood. Everyone turned their attention toward him. "Ladies and gentlemen, the time has come," he said. "Someone once said, 'It takes two to make a marriage a success and only one a failure.' This fleet is now two again, which makes us whole, and I trust a future success. Our merchant and civilian shipping lanes have been plundered and looted for far too long by greedy, self-absorbed people. Lately, these same pirates have begun murdering their victims. Now we have proof of a direct threat by the pirates to the core systems, Earth, and the Confederation government. It seems that they too have learned the benefits of working together. We are here to put a stop to that threat by eliminating a very large part of the pirate fleet currently at New Gloucester. I have formulated a strategy that should accomplish this goal."

Affleck himself had not come up with the current plan of attack—not alone, at any rate. It had been formulated after deliberate and careful consultation with all ships' captains and tactical and intelligence personnel, using available probe data. As the man in charge, however, he accepted complete responsibility for the plan. It would be his head that would roll should things go down the crapper.

The plan of attack called for the flotilla to once again split into two battle groups and hit the pirate fleet simultaneously at opposite ends of the system. Tactically, splitting into two groups could create a host of problems, including the loss of concentrated fire. Each group would only have access to half the

150

available missile load, fighter cover, and missile defenses.

Another concern was the need for no-error timing. Both groups had to coordinate their actions to the nanosecond. A basic AI defensive program within the pirate command structure could launch a counterstrike faster than any human, so timing had to be exact. Getting forces caught in the crossfire also became an issue. In an open-space battle this might not be a major problem. However, in a planetary system, space, while still vast and empty, became just that much smaller. Capital missiles could lock up a target very quickly and mistakes could occur.

There was little maneuvering room in-system when fighting a pitched battle. One missed target due to q computer or targeting error could send a missile off toward friendly forces. Coordination also became an issue when trying to land ground troops from two battle groups. It was a bold plan, with merit.

Three main objectives had to be met for the operation to be a success, and the destruction of the pirate fleet housed in the New Gloucester system was top of the list. Second was the elimination of the pirates' ability to mine raw materials and the production of armaments. This was potentially the most difficult, as it required an assault on both the asteroid belt mines as well as the orbital and ground bases' refining and production facilities. Last of the objectives was the gathering of intel that may lead to identifying the pirates' main base of operations.

In order to do these things, Martin's battle group would slide just outside the primary's gravity well. She would then attack the planet and main fleet and production facilities. Simultaneously, Affleck would bring his group in from the inner ring of the asteroid belt and take out the mining and refining centers.

151

That part was a compromise. The original plan called for Affleck to slide at one AU from the outer belt on the far side of the outer ring. It was safer, but it was decided after some debate that it posed the greater risk of early detection.

The current op had its risks. The biggest one was sliding that close to the inner ring, which could pose a navigational challenge. Launching fighters and missiles so near an asteroid field would also play havoc with target acquisition.

The meeting continued for several hours.

Chapter Thirteen

Walter Hobbin, now Admiral Hobbin, stood on the boat bay of the pirate super-dreadnought *Cape Fear* as it orbited New Gloucester. Hobbin had arrived in-system three days ago but delayed boarding his flagship in order to review planetary defenses. Now that the inspection was out of the way, his next task was to order a complete inventory and shakedown drill of his fleet.

He liked that: *his fleet*. Whenever he heard it, he beamed inside like a young child with a new toy. It was his toy, and no one else could play with it. Of course, Hobbin also remembered that if he broke his new toy, he would suffer in a most grievous way.

"At-ten-tion!" boomed the *Cape Fear*'s captain, James Douglas, to the assembled ship's complement.

A uniformed sea of black coveralls came to attention, but not all at once. There were plenty of waves in that sea.

Hobbin knew how to recognize a smart, sharp drill. It should sound like one clap of thunder as everyone's right leg came up fifteen centimeters and back down, bringing both feet together on the command. This sounded more like mild applause as bodies and feet moved at different times.

Sloppy, thought Hobbin. *I hope it's not this bad on the rest of the fleet. I suppose I shouldn't be surprised, though. Pirates are not known for drill and discipline. Something I will have to work on.*

Douglas turned to Hobbin. "Welcome aboard the *Cape Fear,* admiral."

"Thank you, captain."

The comm feed from the boat bay was being transmitted to all captains in the New Gloucester system; it was vital that they witnessed this. Although this was a pirate navy, Lebakie installed protocols to make certain that there was little or no ambiguity in his command structure.

Hobbin took out a reader from his carry-on bag and read it in his most commanding voice. "By order of your Commander, General Joseph Lebakie, I hereby take immediate command of this fleet, as stationed in New Gloucester."

He lowered the reader and looked at Douglas. "Captain Douglas, please make a note in the log and call a command staff meeting with all ships and dirtside senior officers on the comm in one hour. We have a lot of work to get done in a very short time. Dismiss the men."

Douglas obeyed, dismissing the honor guard and assembled personnel. Again, Hobbin was not impressed with the drill, but he resigned himself to the fact that changing the status quo would be slow.

After signaling his staff to cut the video feed, Hobbin leaned in close to Douglas who was waiting to escort him to his quarters.

He said quietly, "Captain, one more thing, I want a comm-meeting with the captains of" —he looked at the reader again— "the *Maximum*, *Swift*, *Lost Hope*, *Bandit*, and *Slater* in ten minutes. Secure comm feed if you please. I'll take it in my ready room."

Douglas expected the all-ships comm order. That was to be expected. But asking for five battle cruiser captains to meet immediately after Hobbin's arrival on board was out of the ordinary.

"Aye, sir." Douglas hoped his surprise did not show on his face. "I'll have your kit sent to your cabin." He saluted.

Hobbin nodded and returned Douglas's salute. He turned and walked through the open blast doors into the brightly lit corridor, headed for the flag bridge and his ready room. Following closely behind was his executive officer, Major Westbour, staff officers, his clerk, and four very imposing guards wearing a full combat load.

After posting the guards outside and dismissing his staff officers, Hobbin entered his ready room. He examined it with a quick glance. Plain, sparse. *It has potential,* he thought.

Then he got to work with a hand scanner that Westbour passed him. Listening devices placed in a flag officer's quarters, ready room, and even the head were not unheard of.

Hobbin did not want to remove them. He needed to find their operating and transmitting frequencies in order to use them to this own advantage. After all, giving away information could sometimes be extremely useful.

He found three, two of which had separate frequencies. The third was not operational. None were well hidden. *Decoys?* thought Hobbin. A more complete check on multiple frequencies only proved that whoever planted them was not experienced. He did not find any more.

Westbour handed Hobbin a small dark green box with a control screen on one side. Hobbin placed it on a side table and set the screen's frequency range to overlap the ones he found, then turned it on, effectively disabling the bugs. A red LED came on indicating it was working.

He looked at Westbour. "I'm surprised I only found the three."

"I have no doubts that you have several still to find in your quarters and the bridge."

The comm chimed and Douglas's face appeared as Hobbin accepted the call. "Sir, I have the five battle cruisers as you ordered on the line."

"Patch them through on one-oh-four, alpha secure."

"Aye, sir. One-oh-four, alpha secure comm."

Hobbin dismissed the two guards to wait outside with the others and sat down in front of the screen once the hatch was secure. Westbour sat in another chair just outside the comm's field of view. Five confused faces on a split screen amused Hobbin: Captains Appletree of the *Maximum*, Brown from the *Swift*, Jackson from *Lost Hope*, Ganas and Bishop from *Bandit*, and *Slater*.

"Gentlemen, I'm glad you could join me for this meeting. I trust you have not spoken to anyone about this?"

Captain Bishop was the first to speak. "Admiral, it would have been difficult to speak to anyone, considering the speed that this meeting was called. I think I can speak for this group when I say that we are more than a little inquisitive and concerned about the timing and speed with which this meeting was called, and why it only includes the five of us."

The others nodded.

"I can appreciate both the concern and curiosity you all must have right now. Let me start off by assuring all of you that you are not in any kind of trouble. As a matter of fact, it's the exact opposite. I've chosen you and your crew for the upcoming mission."

This drew a surprised look from the five captains.

"The timetable for final op has been moved up. I have been directed to finish preparations, load-out, and crew shakedown in one month. Operation Heart Attack begins shortly after that. The exact time is not being disclosed until then."

This was not all news to the five captains, but the move in the timetable did startle them.

Hobbin continued. "My concern is making any move blindly. I need intel on any problems we may face on the trace and I want it now, before I get sucked into something we're all going to regret."

His tone was starting to change and he caught himself before he lost control of his emotions. After reading the operational order, he knew he was going to be in the thick of it. That part he did not mind. It was what he wanted after all. But being stuck in a position he could avoid—well, that would not do.

"I'm sending the five of you as a reconnaissance-in-force. A light cruiser under stealth with a full sensor package would be the more logical choice to remain undetected, but I want you to be able to fight your way back should it fall into the crapper. Your orders are being transmitted now. Only you and my XO have knowledge of this, and that is how it will stay for the duration."

Hobbin paused and keyed the transmit code. Using a narrow-beam, line-of-sight laser ensured that no one intercepted the comm. The captains reviewed their orders quickly, each with a slightly shocked expression.

Hobbin gave them a few moments to complete their review before continuing. "I have been charged with the success or failure of this mission and I will do everything in my power to ensure it is a profitable, successful venture. It can only be profitable if our losses are minimal. I will not discuss why a reconnaissance of our trace was left off the table, but I am putting it back on."

Hobbin did not say what he truly felt, that leaving off a full recon prior to launch was as boneheaded as it got. *That's first-year cadet training at the TAF Academy,* he thought. The lack of common sense smacked of a hidden agenda.

Captain Brown spoke up. "Sir, what's the chain of command for this?"

"Captain Bishop is the senior captain. I am giving operational command of your group to him. Bishop, you will report to no one but Major Westbour or me. I will leave it up to you how you proceed. There are six navigational waypoints on the trace. In order, they are NGC17246, the Scotia System, Merkley Crossing, IM50216, Lebreton, and Sol Two. If there are no questions, you launch in twenty minutes. Good luck, gentlemen."

At that, Hobbin cut the comm and sat back. He turned to Westbour. "So, any thoughts? I can tell by the look you're wearing that you have several."

"I do, and they have not changed since the last time you asked me. As I said, I believe this to be both a good and bad plan. It has to happen and I can't find fault with the logic for launching the recon. It should have been planned and ready to go or even underway by now. That being said, I have to question why it was left out in the first place, who left it out, and what the consequences are for putting it back in."

"I always say you worry too much, but in this case I have to agree with you. Lebakie must have known. He put the plan together. Shit, King would not have pulled a boneheaded move like this. You and I have both worked with him, and I know his tactics. He was always careful about knowing what was happening around him and his troops. So if it wasn't King, and Lebakie had to have known, then what's he up to?"

"Your guess is as good as mine."

Hobbin leaned forward and keyed the comm. "Sergeant, please have coffee brought in."

The sergeant in the outer office acknowledged as Hobbin leaned back. "I don't want to guess, I want real-time answers, and this force recon should get it for me."

*****

Captain Bishop, still recovering from the order to execute a rushed departure, was sitting on the edge of his bunk reading his new orders when the door chime sounded.

"Come," he said.

"Sir, all stations report ready for departure. Engine room, tactical, and navigation all standing by command," Commander Scott Lawson reported.

"Thank you, commander. Have comm patch me through to the reconnaissance group. I'll take it here in my quarters and I'll be up in a moment. Secure channel, if you please, on that comm."

"Right away, sir."

Lawson stepped out of the door and a minute or two later the comm signal chimed.

"Secure channel ready, sir," reported the communications officer.

Bishop entered his security code, and the faces of the other captains in his recon group flashed to life.

"I think I can read your minds, gentlemen," he began. "We all have the same thoughts and concerns and I doubt that anything else has to be said."

All nodded in agreement. "I am transmitting the order of march now. You'll note that it is based on firepower on our flanks and rear and main sensor sweeps to the front. Captain Jackson, *Lost Hope* has the most updated sensor package, so you are to take the point with myself right behind. Appletree, the *Maximum* and *Swift* will take flanking positions and *Slater* will bring up the rear. We break orbit in five minutes—waypoint alpha is NGC17246. Beta is Scotia, then Merkley Crossing. We will reevaluate our position at that time as I have some concerns about IM50216. I have it on good authority that we may have been compromised there."

Captain Brown spoke up. "Why haven't we heard about this? How have we been compromised?" His voice was strained, heavy with concern and fatigue.

"Like this mission, something stinks. I don't know how, but my source said that we've lost IM50216. It doesn't matter either way. This recon will at least bring some answers to the table and we'll all know what our next moves will be. If there are no other issues at this time, I suggest we get moving."

No one said anything and Bishop cut the comm. Standing, he stretched and walked out of his quarters toward the bridge, his thoughts full of doubt.

Chapter Fourteen

Heather opened her eyes slowly and saw Peter staring back at her.

"You know, staring isn't polite," she said. "How long have you been awake?"

"Not long," replied Peter as he rolled onto his back and sat up straight.

"Does my breath smell or something?" teased Heather, cupping her hand and blowing into it.

"As a matter of fact, it does," he said, adding quickly, "but then, so does mine. How far have we come as a race when medical science can't come up with a good long-lasting breath mint?"

Heather jabbed him in the ribs. "Never tell your lover she has bad breath, no matter how much plaststeel it corrodes off the bulkheads. You may never get lucky again."

"Okay, I give," he said, laughing and grabbing his side. "I'm just glad we had some down time together. I've heard about drilling for an op, but this heavy pace is starting to have negative effects."

Heather kissed his chest and sat up, leaning against the wall. "I know what you mean. The old man must really be worried to push this hard."

Peter said nothing but stared ahead, taking two deep, cleansing breaths.

He looked at Heather and spoke softly. "Until now, the TAF has only gone ship-to-ship with the majority of pirates. There's been very limited contact with any pirate ground forces, especially one this well-entrenched and in an unsurveyed position. There are a lot of unknowns to consider. Pirates as a whole are also very unpredictable, and when greed and power get mixed in the equation, who knows what the outcome will be?"

Heather gave Peter a quizzical look. He was almost starting to sound fatalistic and that worried her. That kind of thinking could cloud your judgment in combat and get you or the people around you killed. She wanted to bring back some levity into their conversation, keeping things lighthearted and moving away from the struggle of life and death.

"Were you not the one who was just complaining about all the drilling and how it's cutting into your love life?"

"Who's complaining?" He paused, his voice rising, only just realizing what Heather had said. "Wait—love life?"

Heather cleared her throat. "You heard me right. Peter, we've been dancing to this tune for some time now and we've never talked about what was next. I'm having much deeper feelings about you. About us." She paused.

Peter took the break to jump in, never taking his eyes off her. "Stop. Before you go on, I have a confession to make."

His mouth was dry. Reaching up on the desk, he grabbed his canteen and took a sip of the now room-temperature water.

"I've spoken to the counselor about you, and how I should approach you about something," he said. "I think I'm in love with you, and have been for some time. I know we agreed to keep this casual, but I can't go on with the thought of you, or me, getting burned and not telling you how I feel."

A tear formed in the edge of Heather's eye. Her emotions spun in unison with her thoughts, threatening to turn her into a babbling schoolgirl.

She tried to wipe the tear away without him noticing, and then said softly, "All this time without saying anything to each other. So what does this mean for the two of us?"

Peter took her in his arms and they kissed. She held on to him, pulling him closer and tighter, knowing that nothing lasts forever. She was going to make the best of it while it did.

***

The flotilla was shaking down nicely and Affleck was looking pleased. Sitting in his command chair, he directed the current exercise as if he were playing a game of chess against the best AI ever created, balancing one move against the next, thinking several moves in advance. He knew there were too many variables to have a hard and fast plan, but he was experienced enough to know that any plan must be flexible enough to compensate for the unexpected.

"Sir, tactical reports a contact from one of our long-range drones. It's faint, but it's there and not part of the exercise."

Affleck wasn't sure he'd heard his tactical officer right at first. They were not expecting any company. "Narrow down the location and patch it through CIC. I want an updated plot in the tank as soon as they have something." This bit of news concerned him, but it would take much more to for him to become completely unglued.

The tactical officer acknowledged, repeating the order. Affleck noticed the odd glance in his direction from several stations on the flag bridge.

"Captain Kugong, recall all drop ships and shuttles. Bring the flotilla to standby alert. Exercise canceled."

Kugong turned to the communications officer, repeated the order, and had the command codes sent to all units. He looked back at the admiral, slightly bent over the comm console. "This is unexpected."

"Life is full of unexpected events. Didn't your parents ever tell you that?" Affleck grinned. "Let's not get too carried away, though. It may be nothing. I want to be sure about this contact—and I don't want to expose myself too much. Bring all weapons and defensive systems on standby, if you please, Mr. Kugong."

Kugong repeated the order as he coordinated events on the flag bridge. It was his job to be the information filter between bridge stations and the admiral, and right now there was a lot of filtering to do. Comm traffic increased tenfold as soon as the alert went out. Half of the ground troops were dirt-side on a small planetoid running through an assault scenario and the fighters were in exercise mode. Launching an attack with lightning speed was easy. Putting all the pieces back together took considerably more time.

***

"Voodoo control, this is Voodoo one-five, confirm recall."

Saunders was pissed. Being recalled was one thing, but being recalled while you were at the opposite end of the system with your ass hanging in the wind all by its lonesome was nuts.

"Voodoo flight, this is Voodoo one-five. End-ex, reform on heading—" She checked her plot. "Four two seven point seven by three eight six point one. Thirty degrees positive. Full burn, people, before we get our sorry butts left behind."

The comm lit up, showing an incoming transmission. "Voodoo one-five, Voodoo control, recall confirmed. Voodoo control out."

Great, at least I can get an early night, she thought.

***

Kugong took the reader from the sensor tech and reviewed the data. He brought his head up and looked at the tech. "This is confirmed?"

"Yes, sir. We've also verified the drones are still running silent and dark."

"Good work, ensign. Thank you." Kugong dismissed the tech, thankful that he had competent people with tremendous expertise.

He comm'd Affleck in his ready room. "Admiral to the bridge."

Drop ships, shuttles and fighters made their way back to their births to re-arm and refuel. Putting the flotilla on standby cleared the way to release the safety lockdown on missile batteries and laser turrets. They would still not fire until the "weapons free" order was given, but it was the final lockout step before that order.

The men and women of flotilla TAFNF25 were ready. The only thing left to do was wait.

"Admiral on the bridge!"

Kugong handed the admiral the reader. Affleck studied it for a moment, then sat in his command chair. He called up the system plot on one screen and the tactical overlay of his ships on another.

"By the cods, this can't be right. Mr. Kugong, I assume you've confirmed with CIC the projected trace?"

"I have, sir, and this data has been updated from our drones in NGC17246. If this is a recon, their next logical waypoint is the Scotia system, based on the intended target of the core systems."

"And into our laps. If we're not careful, this could scuttle our plans for a surprise party," Affleck said. He moved to the edge of the holo tank, a larger two-system image showing both NGC17246 and Scotia along with friendly and projected enemy ships.

"I am concerned, admiral, that we are not able to pin down the exact number and type of ships involved. We weren't able to ascertain that from the drones."

"I can't see them using a large force—two, maybe three ships, and they would most likely be light cruisers. But I agree with you. Let's not take any chances. Get me Admiral Martin, and prep the scouts."

***

Bishop walked onto his bridge to the sound of the alert klaxon, slipping his arm into his tunic sleeve.

"Report!" he barked.

The officer on watch handed Bishop a reader. "Sir, as we were about to transition, tactical picked up a burst transmission. There was a power spike, but not long enough to lock down the location to less than point five AU of its source. I took it upon myself to bring us to alert status and notified the other ships." There was a pang of nervousness in the man's voice.

Bishop reviewed the reader. "There'll be an extra bonus in your credit package on the next upload. Good job. Helm, all stop, go to stealth. Comm, relay the same order to the other ships. Tell them to stand by."

This was unexpected, he thought.

He transferred the data on his reader to one of his command screens. Studying it, he surmised that it may be a system picket running under stealth, but the power spike seemed too low to be a ship.

A drone maybe, but what's it doing in this system? he thought.

"Comm, download the tech data to a message drone and add my last entry from the log. Record logs from this point to download and stand by to launch it back to the fleet. Hold for my order."

The comm officer acknowledged and complied.

"Any more signals?" He knew the answer already.

"None, sir. Incoming from the other ships—they want to know status and next steps. No other ship picked up the signal."

The fact that the other ships did not get a signal capture was not unusual. The relative location of a ship in relationship to the burst source could cause it to be missed by other ships. The worrying thing was that they were supposed to be in safe territory. There was nothing to indicate military or civilian traffic. Then again, they were here on a recon. Better to find out now.

"Signal to all ships, ahead half power to jump point. Sensors on max with the widest gain scan."

He paused, then said to no one but himself, "We may not get a target lock, but if there's something out there, we'll know about it."

NGC17246 was an empty system, devoid of planets. Only a few rogue asteroids drifted about a once great star. The only two existing planets had been long ago engulfed by the star. The red giant was losing its internal fuel and expanding toward its final end. Helium, hydrogen, and other vital elements being eaten up in greater amounts every second. It would not be long before the expansion would end and the star shrunk down to a white dwarf.

Bishop marveled at the surreal beauty of the red giant as he watched it on one of his screens. Over five AUs from the star and at normal magnification it still filled the viewer. He would never peg himself as a romantic; he was too rough around the edges for that. Yet he couldn't help feeling a sense of loss at not being able to appreciate the grandeur of the stars before him.

Activity at the navigation station caught his eye and brought him back to reality.

"Report," he said.

The navigation officer, after downloading his data to a reader, handed it to the officer on watch.

"Nav-comm confirms we slide in thirty mikes, sir."

"Thank you." Taking the reader, Bishop checked the plot one last time and after a few moments, asked for an update on the previous sensor contact.

"No further contact by us or the other ships, sir. CIC does say that a hardware or software fault could have caused it."

Bishop did not like loose ends. "Has anyone been able to reproduce the error, if that's what it was?"

"No, sir. It was also given over to the AI but it was not able to confirm the error. Sir, forgive the forward observation, but if it was anything, a ship or a drone, the burst signal was not long enough to give away any information, and there has not been any subsequent activity. Why sweat over it?"

"Because it's my job to sweat. Shit may run downhill, but that initial impact at high velocity is like a missile being rammed up your ass. That is why I sweat over it. I'm a hundred and nineteen and I'd like to live a few years more and retire wealthy. This operation will allow me to accomplish that goal if we don't screw up." He paused. "All right, ahead full, prepare for slide to the next waypoint. Relay to all ships."

Bishop did not like the idea of leaving the system with any unfinished business, but without any evidence of further contact, time was wasting.

"Aye, aye, captain, relay to all ships, ahead full, prepare for slide."

With that, the young officer turned and the bridge became a flurry of activity. The klaxon sounded and the orders went ship wide. Bishop took a look on his plot and assured himself that everything was going well.

**

Kugong stood at the centre of the bridge on the flagship *York* with an ear and eye on all stations. Station officers on watch went about their duties without notice. Affleck would be notified if anything developed and right now, space was quiet.

Kugong did not like to pace. It was not only undignified for an officer, he also felt it conveyed the wrong message to the men and women serving under

169

him. But he was getting tired just standing there and he admitted to himself that he must look like a mother hen hovering over her flock. Trying not to look too obvious, he sat in the command chair and began to read over reports from the flagship captain and the rest of the flotilla.

Kugong soon found himself caught up in accounts from the various ships. He was fascinated by the different writing styles of the various captains.

The mundane can take you away sometimes, he thought. *I'll comm some of these reports to any ships we come up against. It would put many of them to sleep, at the very least—and it would kill the weaker ones.* A smile crossed his lips.

"Sir!" The tactical officer's voice was hurried, but without panic. "Burst signal from one of the drones, enemy force has transitioned. Time delay puts their slide twelve point five hours ago. CIC is updating a new plot based on departure point. No reports from the drone that they were detected."

"Thank you, lieutenant." Kugong punched in the admiral's comm code right away.

"Sorry to bother you, admiral."

Affleck waved his hand dismissively, inviting Kugong to continue.

"Confirmation from the drone. Enemy ships have transitioned. CIC has begun to project contact vector."

"Good. When was the slide?"

"Twelve and a half hours. Add an additional three hours for comm to reach us. We should have a contact in the next two days, assuming this is their next waypoint."

"Based on the fact that they need uninhabited systems to maintain surprise, and the need for as much speed with their fleet, this is the most logical next slide. Pass the update to all ships, and run through a series of scenarios based on the five most probable entry points. I don't want to spread our resources too thin trying to cover every point, but we should be ready for several contingencies."

Affleck waited for Kugong to acknowledge and then cut the comm. He wanted to get on with it, but waiting was part of life in the service.

***

Heather held onto an outcrop on the rock face with her right hand, dipping her left into a rosin bag strapped to her webbing. She switched hands and repeated the motion.

She loved to climb, but wars and combat duty kept her away from the wall. Every trooper had to be proficient at mountaineering, but Heather excelled at it. She seemed to glide over the rock face as if the laws of gravity were suspended just for her.

During this exercise period in the climbing gym, she was climbing with a full combat load. Almost forty-five kilograms of equipment and personal gear and she still made it look easy.

She reached the midway point on the wall. Above her was an overhang that required her to overextend her reach with one hand, release her footing, and hang with one hand before pulling herself up to take hold of a ledge.

She found a solid hold and tested it, then coated her fingers with a bit of rosin and grabbed hold. She could feel the strain on her shoulder muscles as she did. Blocking out any pain and concentrating on the immediate task, she released one leg, then the other.

Heather now hung at an odd angle. She let go of her lower hand and hung twenty-six meters above the decking, holding on with one hand and taking her weight plus her kit and weapon.

Her mind was focused; she knew the next move in advance, planned out in her mind well before she even reached the overhang. Mustering up her strength, she reached up, at the same time pulling up to grab hold of the ledge. Taking hold, she released her right hand to give it a rest and rosin up before continuing.

As she took hold with both hands, she could feel herself slipping.

"Shit!" she said out loud, though not in a panic.

She moved her left hand over a few centimeters to a dryer spot and pulled herself up, swinging her right leg over the lip of the ledge. She saw a small hold and reached for it with her right hand, at the same time bringing her left leg up so she could sit on the ledge.

That's when she noticed the water where her hand had been. *Someone must have a hole in their canteen,* she thought. *I'll get the little shit when I find out who.*

For the next hour Heather pulled and pushed her way up and down the wall. By the end of her workout cycle she was exhausted and ready for a shower and food.

The Regiment was stood down for forty-eight hours to rest up for the next round of training. That would take place on a small moon and would be the final live fire exercise before the final push into New Gloucester.

Heather's sprits were high. The fitness report for the platoon was the highest it had been in ten months. She ran into other troopers and NCOs coming into the gym area as she was headed out. Everyone else also seemed to be in a good mood.

Chapter Fifteen

Captain Lahaie read the updated orders from the Flag in her ready room. Her steward had just refilled her coffee and warned her about the negative side-effects of too much caffeine and not enough sleep, but there was always something to do that couldn't wait.

She took a sip of the hot beverage and put down the cup. Reaching over to the comm panel, she keyed in her code and called the officer on watch to her ready room. A few minutes later, Lieutenant Provost rang the entry request and entered.

"Sir?"

She handed him the reader and waited for him to skim through the document before saying, "We're about to receive some guests and the admiral wants to move us into the back room."

"Well, transports were always seen as the ugly ducklings of the fleet. We wouldn't want to offend any guests." Provost finished scanning the orders as he spoke. "We won't have much time to sort things out." He handed the reader back.

Taking the reader, Lahaie said, "Plot me a direct course to the RV and coordinate with the other transport. Let's make sure we stay out of the way. I've already passed on a copy of the orders to Colonel Marouf."

"Aye, sir, I'll see to it."

Provost walked out of the ready room, leaving Lahaie to wonder how this would play out.

Surprise is paramount and this enemy recon could scuttle our plans, she thought. *But it might mean intel if we capture their database and comm log intact.*

A change in vibration on the deck plates interrupted Lahaie's thoughts. It was only a slight change, but after spending so much time on the same ship, she knew deep down what every creak, sound, vibration, and rattle meant. In this case, it was a change in course as the big transport accelerated to the rendezvous point out of harm's way, and more importantly, out of sensor range.

The *Athabaskan* and her sister ships *Iroquois*, *Sump*, and *Tembec*, along with the carriers, cruisers, and maintenance tenders, would not be required for this engagement. They would not be able to help the capital ship capture or destroy the recon force. Too many ships could add to the confusion and run the risk of collateral damage.

Better to sit this one out, she thought. *I do want to get stuck in, but not at any price. Besides, Affleck will call us up if needed.*

She turned and reached for the desktop reader's control pad, calling up a tactical plot of the Scotia system on the screen. It was a thing of beauty to watch the flotilla's icons dance.

The plot was tied into the flagship sensors, so the three most probable slide points were blinking an eerie orange. She was not required on the bridge right now so Lahaie ordered some food from her steward. *I'll get an hour in the gym after that*, she thought. There was plenty of time before she would be needed on the bridge again. Her officers were experienced and competent enough to stand watch while they were stood down.

***

It was not easy to predict where a ship would slide. It was more of a guessing game, since there were many points of entry and exit from alternate space. Of course, you also had tactical and navigational restrictions to consider. Sliding too near the gravity well of a star, for example, would put an abrupt end to any trip—as would sliding near or into a well-armed group of ships intent on having your carcass for a doormat.

With so many other options, it was hard to know in advance of a slide—that is, until researchers at the TAF Defense Research Institute discovered that just before a ship transitioned, there was a spike in the gravitational field around the area of slide. Several thousand metric tons of ship about to drop into reality had to disperse the local matter like a wet navy ship displaced water.

Lucky for the navy, bad luck for pirates.

***

After a long wait for any sign of activity, an alert but new and not quite experienced sensor tech on board the super dreadnought *New Terra* almost jumped out of his seat.

"Sir! Gravity spike at twenty eight thousand kilometers off our starboard bow. Two one two point five by five four nine point five, five degrees positive!"

Captain Fitzroy moved quickly to the sensor console. "What kind of displacement are we talking about?"

The tech double-checked his readings. "Sensor shows and AI confirms one hundred to one hundred and forty thousand metric tons, one ship. Slide strength is still low. It looks like the bow push of a battle cruiser. Estimate one-zero point five standard till slide."

"Helm, back us off to sixty thousand kilometers. Comm, transmit to flag and all units the sensor data. XO, bring all tubes to bear and power up my shields. Tactical, put CIC into the loop and plot me a firing sequence based on best guess for quick strike."

Orders went out, repeated and relayed as each command was executed with flawless precision. Fitzroy sat back down and called up a tactical plot on his main screen. Two other ships were now reporting a displacement wave, indicating a ship about to transition into their reality.

***

"Bring the flotilla to alert, if you please. I'm on my way." Affleck quickly dressed and took a last gulp of cold coffee.

He had stood down to get an hour or so of sleep, and had to admit he felt all the better for it. He entered the corridor to the red glare of the battle alert lighting and the ordered flurry of activity as crewmembers readied for action. He made his way to the bridge though the bustle.

On entering the flag bridge, he was handed a reader with updated tactical and navigation information. "Time to transition?" he asked.

The tactical officer, bent over one of his techs, turned his head and said hurriedly, "CIC and our board shows eight minutes, sir."

"XO, flotilla status?"

"All transports and carriers along with tenders are at the RV. Line ships are in place per order of march and report alert status and ready to engage. CIC now confirms we have five contacts, all with

176

similar displacement waves—they have designated them as battle cruisers."

"Right. Comm to all ships from flag, weapons free for non-lethal targeting. Alert the *Athabaskan* and *Tembec*, ready a boarding party, and have them stand by. As soon as we get sensor confirmation of the pirates powering down and closing their missile doors, move the boarding parties in place. Make sure all ships keep a target lock just in case."

"Aye, weapons free for non-lethal targeting. Boarding party to stand by, aye."

The idea was to hit the pirate ships with enough firepower to disable but not destroy the ships. Gathering intelligence at this point was the overriding motive.

Affleck hoped their captains would surrender to the TAF rather than go down fighting for someone else. After all, profit was only worth anything if you survived.

Unfortunately, in Affleck's experience, this theory had not always forecast behavior accurately. Would they fight to the death? He could see their main fleet doing so. What else would they have to lose at that point? But this recon commander may not have the same loyalty while operating on his own.

He needed to know what changes had taken place in New Gloucester and still maintain some level of surprise. It was only dumb luck that permitted this recon in the first place, and he desperately wanted to take advantage of it.

A ship as large as a battle cruiser sliding into reality is a wonder to behold. There would be no marveling this time, however. Each of the five groups of TAF ships had designated target areas, and five seconds before slide, they would let go a massive broadside volley in four waves.

At six seconds prior to the expected slide, Affleck gave the command to open fire. Two hundred and thirty short-range missiles flashed out of their tubes using chemical rockets, taking them three thousand kilometers away before their FTL engines kicked in.

They were limited-yield missiles designed to disable a ship. They did not have enough of a punch to penetrate deep into the heart of a well-armoured hull with shielding, but when they exploded, they released massive amounts of gamma rays that could disrupt sensors and targeting systems and rip human tissue apart.

Such an assault would hopefully be sufficient to instill doubt in the enemy commander. But it was a gamble. The human element was what threw the designers and fleet commanders in the TAF into guessing mode. How would a ship's captain and crew respond when the fight-or-flight instinct was so strong? Backed into a corner, humans and many animals tended to fight first and run afterward.

Destroying a ship, while extremely difficult, was still always easier than taking one whole and with systems intact.

Affleck turned to his tactical officer, "Time to launch *Taciturn* probes. Let's make sure they can't communicate once in-system." He leaned back in his chair.

"Launch *Taciturn* probes, aye."

***

"Countdown to slide," said Captain Appletree on the pirate ship *Maximum*.

His voice was steady but he could feel the sweat roll down the back of his neck. He hated the feeling he got while in alternative space, and welcomed the return to reality.

He was a good actor. The majority of his crew, other than a handful of senior staff, did not know about his discomfort.

As far as he was concerned, pirate life was profitable, while shipboard life offered long-term stability. Appletree had spent several years in the TAF navy but found that he did not make close friends easily. People tended to move from ship to ship and long-lasting relationships did not happen very often. This was one of the reasons he had jumped ship a dozen years earlier and signed on with a renegade captain.

"One minute to slide, sir."

"Ship's status, XO?"

Lieutenant Commander Thaddeus Rubric, the XO, was young and idealistic. He had been with Appletree for the past eight years and was fast moving up the ranks on the ship, proving himself time and time again.

"All departments report standing by. Alert status is high with all tubes loaded and safeties on. Sensors are on maximum forward scan and the AI is up."

Rubric hesitated and looked apprehensive before continuing. "We do have a problem with the fire control system on the anti-missile turrets, and at least half of the close-in weapon systems are not operational. The techs are on it and there're advising it should be corrected within the hour."

"What's the problem with the anti-missile turrets? I thought we had the software problem resolved." Appletree was not happy. One minute before the slide was not the time for him to find out that a good part of his defensive systems were down.

"It's my error, sir," responded Rubric quickly. He had hoped that the problems would be corrected before now, but he readied himself to accept any consequences. "The software issue was resolved, but now it appears to have been only one part of the problem. Our part's supplies are not complete and we have not updated the turret fire control system in the past two years. I did not want to bother you with it until we had a more definitive estimate of the problem. Sorry, sir."

His reasons were valid. The ship had not had any updates to its failing systems in two years, but a recon with the possibility of facing TAF ships was not the time to take this kind of chance.

"Very sloppy, Mr. Rubric, and I am not impressed. Consider yourself on report and your bonus docked. On a recon this far from home and about to slide is no time to fuck around with my ship and tell me that our systems are down. Do you understand?"

Appletree did not want to get loud with his admonishment, especially in public and on the bridge. He did hope, however, that Rubric realized that waiting so long might be costly.

"Yes, sir, I understand and it will not happen again. Sorry."

"Stand by for slide," said the navigational officer, sounding almost bored.

Appletree gripped the armrest on his chair as the big ship slid back into reality. He could feel the ship vibrate and for a moment, he thought that it was an unusually rough slide. It was not until he found himself flying through the air and saw the floor coming up to meet his face that he realized something was wrong.

"What the fuck just happened?" he shouted over the deafening sounds around him as he tasted blood on his upper lip.

Over the sound of the klaxon, the bridge crew was frantically trying to deal with incoming calls from every deck and section head, small fires and blown panels, including injuries and dead crewmembers. Everyone had the same question as they picked themselves up. Even the dead had that questioning look on their faces, frozen in time.

Appletree felt a sharp pain when he touched his head and came away with blood dripping off his hand. He picked himself up, holding onto a support column to steady himself. Looking around, he could see at least two of his men dead, their necks at twisted angles.

"Someone better be able to tell me what just happened!" He had a difficult time trying to keep his voice steady in the chaos around him. His head was beginning to throb with pain.

Rubric had been flung across the bridge but was not hurt. "All stations, damage report!" he barked, then stood slowly and walked over to help move the two dead out of the way.

The main overhead lights flickered and dimmed but provided enough illumination to see. Everyone reflexively focused on post-damage tasks, knowing exactly what to do without thinking. The comm officer busied himself with damage control reports from all over the ship. Rubric hovered close by and relayed the details to Appletree.

"We're dead in the water. Engine room reports all main power is out. The containment bottle is still intact, but the circuits for the main drive are fused and we can't get to the backups. That bulkhead is gone with all hands. Laval said he can get maneuvering thrusters but that's all at this time. Life support is operational but the scrubbers are having a hard time with all the smoke and fumes."

Rubric took a reader from tactical. "Damn!" His look of shock quickly turned to anger. "We've been fucked. We have short-range sensors, captain, but you'll wish we hadn't."

Rubric transferred the data to the captain's screens and called for a live feed to the holo-tank. Both he and Appletree were agog at what they saw. Red TAF icons hovered all around the five battle cruisers and more incoming missiles were headed their way.

Appletree stepped back and paused before asking, "Weapons status?"

Rubric checked. "Seven tubs are down, and we can't open the outer doors. We have eighteen tubes loaded and ready to fire. And we have no point defense."

Rubric felt the scathing look Appletree shot back at that last statement, and burned with the shame of his failure to have the defensive systems operational at a crucial time.

Appletree looked back at the tactical image in the holo tank. The *Swift* was bleeding air, but only the outer decks seemed to be breached. They were also able to get at least one, maybe two broadsides off along with *Bandit* and *Slater*.

"Captain!" shouted Rubric. "We have a firing solution!" He spoke as if the engagement had been going on for hours instead of seconds.

"Fire all available tubes."

Appletree moved back to his chair and sat down, but not before more explosions rocked his ship and damage control teams reported back the bad news. He knew at this point his ship was done for. While the damage was isolated to the outer decks, it was extensive. The engine damage was the worst. It made a quick exit impossible. He could pump out missile after missile but only for two broadsides, and even then he could not count on the targeting AI to hit anything. He was a sitting duck.

Reluctantly he ordered, "Helm, get us the hell out of here. Reverse course, put us on a heading away from the other ships and make best possible speed. Roll the ship and show them our belly."

All eyes now turned to Appletree. Showing their belly was the same as surrendering.

He knew what it could mean for him if they were captured, but the majority of his men would live. A penal colony was better than being dead.

When the helm officer did not move fast enough, he shouted, "Do it! Unless you would rather I order the air locks opened and the ship purged? I don't like this anymore than any of you, but at least this way you live."

That got everyone to turn back to the job at hand. "Aye, captain. Reverse course and roll ship."

**

Heather and her platoon were suited up in preparation for action. They were one of the six platoons in the flotilla getting ready for boarding party duty. Right now, they were watching the ambush of the pirate recon force on monitors in their briefing room. No one took their eyes off the live feed from CIC.

Someone, Heather wasn't sure who, commented that they could scratch one boarding party as one pirate ship was badly damaged and did not look like it would last too much longer.

Cold, but an accurate assessment if things don't change, Heather thought.

She had not seen Peter since yesterday morning. He was not assigned to the boarding party, as power armour tended to do a lot of damage and the plan was to take as much of the ship as possible intact, with prisoners and a functional memory core.

***

"New heading, Mr. Bank. Three five seven point three by six four four point zero, ten degrees negative, ahead flank. I do not want that ship getting away."

Albert Bank, newly promoted to ensign, repeated the order. "Three five seven point three by six four four point zero, ten degrees negative pitch. Ahead flank. Aye."

He did not want the pirate running tail either, and so he was almost at a loss for words when the sensor showed the big ship rotating its aspect and presenting its belly.

Captain Wen handed his XO back the reader he was reviewing, directing his attention toward the fleeing pirate. The *Conqueror* was one of the newer Fort Resolution class super dreadnoughts and in control of one of the seven ship firing groups. His job was to disable and hold for boarding the target identified as Barrel One.

"Sir, Barrel One aspect is changing. It's still running, but he's showing us its belly. They're surrendering, sir!"

Wen brought up the tactical data on one of his monitors. "What the hell is he playing at?"

He was skeptical, and for good reason. This wouldn't be the first time a ship and its crew feigned surrender only to put a round up the kilt of some unsuspecting crew.

"Comm, signal to surrendering ship. Verify—"

"Sir!" interrupted the tactical officer. "Barrel Three is moving to intercept Barrel One!"

A quick glance at his tactical plot verified the change in course, but it also suggested an opportunity. If Barrel One was giving up, the recon commander may not appreciate that and move to take out his own ship.

"Comm, get me the flag, priority one on secure, and include Captain Shark on the comm."

The XO walked over to Wen. "What are you thinking, sir?"

"I'm thinking, XO, that Barrel Three is the recon commander and that he's not changing course to protect Barrel One, but to shoot him in the back for running. We may have to take him out before that happens."

"Captain, flag and Captain Shark on channel two four six."

"Thank you." Wen keyed his access codes and a split screen image of Affleck and Shark appeared.

"Admiral, Kevin, I trust you've seen the change in course for Barrel Three in response to Barrel One's action." They nodded.

"I was about to comm Barrel One when Three made for intercept," Wen went on. "I think Three is the recon commander and is setting up a kill shot. I recommend, admiral, that Captain Shark take Barrel Three out of the picture. It may save B-One and convince the others to stand down."

Shark cut in. "Admiral, I have to concur with Captain Wen. It is unlikely that we will get much from this commander if he is willing to destroy one of his own at this point. We get too close, he seems to be more likely to destroy his own ship than to let us board."

Affleck had already come to the same conclusion.

"Right, gentlemen. Wen, contact B-One and see what aid they need and what their intentions are. Shark, you're in a better position to intercept B-Three. Take him out, but see if you can keep the ship intact. We may still get some data from their core memory. We'll take care of the others."

Affleck cut the signal. Wen sat back hoping Shark could make the kill soon. *Let's get this over with and move on to the real task at hand.*

***

Affleck looked at Kugong. "Comm the other ships. Ready all tubes with ship killers and stand by. Then patch me through on an open channel to the pirates. Alert the transports and close-in defense ships, then get the boarding parties set to launch."

Kugong acknowledged and obeyed. The transports would bring in the boarding parties to within one thousand kilometers and launch the combat shuttles with the troops. A minimum of four boats would be launched per pirate cruiser, gaining access to the four key entry locations. Bridge, engine and engineering levels, weapons control and shuttle bays would all be hit at the same time.

***

On board the *Bandit*, the tac officer was shouting. "Sir, the *Maximum* is moving off! She's making a course away from us at three five seven point three by six four four point zero."

Bishop transferred the nav-comm screen data to his terminal in disbelief. "What the hell is he doing? Comm, get me the *Maximum*."

The ship lurched violently. A split second later the hull breach alarms went off, and damage control crews were dispatched. Most of the missiles fired at them were being intercepted, but the anti-missile fire control computers could not keep up with the onslaught.

Bishop's ship rocked again and two damage-control personnel on the bridge were thrown against a bulkhead. Smoke wafted out of a number of access panels as conduits and fiber melted from small fires and short circuits. Damage control had their work cut out for them.

The comm officer shouted over the noise, "Captain! The *Maximum* does not answer, and the other ships aren't getting any response from her either!"

"Damn them and their coward captain. I won't let the TAF take the data they carry. Nav, plot an intercept course with the *Maximum*—best speed."

Another round of gamma rays penetrated the hull, and this time, it was close. Bishop quickly glanced at the plot to check the status of the recon force.

Fuck this recon, he thought. "Tactical, hold fire on the TAF, plot a firing solution on the *Maximum*. Comm, get me the other captains *now!*"

No one questioned his order to fire on their own ship. They were cowards and did not deserve to live or share in the profits.

The three other captains' faces flashed on screen and Bishop did not waste time getting to the point.

"Appletree has turned tail and run. I'm going to open fire on the *Maximum* as soon as we're in range.

187

Keep these bastards busy—and one last thing: don't get captured. Make every effort to hold until *Maximum* is dead and then we get out of here. When we do break out, head for Merkley Crossing. Questions?" While he did not want to answer much right now, he knew they were inevitable under the circumstances.

Jackson spoke first. "This is bullshit, Bishop! We've been made well and good. What's the point of killing Appletree? It's a waste of time and ammo, neither of which we have an abundance of right now."

"Simple, you idiot," Bishop said with as much sting as possible. "You take orders from me—and even more importantly, there's too much at stake. The profits from this op will more than offset any risks, and you know it. We also have to keep any data Appletree has from falling into TAF hands."

Jackson nodded mutely.

Brown was about to say something when he was thrown from his seat. The *Swift* had taken three missiles on their port side and she was hurt. The connection was cut off and the screen went blank.

"Time to go, gentlemen," snapped Bishop. "Give me enough time to finish the job and stay the fuck away from those missiles. Do not let them get into laser range."

He cut the comm and gave the order to open fire on the *Maximum* when in range. He was going to finish what the TAF had started on Appletree.

***

The speakers crackled to life with a pleasant announce chime, a sound in stark contrast with the announcement. "All boarding shuttles stand by to launch."

There was no draft into the TAF. Planets from around the Confederation sent the brightest and best volunteers to the recruiting centres for selection and training. The reasons for volunteering varied for each person. Some enlisted for adventure, or for a different kind of education; others signed up for a change of life or out of a sense of duty or family traditions in the military.

The selection board vetted the candidates for individual aptitudes. Being selected for training in the ground forces was considered an honor. Ground force troopers required strength, speed, agility, ingenuity, and the ability to think out of the box, improvise, and accept responsibility. Heather had volunteered, and was selected, for ground force assignment right out of university. This was exactly what she wanted to be doing.

Heather's platoon was on the platform, ready to board. As soon as the order was given, they picked up their kit and loaded. Once inside, they locked themselves down and prepared for one of the toughest jobs in the service: boarding a hostile ship with a very pissed off and most likely determined crew in deep space. All this without heavy weapons support.

All Heather could think about was Peter. Why now, as she prepped for a battle? He was on her mind more and more, but right now was not really the time for dreaming. She had to keep her mind focused and clear.

Her section was assigned to board the battle cruiser designated Barrel Three. She did not know one barrel from the next and felt that every one of them would pose an equal risk. But that was her job and she volunteered for it.

Chapter Sixteen

Battle cruisers were big and well-armoured, with an advanced fire control system. They could put out a broadside that could devastate a small moon. They were not invincible, however, and under crushing missile fire pumping gamma rays through plaststeel, ballistic armour, composite ceramics, plastics, clothing and human tissue, a cruiser will fail.

"Admiral, Barrel Four is bleeding air from the port bow and CIC confirms hull breaches in the stern near main engines. They're showing power surges and may be experiencing a containment breach."

Seeing a big ship die with all hands was never easy. Affleck knew they were criminals, but they were still people—part of the human race with hopes and dreams, and this mess had a bile taste to it.

For the actions of a few who lead a cause—in this case, greed—thousands would die.

His thoughts were interrupted when the tactical office exclaimed, "Sir, she's about to blow! Secondary explosions from the hangar deck and aft sections."

"XO?"

"I'm on it, sir."

Affleck wanted to clear his ships out of the blast area. He kept an eye on his plot, but none of his units seemed to be moving fast enough. Once the containment field went on the big cruiser, this system would have a second short-lived sun.

Affleck checked his plot but did not see his ships moving off.

"What's the delay? Get those ships moving, XO!" he said, urgency evident in his tone.

"Sir, all ships are moving now. The delay was due to damage on the main motors of *Provider*. It's been patched for now."

***

Onboard the *Swift*, engineering and damage-control crews worked at a feverish pace to reroute power to stabilize the magnetic containment field.

The cascading power failure had taken out or weakened many of the circuits, eliminating what they had available to work with. Making one connection would cause a conduit, switch, or relay to blow further down the line.

In the end, their efforts were too little too late. The magnetic containment bottle housing the fuel pile on the *Swift* finally let go and allowed the pile to melt down. The crews working on securing it never even realized it before they were dead.

***

Affleck saw the start of the explosion before the filters on the video pickups around the ship cut off the feed. By then the visible light from the exploding ship was too intense to watch with unprotected eyes.

What a waste, he thought. *Twelve, fifteen hundred people in the blink of an eye. Billions of credits gone—and what about all the innocent people these particular pirates hijacked, burgled, and spaced? Their lives wasted? At least this is a better end than some of those poor bastards deserved.*

The command chair began to vibrate and Affleck made sure he was secured. He knew that the concussion wave would reach the flagship, but the strength would depend on their distance from the initial zero point.

Right now they were on a parabolic course with the wave front so they could stay in range of the other four pirates. It also meant they were exposed the blast, and he felt it.

Wave front strength was rated on a sliding scale from one to twenty, with one being the most violent. At this distance, there were experiencing a wave front of twelve. Not enough to destroy a ship, but enough to cause damage that might delay their mission.

The captain's voice boomed through the ship. "All hands brace for impact! All hands brace for impact!"

The TAF ships turned into the wave at the last second in order to minimize the surface area. The dreadnought rocked hard, throwing around anything that was not secured: personal kit, readers, tools and people. It passed quickly, not lasting more than a few seconds, though it felt longer to those experiencing it.

The captain came back on the intercom immediately after the front passed. "All hands secure from impact. Damage control report to bridge. All hands maintain battle stations."

***

The pirates took advantage of the *Swift*'s loss to increase their distance from the TAF force. Appletree knew now that he and his crew had been right to make their exit. Listening to whispered conversations on the bridge and secretly monitoring shipwide comm traffic told him that his crew was also

193

beginning to agree. Spending time on a penal colony was better than knocking at death's door.

Appletree did not appreciate the *Bandit* coming after him. He had no doubts about her intentions. He knew Bishop would have already opened fire if it were not for *Swift's* timely demise.

Bishop should know better than to push this to the death. There's no profit in that extreme.

Now, without self-defense missiles, laser turrets or an AI worth the credits, they were dead in space. He had to get the TAF between him and Bishop to have any chance.

He keyed the comm. "CIC, do we have a firing solution on the *Bandit*?"

"System's just coming back online, sir. That jolt we took played havoc with the targeting computers."

"Good, send it to tactical ASAP." He turned his attention to the tactical officer.

"Tactical, lock on the *Bandit* and fire all available tubes when ready. Best judgment on the firing solution. Helm, after the last round, change course. Plot the shortest distance to the TAF dreadnought that hailed us."

As much as the logic and economics of the action made sense, it was painful. Though the majority of the crew would like, he knew that he, as the captain of a pirate ship, would die for his crimes.

"Port and stern tubes ready to fire. Firing now!"

At that, the tactical officer launched what would probably be his last broadside. He laid out a firing pattern that would progressively slow the *Bandit* down. Without specific firing orders, it was left up to his discretion, and he took pride in the firing sequence.

As in a ground force firing section, he divided his available tubes into left and right sections. He, like everyone else on board, knew they would not be able to destroy the *Bandit*. He intended to make the best use of his assets, however, by first creating a screen two thousand meters in front of the *Bandit*. The screen would help mask their signature and confuse the *Bandit*'s launch computers, making it difficult for them to get an initial target lock on the incoming missiles. It would also mask the second round of missiles he was planning to unleash.

This was intended to be the more lethal barrage. The missiles would acquire a target lock prior to the first set of explosions and punch through at point-blank range. They would only have one chance, so it had to work.

"Firing sequence laid in and we have a solution. Firing second round."

"Get us the hell out of here, helm." Appletree's voice was calm as he stood. He was pleased with his young tactical officer. The firing sequence was sheer brilliance in its simplicity. At the same time, he wondered if it would work.

***

The vibration on the decking was beginning to subside. Bishop picked himself up from the floor and rotated his left shoulder to work out the kinks.

When the *Swift* exploded, she was way too close for Bishop's liking. The wave front passed through the *Bandit,* causing it to rotate out of position. Many of the ship's systems were unaffected, but the human systems were in disarray. Damage control and medical response crews were spread thin. On the bridge were two injured: one with a mild concussion, another with a broken arm. It was a severe break, with part of an upper bone splitting skin and uniform.

195

Blood was splattered all over the environmental station.

"Get the injured off my bridge and get replacements down here!" Bishop yelled, his face flushed with anger. He swung his arm back and forth, stretching it out and rubbing it with his other hand. "Tactical, range to target?"

No one responded right away. Coming through and surviving so close to a ship going nova was cause to both celebrate and make repairs. In this case, with the TAF so close, much of the crew would have preferred to use the blast to make their escape. Profit was a powerful motivator, however, and the hesitation was slight.

"Fifteen thousand kilometers and gaining," said the tactical officer, perspiration pouring from his face. "Tubes six, eight, nine, ten, and twelve are gone along with all crew."

Two hundred men dead.

"More profit for the living," Bishop snapped. "Fire all remaining tubes at ten thousand kay."

The order was acknowledged and relayed. The distance decreased with every second. Bishop wanted to be certain that his missiles fired at point-blank range, leaving Appletree no chance to defend himself. It was personal now.

An old Earth proverb talks about the best-laid plans of men and Bishop remembered it now. At eleven thousand kilometers, his own plan changed when ship killer missiles exploded two thousand meters out from the *Bandit*.

Bishop grinned. *Bad shot, Appletree. You, my cowardly friend, are mine.*

Then Bishop's own world was rocked a second later when two dozen ship killers slammed into his shields.

The main lighting went out and emergency battery backup lamps went on. Smoke filled the bridge and damage control crews jammed the comm system with reports from all over the ship.

***

"Assault shuttle one-one-five, launch when ready."

Heather felt only a slight acceleration in G forces as her shuttle launched from the *Athabaskan*. Assault shuttles did not pull the same Gs as drop ships and fighters, so the feeling was brief. The external monitors in the shuttle flashed on to provide Heather and the boarding party a view of the departure, which would soon be replaced with a destination or forward view. In the inset, a navigation plot showed the shuttle's relative position with the host ship and its target destination. A sliding scale counted down the distance and time to docking.

Their orders were simple: they would board Barrel Three, the battle cruiser designated as the recon command vessel. Other boarding parties would take on the other two combatants while a command and security team would board the surrendering ship.

Heather envied that detail, but in a strange way, she also welcomed the chance for combat in this environment. Self-preservation told her that this was contradictory to survival, but she felt a sense of completeness in battle with her squad. She filed that observation away. Something she would have to speak to the counselor about.

That would have to wait, however, as the assault shuttle pitched and changed direction in preparation for boarding. This was the most dangerous part of this type of action. One shot and they would be part of the cosmic dust that drifted through space and time. Their briefing packet indicated that the battle cruiser was disabled, but that assessment could not guarantee that the self-defense and close-in guns and lasers were down.

No major power emissions were being detected from the huge ship, but there was still some activity. Heather was certain that damage control crews were feverishly repairing the destruction.

***

Bishop coughed and spat blood as he picked up a dead crewman from the tactical console and tossed him on the floor.

"I want the dead off my bridge and power restored!" he roared. "XO! Get me tactical and sensors! I want to know what's happening!"

No one responded right away. They were all busy, trying to repair the damage caused by the last missile strike fired by the *Maximum*. Display panels were blown out and smoke was coming out of several panels. Damage control crews worked feverishly to control two small fires ignited by power conduits that overloaded when the breakers did not give.

A crewman took the tactical seat and tried to call up data but nothing happened. "Captain, tactical is down and I don't have any power at this station."

Bishop lunged at the ensign and hit him in the back of the head with an open hand.

"Get up and find another terminal then, you idiot!" he shouted and spat at the same time.

Leaning over to steady himself on the back of a chair, he fought to catch his breath. Smoke, saliva, and blood filled his throat and lungs, but he was determined to keep after Appletree and he needed a functional ship to do that.

The ensign got up quickly and nearly tripped over Bishop on his way to another open terminal. Two seats over, he found one that had power and transferred the tactical protocols in order to access the external sensors.

What he saw only added to his fear.

"Captain, incoming targets—five assault shuttles on a vector to us." His voice was calmer than he thought he could muster, and it surprised him.

Bishop seemed even more surprised. He ordered the close-in weapons systems activated to target the shuttles. "Range on the shuttles and blow them out of my space, mister."

"I can't, sir. Only one turret is sending feedback. The others are down and I can't raise any crew in the area to man them." The ensign's voice was becoming shaky and strained.

"Then fire what we do have and get me internal comm!" replied the infuriated Bishop. He suddenly felt tired, and his legs were beginning to give out. He sat back in his command chair. The comm officer looked over and signaled that he had internal shipwide communications.

"All hands, this is the captain," Bishop announced. "We're going to have company very soon, and you need to know that if you don't kill the TAF who are about to board us, I'll kill you myself."

He cut the signal and said to the comm officer coldly, "Sound general quarters—repel boarders."

Under his breath, he added, "I won't let this stop me, Appletree. You'll be dead by my hand when I catch you."

He coughed again, spitting more blood on the floor, then wiped his mouth with the back of his hand.

*　*　*

Heather's shuttle was one of five that would hit the battle cruiser at different entry points simultaneously. Her squad was tasked with taking the bridge, the forward data banks, and the forward weapons lock-up. Other squads would take the auxiliary bridge, aft weapons storage, CIC, engineering, torpedo and missile bays, and the shuttle launch bay.

Everyone would be on crew suppression. Their orders were to take prisoners if possible, securing them with sub-dermal locator tags and knockout drugs. The tags were to be injected under the fatty layers of skin near the neck. Nanobot technology would then send back a signal to a central location. It was a highly effective way of monitoring a prisoner. If one moved out of an established location, an alarm sounded.

If the pirates did not respond well to the hospitality of the TAF, then Heather and her squad was authorized to use deadly force—a phrase Heather thought sounded like it came from a bad holo drama. She hoped the writers of *this* drama had a better ending that those of the photoplays she had had the misfortune of watching.

Dead or alive. What other outcome was there? she thought.

She watched the tactical plot and the countdown timer. Barrel Two and Four had been targeted with ship killers, and by the look of their aft areas, the engines were down. Point defense seemed to be still functional and one TAF shuttle had been blown apart. Heather could not tell if there were any survivors, but it did not look promising.

Another shuttle suffered some damage but continued on. All shuttles were executing an evasive pattern to avoid the lasers. Once they got close enough, the lasers would become ineffective, allowing them a chance to dock.

Sergeant Taylor brought everyone back to the here and now. "Stand up! Ready for boarding!"

Everyone stood in the tight compartment. Each trooper checked the kit of the one in front, with Taylor checking the last man.

The monitor would shut down soon, so Heather glanced over and noticed the distance to target indicator closing to two hundred meters.

"Helmets on, weapons charged," Taylor said.

Everyone obeyed just as the external feed to the monitors was cut. Their internal combat suit power came online and Heather checked her telltales and suit status.

"CIC confirms no active power source from main motors and close-in weapons. You all know the drill, so I do not want to see any fuck-ups. Let's make this clean. These bastards will fight it out so let's be ready. Comm check in one."

Taylor hated the pep talk before an op. He always thought it sounded corny. *Besides, everyone knows their job by now or they wouldn't be here*, he thought—but he also knew that some of the troopers needed it.

Heather felt the adrenaline rush sweeping over her now. It was a comfortable, warm, familiar feeling, a natural high that no synthetic drug could ever replicate. She remembered again why she loved her job—that feeling, the sensation of familiarity and power mixed with a sense of home. It would have been hard for her to explain to someone who had never experienced it.

The shuttle pilot made one last evasive maneuver before docking, lining up the access hatch with their docking clamp. It would be normal for a defending ship's crew to get people to these areas in order to defend access and repel boarders.

In the past, many troopers lost their lives boarding a ship, since they became cannon fodder. The first off the assault shuttle were usually mowed down until the boarders could overwhelm the defenders, setting up a defensive perimeter. The TAF had developed a solution to this problem in the form of a massive plasma discharge outside the hatch just before the door was blown. It was messy but effective, and often deadly.

Heather felt the shuttle rock as the plasma discharge cleared their way into the pirates' hull. Anything that had been human was now nothing but overcooked meat and cinders mixed with molten plastic.

The hatch slid back into its recessed space and Heather moved quickly out with the rest of the boarding party. She moved forward, stepping over four bodies toward an unmarked hatch that was partly opened and scorched from the plasma blast.

The passageway was smoke-filled and the main lighting was offline. Emergency lighting wasn't working much better. Much was in disrepair. Heather noticed several maintenance and access panels opened or missing along the corridor, as well as unrepaired equipment and damage to local systems.

As Heather's helmet display came online with a schematic of the pirate hull, she could see where the other teams were entering the ship. Seeing the overall operation was fine for a commander, but she needed to narrow the field of view.

With a few practiced eye movements, she dialed down the field to show just the immediate vicinity with an overlay of the main objectives. Her thermal image system showed the hall clear of targets to her front. She checked the room on the other side of the broken doorway. It looked like crew quarters with a bunk, table, and storage cabinets, but it was empty and did not look as if it had been lived in for some time.

"Sergeant, north corridor clear."

Taylor needed to get this phase of the operation moving. "Brassard, you and Bird with Brown, clear one hundred meters down the north corridor. Carmichael, take Williams and Ratte. Clear the south end. Same distance and hold."

Heather and Carmichael acknowledged and started to move with their charges. Taylor held with the rest of the squad in reserve in case they had to respond.

Platoon and squad composition were different on a boarding party. Only troopers with special training were invited to the party—those with detailed knowledge of shipboard systems and configurations. It was vital to everyone's survival, because shooting out the wrong power conduit or circuit could result in loss of air or gravity, or even flood the compartment with toxic gas.

Maneuvering room in such a confined space was limited, so squads often needed to break into small groups of two to five troopers—a strategy not needed usually in larger, more open side operations. Booby traps and ambushes were also more dangerous onboard a ship. A small explosion could do more damage in such confined spaces, and ambushes could kill more people and be set up very quickly in more areas.

Heather made sure her arc of fire was clear and signaled for Bird and Brown to move forward. Brown took a position ten meters to the right in a doorway that was half open. Signaling "all clear," he motioned for Bird to move forward.

The troopers moved slowly, ensuring that the way was clear before a step was taken. They did not want to get caught in a vulnerable position.

After almost seventy meters, everything was going well. The smoke and dust from the initial boarding was starting to clear, and visibility was improving. There was a slight bend to the right in the hall so Bird moved with deliberate speed to see around the corner. Hugging the left side, he slowed when he neared the crest.

"Hey, Brassard, this is weird. The lighting is offline just ahead but it's too dark. Even with the damage to the ship there should be some emergency lighting. There's nothing here."

Brown keyed the mike as he took up a better position. "Hey, Bird, you afraid of the dark?"

Heather moved parallel with Brown and waited for Bird to get settled. He was about twenty meters up and holding, trying to get a better angle.

"What about thermal? Any signatures?" asked Heather.

"That's the other strange thing. I'm not getting anything. No thermal signature of any kind. At the very least I should be seeing some hotspots. They must be masked. I should be getting something even off the wall monitors."

Bird crawled forward a meter, still hidden from any direct fire that might come his way. "I'm tossing a grenade. Fire in the hole!" he announced as he shot one into the darkness from his launcher.

As soon as he did, someone fired back. Rounds smashed into the wall above his head.

"Shit!" Bird rolled to the right. As he did, he extended his left arm and pushed off with his right to flip back.

The rounds traversed toward him. He was just able to push back and flip in time to feel a sting in his left arm.

"I'm hit! It's not bad—my left arm, but it's only grazed," he gasped.

Brown moved forward to grab Bird and pull him to relative safety. "Trying to get another medal or just want to visit that captivating nurse in the med lab?" he joked.

Bird's grenade exploded, but fire continued to come from around the corner. Heather pulled up her schematic on her helmet display, then called Taylor on the squad frequency and gave him a sit-rep.

"Sergeant, contact at seventy-five meters at the right bend. Unknown number, well-armed and determined. Bird's left arm was hit but he can continue. We fired off one grenade but they must have knocked it into an empty room off on their right. They also have the lighting off in that section, and we didn't pick up any thermal signatures."

Taylor responded instantly. "I'm bringing up the team. Carmichael came up blank at his end and we have to push forward in your direction anyway. I'm guessing they have thermal suits and heat suppressors, which explains the lack of signatures. Hold on..."

Heather turned and saw Taylor coming up the corridor behind her. Firing had stopped from around the bend. Once Taylor reached them, he would take over, and she was fine with that.

Brown motioned ahead. "Movement," he whispered—though no one but Heather could hear him even if he shouted. He pointed, and she saw a quick shadow on the left side of the wall.

People and—

Before the thought was completed, she realized the pirates were about to launch a smart bomb. A man-portable missile normally used against light armour, it would prove even more deadly in the confined space of a ship.

"Smart bomb incoming!" she screamed.

A few troopers dropped or ducked into alcoves while others dropped back to take cover in an empty room. Heather picked up her weapon and flipped the selector to full auto, ejected the half magazine, and dropped in a full one. At the same time she stood, bracing herself against the wall.

She took two running leaps forward and dove for the left side of the hall near where Bird was hit. As she flung herself forward, she aimed at the general direction of the launcher and fired, holding her finger on the trigger until the magazine was empty.

One hundred rounds of ten-millimeter darts fired on full auto. It did not take long to empty the magazine, but the damage it did in such a tight confined space was enough to bring the ambushing pirates to their knees.

"Hold your fire! We yield—we give up!" one pirate screamed, coughing and spitting blood,

Bird and Brown, closest to Heather, ran forward and around the bend. The two people who had been about to launch the small missile were barely recognizable as human. The darts had torn through them and left large holes behind with bits of flesh, bone, and blood on the floor and walls. Several others, hiding behind debris, were bleeding from multiple injuries. Others were moaning or holding arms, legs, and faces that had received some of the darts, compliments of Heather Brassard.

Brown collected the weapons from surrendering or wounded pirates and passed them back to the other troopers now joining them from the main group. Bird and another trooper started to check the dead and near-dead as well as the makeshift barricade for any booby traps or intel, while medics treated the wounded.

Taylor assessed the situation quickly. "Burnaby, you and Douglas take our guests and secure them in the last room we passed on the right. Matheson, start processing them."

The three troopers acknowledged and began to direct the surrendering pirates toward their new temporary home. Matheson was the medic who would tag and put to sleep the eight surviving ambushers, including the wounded. The eight men ranged in age from fifty to eighty years and appeared to be in good physical shape. They held their heads low when their hands were bound, showing little, if any, fight left.

Taylor now looked at Heather, who was crouched, leaning with her back against a bulkhead. She was breathing heavily but alert.

"Nice job, Brassard. You just saved our butts. Now, do you mind telling me what the hell you were thinking?"

Winded, she panted, "Launching that thing would have fried any pirate in proximity to the back blast. They would've had to take cover first. I know it was a long shot, but I figured I only had a second or two to react before they were ready."

"Damn good show, Brassard, but give me some warning when you're going to give me heart failure." He smiled and stretched out his hand to help her on her feet.

She stood with his help and switched her now empty mag for a fresh one, placing the empty magazine in its pouch on her webbing.

"No problem, sergeant. Just part of the job." She smiled and took a deep breath as she prepared mentally for the remainder of the operation. She was not fazed by what happened, but the latest adrenaline rush on top of her already heightened state of alertness left her on more of an edge than she wanted to be. Overstimulation could prevent clear thinking, and that could be lethal.

"I'll be fine," she reassured Taylor—and herself.

Taylor was already concentrating on the next leg of the operation. This would be the most difficult part, since the squad would need to split into two in order to meet the timings and secure the forward data banks and weapons lock-up.

While securing the computer core and lock-up was not going to be a walk-through, it would be the least of his problems. The toughest area to take was going to be the bridge. For that, Taylor would have to meet up with another squad and hit it from two different entry points. First things first, however, and that was to secure and lock out the data banks in the computer's core.

"Hickson and Williams, take point. We move forward to this junction." He highlighted the T-intersection on their helmet displays.

"The data terminal access port is on the right corridor about two hundred meters, and the forward weapon's lock-up is on the left, three hundred meters and up two levels. Hold at the junction and send back a sit-rep. I'll give you…" Taylor paused and checked the chronometer in his helmet display. "Ten minutes to get there. We'll hold here. Any questions?"

Neither did. They checked their weapons and left. The corridor was still dark and they could not see past the current bend to the right.

The two separated themselves by ten meters and moved out, with Williams taking the lead point on the right side and Hickson on the left. The separation would allow them to react to any surprises and respond without both of them getting killed. In the meantime, the rest of the squad would assess any damage to their equipment, finish securing the prisoners, and check in with the other boarding parties.

Taylor finished talking to the other squads. "The other sections have seen about the same amount of resistance as we have. There had also been some sporadic hit-and-runs, but nothing serious," he announced. It was always good to keep everyone updated on the big picture. "We've taken some casualties, though: three dead and seven wounded, bad enough to be evacuated. Still, we've gotten off lucky considering the op."

No one spoke. Everyone had known and accepted the risks.

After ten minutes, Taylor verified the time and pulled up the map overlay showing the green icons representing Williams and Hickson making their way along the long corridor.

"All right, people, let's move," he said and stood.

Chapter Seventeen

Williams comm'd Taylor. "Sergeant, we're twenty meters from the junction and no contact. There's no cover or hatchways to duck into from here to the corner, so I'm going to use a stun grenade. We'll toss two on each side."

"Go ahead, and watch yourself."

Williams and Hickson took out two stun grenades each—nothing more than smoke, flash, and lots of noise. They set the timer on the first to one second, the second to one point five, and launched them around each corner.

The small grenades had just cleared the edge of the intersection when they exploded in a flash and bang that would have woken the dead, if any were around. No fire returned so the two ran forward and cautiously checked around the corner. No pirates or other thermal signatures.

"Sergeant, all clear. Come on up."

"Right, we can see you now."

Taylor and the squad reached Williams and Hickson a minute later. He sent part of the squad with Carmichael to the forward data bank to secure the memory core and isolate it so no one could destroy hopefully valuable data. They would also set up a guard with four troopers to hold it.

***

Carmichael and his contingent reached the data terminals easily. He put Erin Longwood to work securing and locking out the memory banks, keeping them from being erased.

210

Longwood was a newbie to the TAF, but when he was in his late eighties he was considered one of the best computer techs of his time. He had trouble articulating what drew him to TAF. He certainly hadn't joined for the adventure—adventure in many forms terrified him. And joining the TAF for the money, or saying you had, would only get you a term as a resident in a psych facility on a distant colony planet.

Longwood only knew that deep down he felt that he had a duty to serve a greater cause. It encompassed who he was and his place in the universe. It was as if there was emptiness around him, and his place in the grand scheme of things was being part of the TAF. It gave him a sense of completeness he needed.

Carmichael set up two guards on either end of the short access passageway to watch for visitors while Longwood worked on gaining access to the secure room housing the memory core. The hall was dimly lit with only emergency lighting, which cast a shadowy glow on the troopers.

Longwood had to turn up the cooling on his environment controls as sweat started to form on his brow and eyelids.

"Is it hot in here?" he asked out loud, not realizing his mike was tuned to section frequency.

Carmichael grinned. "Erin, you'd work up a sweat taking a cold bath. Relax and just concentrate. We have plenty of time."

"I'm almost through the initial security lock. It should be just one level of—"

Longwood hadn't even finished as the lock on the hatch cycled and slid into its recess.

"Okay, then," he said with a confident smile. "If the lockouts on the core are this easy, we should have no problem isolating it from the bridge."

"Great, let's get on with it then." Carmichael did not want to give the crew time to wipe data that might give them an edge when they hit New Gloucester.

Longwood unclipped his portable terminal from the hatch security panel and walked through into the data core. It was a narrow room with data banks on either side of the passage. The passage itself was only a meter wide and six meters deep.

His eyes scanned the several monitors that lined the left side until he reached the desired section. Taking his portable terminal and placing it on a pull out shelf, he plugged the lead into the access port and started to type in commands.

Carmichael watched Longwood with interest before realizing he had not checked on his sentries.

"Small and Warburton, sit-rep."

"No contact," was the response from both.

Carmichael felt relieved, but knew the longer they took, the more likely they were to be discovered. He sent two other troopers to set up snoopers further up the corridors leading to the data room and to add a few booby traps that would slow down anyone who wanted to crash his party.

"How much longer, Erin?" he asked on the section net.

"Not much. This is better secured than the door, so it will take a little more time. I've managed to isolate two of the locks but I have no clue how many they have in place. Without the command codes, it's going to take time."

"Great." Carmichael switched frequencies and reported back to Taylor, who was waiting for a status report. He watched Longwood in silence. Carmichael had never had the aptitude for computer or technical fields, although it interested him greatly. He envied the tech's specialized knowledge.

Longwood's fingers flew over the keyboard as his eyes moved between the portable terminal and the data monitor.

"I've opened up five of the keys now, and I'm thinking that there are only six. That should be it." He beamed with pride.

Carmichael looked at him wryly. "You unlocked a computer. You didn't crack the codes to the palace fortune."

"Let's see you do it," retorted Longwood, undaunted.

"With several years of school I could, but right now, just input the new codes and make sure that you put in more than six lockouts. I don't want to make the same mistake they did."

"Already started. It would take the captain of this tub and an army of techs months to gain access to the core now."

Carmichael reported the success to Taylor and prepared to pull back and rejoin the rest of the squad. He would leave four of the troopers to guard the data core along with some remote squad automatic weapons that were set up along the passage. The guns would blast any movement that did not send back a friendly signal. If that failed to discourage the pirates, the four troopers would have enough firepower to hold off a small army. By then, the ship would be the property of the TAF.

***

213

Heather, the rear guard, noticed Carmichael's section approach. She called Taylor and gave him a heads-up.

Taylor got on the squad frequency and ordered the team up and moving to the next objective: the forward weapons lockup. He had a feeling that they would meet some resistance at that point. It would make tactical sense for the ship's crew to hold not only the bridge, but also access weapons in order to hold the ship. He called up the schematic to see what options he had to reach the weapons.

Of the three routes that he could take, he rejected the most obvious. It posed too much of a risk for ambush and narrowed the entry route where automatic and sentry guns could cut down his people. The other two routes, though less direct, would give them better access.

They would have to move fast, as they had a fair distance to travel. Again, he would have to split his team and hit the target from two sides simultaneously.

Taylor gave the orders to get them up and moving toward the forward weapons lockup. The point guard watched for booby traps, ambushes, and targets of opportunity. It was always possible to run into an officer, crewmember, or piece of equipment that might yield intelligence.

As they passed several doorways, they could see damage from neglect. Ceiling covers and wall panels lay on the floor or leaned against the walls. Lighting did not work or flickered on and off.

The squad also saw damage indicating a previous fight with small arms. That was peculiar, as it had to have occurred pre-boarding. Perhaps it had come from those who had inhabited the ship prior to the pirates, or from an internal power struggle.

Taylor made a mental note of it. He also ordered Carmichael to record the damage and begin a log outlining items of special interest.

The point guards reached a locked door and marked it for Taylor to deal with. There was little time for the diversion.

When Taylor reached the marked door, he configured a portable scanner to deep scan, a setting normally used to search for mines buried deep in soil and rock. The scanner should have no problem penetrating the thinner bulkhead.

As he activated the unit, he was caught off guard by the scene. Silhouetted in the scanner screen was a washed greyscale image of two people in the throes of passion..

Heather, also looking at the scanner and then glancing at Taylor's reaction, began to laugh.

Taylor looked up. "What's so funny?"

"It's not what you think, sergeant. Take another look."

Taylor looked at the image again and almost broke out laughing himself. The image was showing two *men* having a romp.

"Okay, so I almost jumped the gun," he said with more composure. "Time to lock these two in for the night. Blow the door and…" He looked around, "Matheson, give them the treatment and let's get moving." He was still amused at the scene and its contrast to the situation around them.

Two troopers with welders cut the door away and two others went in to secure the surprised lovers. Matheson implanted the locator nano and almost with reluctance, put them to sleep. These two were more likely to carry on with what they were doing than to run or cause trouble, but why take the chance?

The squad secured the doors again and marked it as occupied before starting again. Taylor got situation reports from the other squads. Things were looking up. Resistance was becoming less intense—but the big assault on the bridge was still to come and they were falling behind their timetable.

***

On board the *York*, Affleck could not sleep any longer. Too many nightmarish dreams to deal with.

The ship's doctor had finally ordered him to bed during the boarding operation. "An exhausted admiral running a battle is no good to any of us. I will relieve you under a medical chit if you do not get some sleep on your own," he warned Affleck in the briefing room.

Affleck now regretted asking for medication for a headache. Doctors had an enormous amount of power over military officers, especially if there was any question of reduced mental or physical ability. An admiral who had not slept in two days and had operational control over combat troops could start to make decisions that might not be sound, and could cause the needless loss of lives and resources.

Affleck knew this and so did not argue too much with his doctor. Besides, the boarding party was not his party. Operational control for that phase fell to the regimental commander and his staff.

Lying on his back, he turned to see the chronometer. He had fallen asleep almost as soon as his head hit the bed, but the dreams he was having disturbed him.

He tried to make sense of them, but was at a loss. In one dream he awoke on a bleak, rocky, barren planet. Massive rocks jutted from the ground and ended in sharp edges and knifepoint tips. He had looked around and shouted, but there was no response and no one around. He began to walk, tripping over boulders and cracks in the earth.

In the distance were more mountains, but no trees, grass, or scrub. No birds, animals, or insects. Nothing living. He felt out of place and small in the vast space. He looked down, but even his clothes looked unfamiliar. He couldn't tell how warm or cold it was. He stopped, picked up a small rock, and looked at it carefully. Nothing. He scraped the rock on his arm and drew a small amount of blood but felt no pain. It was only now he realized that with each step he never felt the rocky ground.

He spotted smoke in the distance and felt a surge of hope. Someone to tell him what was happening and where he was! He dropped the rock and began to run toward the smoke.

As he approached, he began to experience feelings of fear, outrage, loathing, and disgust along with more confusion. As he got closer, he saw something on the ground. After a few more tentative steps, he made out the form of a body.

He ran toward it and grabbed the shoulder and arm, rolling it toward him. The sight that greeted him caused him to jump and fall backward, pushing himself away on hands and feet.

There was no face. Smooth skin was stretched across where a human face should be.

He began to walk and then saw other bodies, and then even more, some dressed in battle gear. Their helmets were on and the face shields lowered, hiding the faces. First he passed one or two, then five and ten and twenty, fifty, a hundred, thousands. It went on and on—all of them dead, all faceless.

Dread passed over him like a deluge. He knew he was the one responsible. The blame lay squarely on his shoulders.

Affleck had awoken in a sweat. The men and women he sent off to fight and die were his responsibility and his alone. Civilian leaders and generals higher up might have given the initial command to deploy, but it was his order that sent ships and personnel into the fight.

He sat up and put his feet on the soft rug by his bed, steadied himself, and stood, stretching. He still had time for a quick shower before he had to get back to the flag bridge. Until then, the XO and regimental commander could handle things.

Colonel Marouf is a good man and an excellent commander, he thought. *His people are the best for this type of operation. I don't have anything to worry about—right* now.

Chapter Eighteen

"The generators must be going offline again," snarled one of the pirates setting up defensive line near the bridge of the *Bandit*. He pointed to the pocket lights that functioned as emergency lighting.

His partner glanced over, not really paying attention. Sub-Lieutenant Terry Karparov had other things on his mind.

"What?" he asked, his Russian accent heavy. He was the third generation born outside of Earth, but his original family line, so he claimed, could be traced back to the European Federated Union on Earth, in the Russian sector. Much of his family still spoke both English and Old Russian, so he maintained his accent.

"The lights! They haven't been on steady for the past hour!"

"It'll make our lives easier," Karparov responded. He wanted to tell his shipmate to shut it, but he knew it was just nerves. "They can't see us that way, so enjoy it. Just keep your eyes and ears open and aim well. We'll get through this and reap the profits in the end."

In truth, he had stopped believing that a long time ago, but it sounded good.

Seven other pirates joined them from a maintenance access tube that carried fiber, power, and life support throughout the ship, adjacent to a missile loading and transport channel. Each carried his weapon and spare ammo, and two carried man-portable missile launchers.

"I hope you have the safety on those things!" Karparov barked, angry that they would draw a weapon so unsuitable for internal ship defense. "Do not, and I repeat, do *not* use those missiles unless I say so and give you the word. Don't even think about unpacking them. One wrong shot and we're all dead."

Karparov was assigned the task of holding one of the routes to the bridge, which was fine with him. His main job was weapons officer and his station was on the bridge, but right now it was not the most pleasant place to be.

Besides, he thought, *this is not the most likely route the TAF will take. It's too roundabout and they probably have a time restriction.*

His comm cracked with a scream and sounds of weapons fire in the background.

"Bridge, this is weapons lock one!" The voice was rushed, panicked, and almost screaming. "We're being—" and then it went silent.

Another voice: "Eliot's dead—the bastards are still coming and we can't hold!"

This time, the captain came on, "Hold that lock up, you cowards! It's the end if you let it fall. I'll send out more people to reinforce your position. Out."

Karparov knew there would not be any more reinforcements. They were on their own and from what he'd seen before leaving the bridge, the entire recon force was in the same mess. He had been hearing reports from all over the ship since the boarding began. Whole sections were being overrun and his shipmates killed or captured. He knew it was only a matter of time until it was all over.

He recalled his childhood fantasy of striking it rich as a pirate. Growing up on a fringe colony world was not easy, and he'd always blamed his parents for dragging him off to some far-flung rock in space. It was tough to be ten years old on a world that seemed to have more predators than humans, with the humans at the bottom of the food chain.

It became natural that all his childhood games featured him as the one to win, to get the bounty and prevail over others. They gave him a sense of achievement as a child without the power to direct his own life and destiny.

He'd left his home and family at the age of twenty after he'd earned enough credits to buy passage on a tramp hauler. As luck would have it, that ship was boarded by a group of pirates, who stole its cargo. Crews and passengers were not yet being spaced, so he managed to convince the pirate captain to take him onboard as junior crew.

Now, that childhood dream was fading.

"There have been riches and it was a good run, but now it's more likely that I will spend the next few years on a penal colony," he said to no one as he stared down the corridor.

***

Heather knelt and removed the ID disk from Ratte's body. He had a hole in the side of his head where the ten-millimeter dart had hit him as he tried to get to better cover. She stood and handed the disk to Taylor, who had two other disks in his hand.

She helped zip Ratte into a body bag as the rest of the squad made sure that there were no pirates still alive in the jumble that was once the forward weapons lockup. It was a fierce battle but short-lived, and Heather was thankful for that.

The weapons lockup now belonged to the TAF, as did most of the ship. Other squads had taken the majority of the crew into custody and secured them.

The wounded were taken to the shuttle bays for evac to the medical ship.

The firefight had left several holes in the walls and bulkhead at the far end of the companion-way. Scorch marks lined the floor and the lighting was almost completely gone as the last of the pirate crew surrendered. Heather counted eighteen pirates dead as she collected intel in documents, readers, and identification chips.

Taylor clicked on the squad frequency. "Okay, people, time to go. We have a deadline to meet, places to go, and people to see, and we're not going to get there by standing around here."

He recalled the security pickets and transferred the order of march through the data link in everyone's helmet. Taylor's squad would have to cross over to the portside maintenance companionway and climb four levels to reach the bridge. One other squad would make their way along a small but passable missile-loading channel, used to move missiles from storage magazines to launch tubes. One of the channels passed close to the bridge deck, where the team would enter twenty meters from the bridge's rear entrance.

Chapter Nineteen

Karparov was watching his scanner when it flashed a quick signal showing movement. He only saw it for a split second, and at first he thought his eyes were playing tricks on his brain. He glanced up to curse the lights, which were now more off than on.

"Stay alert, everyone. It's been too long since we've had any word from the rest of our people." His voice was not as steady as he'd wanted.

His lips were also dry. Taking a sip of water from his canteen, he rechecked the scanner by replaying its flash memory. His heart began to pound even harder as he confirmed movement up ahead. It did not last long, but it was there. Karparov changed the scan to look for heat and biological signatures in an effort to narrow down the location and size of the possible target.

Ten minutes went by, but no other signal appeared.

"It must have been an error or a piece of the ceiling panel falling," he muttered to reassure himself.

As he spoke, however, the hair on the back of his neck stood up, and he shivered. Fear like he had never felt before gripped him as his ears registered a sound behind him.

Then the maintenance door to the missile channel was blown out and slammed into his makeshift barricade and three of his men. He turned and hauled himself over the other side of the barricade as darts slammed into his men before they had the chance to scream.

223

Smoke filled the corridor as the remaining lights went out, adding to the confusion. Karparov tried to fire at the uniformed troopers piling through the blown door, but every time he took aim, rounds smashed into the debris of spare parts and furniture around him, throwing dust, plastic, and other materials into his face.

He may not have liked his parents for dragging him off to a world where he had nothing, but he did thank them for raising him to have a passion for life. He decided, in that very brief moment, to not to throw it away for a lost cause.

He waited for a pause in the firing, then shouted, "Hold your fire! I'm throwing my weapon down."

A deep but feminine voice, amplified by the trooper's internal helmet mike, responded. "If there's anyone left alive, stand now with your hands interlocked behind your head. Have your backs turned toward us. Now!"

Karparov complied. He heard the same voice ask, "Who's in charge of this group?"

"I am—Sub-Lieutenant Terry Karparov."

Two TAF troopers made their way over and scanned him for any biological or mechanical booby traps. Detecting none, they conducted a physical search, turning out his pockets and uniform. They then secured his hands with binders and led him over the barricade toward the leader of the squad.

A deep, no-nonsense, don't-piss-me-off voice said, "I'm only going to ask you this once. How many people are on the bridge, what are their weapons, and what is the status of the captain?"

Karparov saw medics were already treating his wounded without being harsh or abusive. He looked back at the sergeant in front of him.

"When I left the bridge, there were a dozen people," he said readily. "Officers and NCOs, all of them armed with five-mil autos. I don't know how many rounds. The captain is an asshole who's gone ballistic with revenge for Captain Appletree and I'm not sure what he'll do with his back to the wall."

***

Taylor received a comm from his counterpart in the bridge assault. They had already taken the back door. Now it was his turn to finish off the side entrance, which was not going as easily as he would have liked.

Right now, he was in a storage room just outside the bridge entrance, pinned down by a twenty-millimeter sentry gun trying to give him and the five troopers with him an early retirement.

"Brown, twenty-five meters portside, sentry gun, take it out."

Brown crawled to a better position and fired off a grenade.

"Fire in the hole!" he announced on the squad frequency.

The explosion went off right under the gun, blowing it up and across the deck, smashing into a pirate and crushing him. Only sporadic fire came now from the pirates and Taylor had just about had enough. He did one final check of the thermal signatures and ordered Heather and her section to move forward while he flanked the holdouts from his position.

Heather reloaded her magazine and started to move under cover from Carmichael's section. Darts flew through the air with the buzzing of a swarm of hungry fire wasps. The pirates could not get off any shots unless they wanted to have a head blown off. Three of them had tried and paid the price.

By the end, only one pirate was left alive, and only barely. Taylor got on the squad net to update everyone. The ship was almost theirs; tech crews had already landed and disarmed the self-destruct, sensors, and weapons. The captain was now completely blind. One last push and the bridge would be theirs.

Taylor called for a door charge, a flexible cable filled with a chemical mix that would burn fast and at an extremely high temperature, but would leave the bridge reasonably intact. It would slice through the door that barred their entrance to the bridge. His counterpart in the other section would do the same on the other side of the bridge.

Once the charges were set, they ignited it. An electrical current raced along the fiber cable to the charge. Within a matter of seconds, both doors had been burned off the tracks.

As soon as there was an opening, even before the door hit the floor, both squads tossed in several flash-bang grenades set to go off a fraction of a section apart. This would ensure that the occupants of the bridge did not have time to recover before the troopers made their way in. The troopers would be using stun guns and not automatic rifles with darts, another attempt to preserve the bridge and therefore potentially valuable intel.

Friendly fire was not a concern as all TAF weapons, were, in effect, smart weapons engineered to send out a laser signal to the target. If the target was another trooper with current ID tags, the weapon would not fire. At the speed of light, the "friend or foe" signal eliminated the type of accident responsible for the deaths of thousands of soldiers in centuries past.

***

Bishop sat dejected in his command chair as reports came in, indicating an ever-advancing ring of TAF forces overtaking his ship.

He had never contemplated this happening, always seeing his end in a true test of navy battle, in space between ships so powerful, that whole planets cowered before them. Bishop had also envisioned the vast sum of credits his ventures would bring in.

"A battleship captain should not be allowed to end his career like this," he murmured.

He looked around. His crew was doing everything possible to stave off the inevitable, including welding the three bridge access doors shut and handing out weapons and ammunition. They set up portable dampers to offset the biosensors the TAF used and even cut any remaining systems, trying to slow the onslaught of troopers heading their way. Nothing was working and he knew it.

Bishop had always been afraid that if he equipped his bridge crew with small arms, they would use those weapons against him. He had tried once before, several years back, to dismal failure; he'd only trusted a few special people to have access to armaments onboard since then.

Now he hoped that one of them *would* use a weapon against him.

He made one last attempt to access the ship's internal and external scanners, to no avail. He even tried to initiate a self-destruct overload on the main engines but he had been locked out. Not even his communication was available.

Bishop stood and made his way to the centre of the bridge, trying to look confident. It was an act and he knew it. So did his crew, who now showed only contempt for him.

It was quiet now. All activity on the bridge had ended, with everyone holding a weapon, waiting for something to happen. Bishop was not sure how long it would be before the rear and auxiliary bridge access doors were suddenly cut away.

He watched it all happen as time slowed down for him. He saw every flicker and shard of the plaststeel doors fly away in a shower of sparks before they fell to the deck to cool and fade.

Bishop now saw his life with a clarity that surprised him. He viewed his experiences like the door that was burned away: solid, allowing no one to pass unless he opened and let them inside. Like the compound that it was made of, he would not rust or age and be discarded in the knacker's yard. It would take an act of total destruction and sudden force to remove his barrier and open up his inner self. And like the door, he would not be broken down easily. He would not let them take his mind apart.

Bishop watched the door fall to the deck.

It's time, he told himself. Then he held the pistol to his head and pulled the trigger.

***

"Colonel, incoming transmission from the boarding party commander," said the comm officer on watch in the CIC.

"I'll take it here."

Marouf knew what the report would include since he'd been monitoring all the comm traffic since the beginning of the boarding. He knew how many men and women he'd lost and the moment they died by watching the medical telemetry. He knew them all by name and family background.

The signal was not clear due to radiation leaking from the damaged ships but he could make out the boarding party commander's voice.

"Colonel, all boarding parties report objectivities taken and secured. Pirate crews are tagged and sedated, locked in various compartments onboard. Barrel Three was taken but we lost their captain—he suicided just before the bridge was breached. Tech teams have boarded all ships and are downloading navigation, comm, and other intel. Colonel, there's a lot of data—more than what we had originally hoped for. I'm securing the boarding detail now and will be assigning crews to guard all ships. Navy personnel are en route with prize crews to repair and ferry the ships back to the nearest friendly system."

The commander sounded pleased, thought Marouf. *I should be, too, but it's a hollow victory when we have seventy-six dead and thirty-five wounded. Mind you, it could have been worse. For that, I am thankful.*

"Thank you, commander," he said aloud. "Let your people know how proud I am of their work, and I'll see you back on board for the pre-launch briefing. Marouf out."

He paused. "Comm, get me Admiral Affleck."

***

Affleck was on the flag bridge when he received word from Marouf. He looked forward to reading the full report being compiled from the data and intel collected. This crucial information could swing the odds in their favor for the final operation in New

Gloucester. The number of dead and wounded greatly disturbed him, especially in light of the dreams he was having, but that was his burden to work through.

"XO, call a command staff meeting for eighteen hundred tomorrow. Make sure that everyone has readers with the new data," he said. "I want to get this operation going ASAP, so let's get the order of march updated as soon as the troopers return and the prize crews are supplied and sent on their way. I'll be in my quarters if you need me."

Affleck left the flag bridge feeling a little better than he did when he got there.

Chapter Twenty

The large briefing room on the flagship was packed with officers from around the flotilla. The external comm monitors lining the walls showed those who could not attend. The last few months had been leading up to this moment—and it was about time, in the view of many. Readers were passed out with a synopsis of the intelligence gathered from the captured ships, their crew, and the captain of the surrendering pirate battleship.

The complexity and organization of the pirates under the leadership of Joseph Lebakie was a shock to most people in the room. Lebakie had managed to unite more than a dozen pirate groups and several hundred ships and their crews in less than five years. For three years, no one in the Confederation had a clue what was happening, and only now was the full scope revealed.

In a sense, it was an amazing accomplishment: Lebakie had successfully organized every ship's captain and faction leader, along with all crews down to the cooks, around a singular purpose. An iron hand was used by the best pirate captains, but they did so with the tacit agreement of their crews. Lebakie had achieved this with a promise that also stunned the assembled group: "Join with me, and I will give you Earth and the wealth and power that come with it."

The report did leave out one piece of the puzzle: why? There was no indication in the captured ship's computer memory or among the crew or officers why Lebakie did the impossible. He already ran one of the largest pirate and privateer assemblages and was doing well for himself in the fringe colonies. So why

231

escalate to this level, with the enormous risk involved?

The other piece of missing intel was Lebakie's location. Murmured theories hummed around the gathering, with some even suggesting that Lebakie was a fictitious character invented to bring the pirates together. The TAF leadership had initially assumed he was running the show from New Gloucester and simultaneously leading the assault on the central core and Earth. Now it seemed that a different figure was in charge and Lebakie was held up in another location. At this point, it wasn't even clear if Lebakie was ever at New Gloucester.

In the hall just outside the briefing room, Affleck ran into Martin. "Rear-Admiral Martin, good to see you again. It's been so long," he joked.

"I'm happy you were able to make it, too," replied Martin.

"You're very funny today, admiral. I'm glad to see you haven't lost your ever-present wit."

She would have liked to poke more fun at Affleck, but not in the mixed company of aides and JTF security troopers. "Why don't we get together for supper after this meeting, before I head back to the *Montebello*?"

"That sounds great—we can talk more then."

Martin entered the room. Affleck paused for a few seconds, then proceeded.

As he entered, someone shouted, "Room!" Conversation ended as everyone stood to attention.

"At ease, ladies and gentlemen," he said. "We have a lot to accomplish at this meeting so we won't waste time on too much formality."

Affleck removed two small readers from his trouser pocket and accepted a larger reader from an aid. After placing all three on the podium, he made eye contact with as many in the crowd as he could before continuing.

"First of all, I want to personally thank each of you, your officers, crews, and troopers for a job well done. It's been a difficult slog so far and we've been pushed close to breaking, but you have all accomplished so much. It has been my extreme pleasure to serve with everyone in this flotilla and I wouldn't have it any other way.

"Second, we have just completed operation Barrel Roll—the capture of the recon ships that was dropped into our laps by fate, the gods, or dumb luck. Take your pick."

That brought a smattering of laughter. Affleck was smiling as he continued.

"Our spooks are still reviewing the material, but we have the best picture yet of how these pirates have organized, and the best estimated strength level of the New Gloucester system and obstacles we will encounter in taking our objective. We still—and I must emphasize this—we still have many questions to answer, but we are ahead of the game, with the odds now better than when we began this operation."

Affleck spent the remainder of the meeting outlining the intelligence they had gathered. The original operation plan was fleshed out, refined, and vetted against the newly acquired information. The captains and commanders also assigned timings and confirmed the order of march. Affleck was pleased.

Halfway through the meeting, attendees broke into clusters to finalize details on individual operation orders. When they were done, Affleck dismissed them to get a quick bite to eat and rest.

***

233

Heather and her squad had returned to the *Athabaskan*, and after cleaning and returning their squad and personal equipment, they were dismissed to take some much-needed down time.

The squad was debriefed and various accounts of action and contact repeated to intelligence officers, who wanted details or specifics that might have been left out in the computer recorded logs, videos, and interrogations. It was always good to have verbal accounts of an operation from the troopers involved, as the human brain might pick up on a point that could have been overlooked as trivial by the computers.

One of the officers interviewing Heather seemed most interested in the blast and weapons damage noted by Taylor and several other troopers. Heather gathered that every ship captured had similar damage. Interrogation of the prisoners indicated a short-lived mutiny some time ago by a splinter group within the pirate ranks. How long ago, and how widespread the mutiny had been, was unclear.

Heather wasn't sure how the powers that be could use this to their advantage, so she put it out of mind and concentrated on finding Peter.

***

Affleck ate, more out of reflex than hunger. His mind was far away—so far that he took no notice of his dinner guest, Leslie Martin.

"Credit for your thoughts?" she prodded.

Affleck did not respond.

"I'm pregnant and having your child," she declared.

"Wh-what?"

"Oh, I see, I have your partial attention now. Well, I won't bore you with the details. Suffice it to say it involved alien technology, several anal probes, and some engineer named Scotty." She smiled.

"What? How's your dinner?" Affleck knew he was busted. He tried to sound engaged.

"I have been trying to get your attention for ten minutes to no avail, my dear friend, and I must say that I am horrified at the way you treat such a fragile woman." Her tone was mocking and playful.

"You, madam, are no mere woman and certainly not fragile. You are a viper in the skin of a war goddess who knows no mercy. One who takes innocent men and after having your way with them, devours them."

"Don't hold back. What do you really think?" She picked up a glass and leaned back in her chair as they both laughed out loud.

"You've become a poet, my dear friend," she added. "I haven't seen this side of you in some time."

"It's been too long since I felt this good, Leslie. It seems like it's been one setback after another with the fleet and the TAF in general. Every time we try to do some good, we're hamstringed by a bloated bureaucracy. For centuries, democratic governments have gone to the polls and the people have voted for and elected one political party or individual only to find out nothing changes. All that time, we've been fooled to believe in the democratic system when it's the bureaucracy that's been in control. But now we've finally elected members of the Confederation that have taken control of the corruption and tossed it out on its ear."

Affleck knew he was ranting, but he felt good about the situation and truly was happy for the future. He looked across the table and smiled.

"Enough about me. How about you and Jim? What have you two been up to—and the kids, how old are they now?"

"Jim's doing fine. He's the director of the sub-aquatic life sciences section at the university. It's been good for him. The children are missing their mom—or I'd like to think they are." She beamed with pride. "They are ten and seven and behaving as if they were twenty years older."

She paused. "It's been enjoyable catching up like this. Things have been hectic lately and having a moment to just reminisce and chat is healthy for the soul. I can see from the chrono that it's getting late, though, and I have to get back to the *Montebello* before my exec marks me as AWOL."

The two stood and shook hands. Martin gave Affleck a warm hug and a brief kiss on the cheek. He returned the gesture.

They walked toward the lift, where Martin would head for the shuttle bays. Affleck paused at the door. "Let's do this again when this mission is over. I'd like to see the kids and Jim again."

"That sounds good to me. I'll let him know to clean up the place before we get home. Admiral."

Martin saluted and stepped into the lift.

Chapter Twenty-One

"All ships report ready to transit to New Gloucester, admiral. System picket and recon drones have been deployed." The comm officer wiped her palms free of sweat.

The flag bridge was quiet, mirroring every other ship's bridge in the flotilla. Everybody wanted to get on with the job at hand and nerves were tight.

Affleck turned to one of the darkened monitors around his command chair and took note of his reflection. It surprised him to see a smile on his lips. He'd never realized he was smiling.

He was happy with the drills and simulations that they had run over and over again. In the beginning, he had thought they were rusty. Captains, crews, and troopers had been working so hard on developing small unit tactics that the larger structure was all but ignored. But initial drills showed them to be fully operational and combat-ready when it came to combined arms against a very large target. In the end and after a week of intense work, they had shaken out the bugs, and he was pleased with the outcome.

"Okay, comm, relay to all ships, stand by to transit on my mark. Mark."

To himself and without emotion, Affleck said, "Once more into the breach."

***

"How long before we get back to real space, sir?" Heather, sitting mid-row in the platoon briefing room, had just voiced the burning question on everyone's mind.

Fitzpatrick had already received his briefing and was now passing on specific platoon and squad orders for a multi-operation mission, with combat taking place over several thousand kilometers. He had never seen anything like it. Even within the Regiment, only a couple dozen senior officers and a hundred or so veterans had. In Fitzpatrick's platoon, he only had eighteen troopers and NCOs who had taken part in an operation this large.

"Before I answer that, let me give you an idea of the complexity of this mission," Fitzgerald said. "First off, it's big—and I mean *big*. The flotilla will split into two battle groups and hit New Gloucester from two entry points. We're talking about a solar system-sized combat mission involving multiple ground-based drops with some squads in reserve while others are held for ship boarding parties.

"Rear-Admiral Martin's battle group is designated group Alpha and will slide in ten hours to take on planet defenses and the main pirate group stationed there. The second group, Bravo, which is us, for those of you still asleep—someone want to wake Richards?—will slide in eleven hours and enter the system inside the asteroid belt. The one-hour gap will, it's hoped, cause mass confusion among the pirate command.

"By then, they should have committed their forces all on one side, giving us the opportunity to attack with little resistance and restrict their ability to respond in force. Bravo's task will be to take out the main pirate fleet massing there along with the mining and processing facility."

He paused and checked his reader. "Our job will be to drop platoons on the mining and processing

238

facilities located on New Gloucester's third moon. Intel shows that the pirates have been using this as a base for their ground forces, and data collected from the capture of their recon force also shows that the system commander has moved his HQ to that location for security reasons. According to Captain Appletree, the surrendering ship's captain, the new commander is an Admiral Walter Hobbin. He splits his time between the base and the *Cape Fear*, a super-dreadnought."

Heather glanced around at the faces and saw hunger for the upcoming action. She looked over at Peter and caught him looking back at her with a childish grin. They had spent all of their off time together since she'd returned from the boarding party.

Two other things awaited her on her return, both of which gave her a feeling of satisfaction and peace. Her leave had been approved, and she was ecstatic. Both she and Peter would get time off together. was And she had received a letter from her parents.

Mail was an important commodity in the TAF. Whenever message packets arrived, the TAF endeavored to deliver personal letters as well. Her parents' letter had arrived on the last packet, and she'd spent the morning reading and rereading it.

Her parents were concerned for her welfare and pleased about her relationship with Peter. They told Heather that everyone was looking forward to her visit. News and gossip about family and friends peppered the message, as well as news clippings from her home planet.

Heather shook herself free of her thoughts when someone jabbed her with an elbow. She looked up and realized that the speaker had changed. The platoon master sergeant was now giving his orders.

She noted the time: eight hours and sixteen minutes until the slide.

***

Affleck did not sleep well, bizarre disembodied images swirling around his head. Those strange dreams had him tossing and turning, but he did awake alert this time. He stood in the lift on his way to the flag bridge, removing a small white speck of lint from his tunic.

The doors opened and he stepped onto the bridge. He was approached by an aide who handed him a reader with a readiness update. The flotilla had stopped once en route to do a final shakedown, a last-minute addition, but it did not cause a delay. Now they were ready, and at the prescribed time, the flagship's captain sounded general quarters.

"Time for Alpha to slide into normal space?" asked Affleck.

"Group Alpha slides in six minutes, sir."

***

Onboard the flag bridge of the *Montebello*, Martin leaned forward in her seat and tightened her grip on the armrest. The chronometer was counting down the time to slide for Alpha, and she watched it decrease.

Normal space is about to become anything but, she thought.

As it reached zero plus one she ordered, "Launch drones, launch fighters and long-range recon. Bear on all targets and fire when in range."

As each ship in her battle group flashed back into real space, they followed the same protocol.

Long-range recon stealth fighters were launched toward predetermined waypoints, and sensor and target drones were sent scattering the system to seek out and paint their targets: the pirate ships, mines and any other defenses encountered.

Jamming and electronic warfare drones sent out a mix of false signals, hopefully fooling the enemy's sensors into seeing a fleet instead of a battle group. Combat fighters took off to defend the battle group and provide a combat air patrol to the ground forces about to launch in drop ships.

The battle group sorted itself out within a few minutes of sliding, with dreadnoughts and super-dreadnoughts leading the charge.

Martin moved to the big holo tank in the middle of the bridge and watched. Her orders were now being executed.

What she saw was close to the projected pirate force, so that was no surprise. What *was* a surprise was the layout and assembly of the force. They were closer to launching their attack than anticipated. She concentrated on the pirate fleet.

The targeting computers had already identified the super-dreadnought *Cape Fear*, the second home of Admiral Hobbin, and tagged it as Bonfire One. She noted that it took three minutes before the *Cape Fear* powered up its main engines and began to move into position with escorts following, creating a screen.

That was a good start; it meant their engines were already hot and on standby, which took an immense amount of fuel and resources.

"Send the *Ottawa, Goth, Chieftan,* and *Torbay* in a blocking and delaying action against the *Cape Fear*," she said to her operations officer.

"Sir, they will not be able to get into position before it reaches maximum speed."

Martin looked at the speed and power indicator. The *Ottawa* and her escorts were out of position to begin the blocking action that would hold the pirates command ship for Affleck's battle group. *Nothing ever goes as expected,* she thought.

"You're right," she said, frustration in her voice. She did a quick calculation. "Re-arm the ready squadron with ship killers and launch. They can fire in standoff mode ahead of the *Fear*. If we get lucky, they'll take the bait—at least until the *Ottawa* can get turned around. I don't want them getting in behind us or out too far toward the belt. At least not till Admiral Affleck slides and gets into position."

"Aye, sir."

"Time to slide for Bravo?"

"Thirty-seven minutes," came the reply.

***

Hobbin woke after several hours' sleep.

"Rank does have its privileges," he said to himself as he stretched. He knew that very few others in his fleet would get that much sleep.

He sat up and checked the chronometer on the desk, then hit the intercom for his steward.

"Bring me some coffee and breakfast."

Before the steward could respond, the klaxon sounded the alert. "Belay that." He cut the comm and connected with his flag bridge.

"Report! Why have we gone to combat alert?"

The *Cape Fear* lurched, throwing Hobbin against the bulkhead, answering the question he'd just asked.

The officer on watch replied quickly. "TAF forces are entering the inner system and taking up positions. They've launched missiles."

Hobbin could hear the fear in his voice. This was not supposed to happen—not when they were so close to launching against the Confederation.

"I'm on my way. Power up and get ready to move. Have the fleet come to action stations." He grabbed his uniform and dressed quickly, forgoing his tunic.

The bridge was a chaotic hive of activity. Ships' captains were calling for instructions and planet defenses were in a panic. The ship rocked again as a missile impacted near the stern.

"Main motors are up. Full power, ready for action, sir," said the helm officer.

"Flank speed, set course for four five seven point three by oh oh nine point three, same plane. Comm, inform the escorts to follow our lead."

***

"We're up, boys and girls. Let's move it!" shouted Flight Lieutenant Sullivan as he and his ready squadron ran for their fighters.

The flight line was jammed with crews swapping the long- and short-range air-to-air and air-to-ground missiles with ship killers. The swap meant two shifts on deck, plus the pilots and their aides jostling for space while the missiles were loaded.

"Your nav-comms have been uploaded with new targeting data," Sullivan informed his pilots.

He reached his fighter and climbed the short ladder, slid into his seat, and was secured in place by his ground crew support.

"Have a good one, sir."

"I will, Tom, and thanks."

Sullivan pressed the button to close the fighter's canopy and pressurize the confined cockpit. His systems were already powered up and the ground weapons crew was just finishing locking down the new load of missiles.

"All ships three-one, this is three-zero, report when ready."

Within forty seconds all pilots reported ready. The ground crews secured their kit in the bay and ran for cover behind blast doors. Sullivan was given the launch command from the carriers launch control officer, and the small sleek fighters blasted out of the launch bay.

Sullivan's squadron flew the newer star-fighters, which had a longer overall profile than the Voodoos but carried a bigger payload. They improved on the Voodoo in many ways, including range, speed, and an increased computing power that allowed for a more extensive and robust targeting system.

Still, the ground crews had reservations about the new design because some of the access panels did not allow full admittance to some systems on the fly, delaying repairs in combat. It still needed testing in heavy combat situations when fighters would be coming in hot and needed to be sent back out quickly.

The pilots also had mixed reviews. Many still preferred the older Voodoo, and the upgraded Voodoo Two models, but they quickly got used to the improved avionics package.

As soon as the star-fighters left the launch tube, Sullivan's squadron throttled up and raced out to intercept the *Cape Fear*. Its red icon glowed in the HUD, and it was moving fast.

The squadron would have to use over forty percent of their fuel to reach the target and launch the ship killer missiles. If there were any other contacts between here and the missile launch point, return could be a problem. They could refuel mid-flight, but in a combat zone that would be suicide for the tanker crews.

Stars and streaks of light flashed past in the distance, and dust clouds partially obscured several small nebulas in the vastness of space. The colours were a mix of hues that many humans had never seen. Here in the fringe systems were things the human brain had never dreamed of.

Yet Sullivan paid no attention. His focus was on the *Cape Fear* and stopping it.

"We only have one shot at this, boys and girls, so double-check your targeting computers. We have to slow them down or stop them for the *Ottawa* to get into place—but let's not have any heroics. Once you shoot your load, regroup and head back home to re-arm. Jenkins and Rim, you're in first, then hold high as CAP. I don't want to miss anything that may be coming our way."

He knew it was a long shot, but it wasn't his job to second-guess the officers that sent him out here.

Three quarters of the way there, the *Cape Fear* and her protection began to take notice of Sullivan's fighters, the close-in weapons targeting and letting loose a barrage of flak. *Time to go,* he thought as he keyed his comm.

"This is three-zero, evasive—now. Tie into my targeting and stand by."

The pilots began to spread out into a more aggressive flight path to avoid the barrage. Simultaneously they punched in the code to synchronize their missile firing and targeting with

245

Sullivan. This would give them the same point of aim regardless of their position in space. If this was done manually, there would be a delay in firing between ships, and considering the size of the target, unsynchronized impacts would have little effect. They needed to deliver a massive impact to slow the *Cape Fear* down.

"On my mark. Three, two, one—mark!" Sullivan flipped the toggle on his control stick and pressed the button. Ship killer missiles streaked out from each of the fighters, aimed at a point just ahead of the big dreadnought.

Sullivan didn't have to wait long before the first wave of ship killers exploded. The bright light against the backdrop of deep space would have blinded Sullivan if not for the reactive blast shield on his visor.

Cape Fear was not hurt yet, however, and the gigantic super-dreadnought and her escorts were still expelling immense amounts of flak as it ploughed through the vacuum of space.

"Let's get the hell out of here, people. Turn for home."

The pilots cranked to turn for their carrier. As they did, three fighters had the misfortune of flying through a cloud of darts fired from one of the escorts. The first fighter disintegrated on impact, while the second had the nose section blown off, sending it spinning. The third lost part of the starboard wing pod and landing gear. It, too, went spinning but the pilot was able to fire stabilizing jets.

Both pilots ejected and Sullivan marked their position on his plot. They would not activate their beacon in the middle of a combat zone, but that also made rescue harder and in many cases, impossible.

All Sullivan could do was hope the rescue shuttle would be able to find them after the battle was over.

***

On board the *Cape Fear*, Hobbin saw the incoming missile strike aimed at him. The icons on the screen seemed to have his name emblazoned on each symbol, but he reacted quickly.

"Helm, eighty degrees positive angle, steer to course two six oh by oh oh five."

The order repeated and executed, the *Cape Fear* climbed sharply relative to their original axis and position, their escorts following. Hobbin knew nonetheless that he would get hit. A big ship with that kind of mass could not stop or change directions as fast as he needed.

He did a quick calculation and ordered three of his missile defense escorts to intercept the incoming onslaught as he coordinated the battle. His anger at the unexpected attack was showing, and watching the battle in space only added to his rage.

Something isn't right with the plot, he thought. Eight of his smaller escorts and two dreadnoughts were destroyed early in the battle. The surprise complete, the TAF had launched into the heart of the system, catching them with their pants down.

Hobbin ordered other elements of his fleet to disperse or move to cover key sectors. He watched for the launch of assault shuttles and drop ships he knew would happen, targeting the planet and its installations.

Then it hit him. There were not as many TAF ships as there should be! Hobbin had many years of training and experience in the TAF, and for an operation this size, there should be at least a flotilla or larger. What confronted him was a battle group, and it didn't seem to be complete. *Where was the other battle group?*

"Comm, to all ships from flag, withdraw to the inner asteroid belt and stand by. Second TAF wave expected—direction unknown. Send now, comm!"

There was an edge to his voice as he sent out the orders. He had to figure out where they would make their move.

"Comm, send to ground defenses, stand by to repel drop ships. Set up a second line and be prepared for a counterattack after they drop. Helm, new course. Set up for an RV with the withdrawing ships."

He wanted to pace, and would have if it would have helped and he had had the room. He had been assigned to command this force because he was good and could make the operation work. Now he had to defend his own position, and his confidence had fallen a notch.

"Sir, I have three—no, four ships leaving the system and they're not answering hail."

"Those bastards! They're trying to run—well, the TAF can have 'em. I have my own problems. No! Wait…"

Looking at the holo table he spotted a dreadnought on the fringe of the battle, close to the running ships.

"Send the *Crossing* to intercept them and blow them back to hell. Maybe we can use this to our advantage. It may just distract the TAF long enough for us to regroup."

He showed no emotion. His tone was self-assured now as he tried to project a sense of victory. His crew looked up to him as their commander, and since he took over the operation, there was a general sense of imminent success, of the profit, wealth, and power that would come with a win.

This was partly because Hobbin, apprehensive at first, had come to see this as a feasible endeavor. The TAF and the Confederation had become bloated with greed and corruption and would only implode if nothing was done. It was now their turn for a piece of the pie.

***

"Slide in five, four, three, two. Slide now!"

Affleck stood, holding on to the armrest of the command chair to steady himself after the slide.

"Engage targeting computers and get me a firing solution on—wait."

He checked the plot, looking at the battle unfolding. The data link from the *Montebello* was already slaved to his sensors so he could get real-time data. At this distance all he could see on the screen were small pinpoints of lights when a ship died. Martin had already chosen one special target for him and he saw why.

He also noted a dozen or more ships headed his way. *So much for a complete surprise,* he thought.

"Bonfire One is the primary," he barked. "Dispatch the other elements to change course and intercept."

Affleck watched the plot as smaller anti-missile escort ships moved to put a screen around the Bonfire One target. They were more mobile than the line ships, able to execute a turn-and-burn in a smaller volume of space. They moved to intercept incoming missiles, sending up a wall of darts penetrate and detonate the ship killers.

Still, some missiles reached their targets. Several pirate ships received lethal impacts and exploded or leaked air as they went careening out of the system.

"Bring in the carriers and launch the assault," said Affleck while he watched the icons dance in the holo-table.

A thin-beam communications laser sent out a line of sight message to the *Montebello*, where Martin also launched her main carrier force and brought up her assault carriers.

***

Heather loaded on the drop ship with her weapon, securing her kit and equipment along with the rest of her platoon. The drop bay was crowded as the whole regiment prepared to drop on the main command base on the small moon.

Intelligence briefings showed that it was guarded by at least two platoons, and less than ten kilometers away, a battalion-sized garrison of pirate troops stood ready to load on transports. With the main attack going on, they would stay on the ground, but that meant Heather's regiment would be fighting a substantial and largely unknown force.

Just as she was entering her transport, Heather noticed Fitzpatrick giving last-minute orders to the squad leaders. He looked confident and secure, and that gave her a good feeling. Seeing a worried platoon commander would have given her the jitters, and now was not the time for any uncertainty.

Commanders had long since given up the notion that a particular god or deity was on their side in battle. You fought for what you believed in, and right or wrong, you did your best to inflict more damage to the other side than they gave back to you. TAF troopers knew this all too well, and that helped to drive them forward.

Heather caught sight of two of the newer NCC-class drop ships getting ready to launch at the end of the bay, their ramps already drawn up and the swing arm being moved into place. She knew that the only group in this flotilla to use those ships was the JTF.

JTF units were always used on high-value missions. Their ability to get in and out of tight spots unnoticed made them a valuable asset. For a mission this size, they could be used to paint targets behind enemy lines for artillery or air-delivered munitions, sniper duties, or grab-and-snatch missions.

This is going to be some op, she thought. *I wonder what poor bastards are going to get a visit from the JTF. Whoever it is, I feel sorry for them— well, almost.*

Heather quickly moved into the drop ship, her mind focused on the job ahead.

***

The *Cape Fear* converged with Hobbin's reserve force ships just as they entered missile range of Affleck's battle group. Hobbin stood with both hands holding onto the holo table, his feet firmly planted. He was watching two separate battles: the first in and around New Gloucester, and the second about to commence in earnest near the inner asteroid belt. He still had three TAF battle cruisers headed his way and he was going to meet with more.

If I ever see that bastard Lebakie again, I'll kill him. Life really is a bitch. Hobbin tasted bile that was working up from his belly.

He bit down on his lower lip and cursed Lebakie several more times, simultaneously surprised at the amount of planning that must have gone into this operation. It was the largest even he had seen.

Well, no one ever said that life was going to be easy, and sure as shit, death was even harder.

The shout from the tactical station officer brought Hobbin back. "We're being painted—confirmed—weapons lock!"

"Helm, new heading, two five five by oh one one, twenty degree negative and slow to one third. Comm, signal to reserve force, link fire control in effect, report when ready." The pupils in Hobbin's eyes expanded as he watched the green and red icons begin to intertwine on his plot. He wanted to ensure that all the ships in the reserve group linked their fire control AI with his. The *Cape Fear* had a more advanced system than most of the ships, which would guarantee a higher accuracy rate.

Hobbin was just beginning to feel better about his chances when: "Sir, new group of signals coming in to sensor range—Carriers! And there're launching!"

The sight of the new incoming icons drove the dagger in hard, and Hobbin gripped the side of the table even harder, feeling as though the steel would come away in his hand at any time. Then he saw the other signals coming into view from the first battle group around the planet.

He held up his hand as the tactical officer began to say something. "Don't bother telling me—I can see it. Has CIC made an estimate of strength?"

A moment later: "Not yet, sir—at least, nothing confirmed. They have to tie in with the first group and confirm what numbers they have. However, they have a preliminary figure of three hundred fighters and fighter bombers between both groups."

The flag bridge went silent. That many small maneuverable fighters with incoming missiles meant a problem that wasn't going away anytime soon.

***

"Voodoo flight, this is Voodoo control. You are cleared to start your attack run. Nav-comm has been updated. Good luck."

"Voodoo control, this is Voodoo one-five, thanks and keep the lamp burning." Saunders cut in the flight frequency and gave her pilots the weapons-free call they had been waiting for.

Coming in at mach five, they would accelerate to mach nine at full throttle, aiming their fighters like darts toward the pirate ships in the distance, still invisible to the unaided eye.

"Voodoo flight, this is Voodoo one-five, watch for flak and don't run into our own ship killers. They're right behind us and will pass in...three minutes, on my mark. Mark."

The flak was starting to show on their screens. Just as in past Earth wars and other dirt-side battles, flak was intended to kill, disrupt, or divert an airborne assault. The small darts were fired from the head of an anti-fighter missile, or AFM. The more AFM, the more flak, and the harder it was to get to your target alive.

The lead elements would soon have to pass through it or alter course and neither option was good. Passing through it, even at this distance, would kill or disable many pilots and their ships. Going around would put the flight off course with little time to correct.

On a planet with atmosphere, flak had a finite effective range. Drag through air and gravity prevented its launch until the last minute. In space, no drag meant the range could be infinite.

*** *

Heather locked herself in the shock frame, then indicated "go" to Taylor, who took the same signal from the other troopers before locking himself in. Telltales showed green, meaning that each trooper was ready for action.

The standby alarm sounded and navy ground crews ran for cover behind blast doors. Drop ships were secured and their massive swing arms reached out as the first doors opened below them. As the ships were lowered, the second warning alarm went off and the atmosphere was drained from the boat bay, leaving it in a vacuum. Heather felt a slight shake as *Eagle 302* was lowered.

The intercom came on line with the AI voice, "Stand by—in five—four—three—two—launch— now!"

The *Athabaskan* and her fighter escorts had made it to within four hundred thousand kilometers of the third moon, just over the distance from Earth to its moon. This moon was named NGM3—not a flowery name, but then again, it was not a flowery sort of moon.

It was larger then Earth's moon; with a diameter of six thousand kilometers, it was closer in size to Mars. The atmosphere was barely breathable by human standards, and there was no water. The terrain was a mix of flat plains, sand dunes weathered by constant winds, and mountain ranges as high as twenty-five hundred meters. Strange rocks and columns jutted up from the ground in areas, shaped and sculpted by wind and time.

This was a full regimental assault and *Eagle 302* with Heather's squad was only one of the one hundred and twenty six drop ships that blasted away from the *Athabaskan*. An equal number of drop ships launched from the *Iroquois,* headed for the planet itself.

Warrant Zachary Clarke, *Eagle 302*'s pilot, banked slightly to port as he lined up for his approach run along with the rest of the flight. Still over a hundred thousand kilometers away, Clarke was beginning to pick up new sensor signals on an intercept with the flight.

"*Eagle* flight, this is *Eagle* control," came a voice on the comm. "Interceptor missiles headed your way. Fifty thousand kay and closing. Stand by to launch counter measures"

Clarke cut into the squad frequency. "Incoming. Stand by for evasive and countermeasures."

Heather used both hands to tighten her shock frame. She always felt as if she had both hands and legs bound together and her eyes blindfolded at times like this. There was a feeling of being back in the womb: things were safe inside, and outside represented the unknown, fraught with danger.

Sometimes she wondered why they provided status reports of an attack run. It was almost better off not knowing you were about to die before you even left the ship.

No matter how many times I do this I still get the chills, she thought.

She cut to a private frequency she had set up with Peter. He sat in his harness quietly, his head inclined to his right side and both arms hanging loosely.

"I'll bet you're sleeping, you butthead," she said.

With her face shield down, only he could hear her.

"I'm not, you know. I'm in quiet contemplation of the meaning of life. That, and thinking about what's for dinner when we get back. I should have eaten before we boarded."

Heather chuckled. Peter was good at breaking the tension that way for her. "Ahh, if memory serves, you did eat and you enjoyed it."

"Yes, but I didn't mean *you*. You were dessert, and I missed the main course."

"You hurt me, sir, and I demand satisfaction."

"You'll get your satisfaction when we get back and not a moment before."

"I can't wait." Heather clicked off the comm. She felt content. She had the TAF and her family on one hand and Peter on the other. Life for her was truly complete, yet not finished.

She became serious again when Clarke came on the comm. "Stand by, we're about to pass joy."

Joy was the commit line where the drop ship flight would be past the halfway point and committed to the assault. There was no backing out now.

Chapter Twenty-Two

"Roll sixty to starboard, flank speed!" Hobbin shouted, his ship hit from two sides.

"Damage control, report to auxiliary bridge. Weapons officer, what still works?"

As the *Cape Fear* rolled, it presented a smaller aspect to the onslaught of missiles fired by the TAF.

"Shield generators are losing power—we're not going to be able to hold at this level for much longer." The tactical officer was almost shouting to be heard over the noise of the injured, klaxon, and crew trying to contain the situation.

"Admiral, the auxiliary bridge is not responding; damage control is trying to reach them now. As for weapons control, Sanchez is dead and Hussain is trying to reroute power and data to another station."

Hobbin did not notice that his weapons officer was without a head, his lower body burned to a cinder, smoke still rising from what was left of his uniform. The weapons station was also smoking and sparking. A ceiling conduit had fallen, severing the head from body and smashing the station. Blood and brain matter had splattered all over the console and the two other crewmen sitting near by.

"Shut that damn klaxon off," Hobbin screamed.

He quickly calculated a new course. "Helm control, new heading. Zero one zero point one five by five three three point zero three. Cut power to all non-combat systems and basic life support, reroute saved power to shield generators and get a special team down there. Comm, get me the base. General Wadas."

"Aye, steer new heading zero one zero point one five by five three three point zero three. General Wadas is being patched through to your chair, sir."

The *Cape Fear* was bleeding from several holes in its hull, frozen bodies of pirates spinning off into deep space, blown out from both internal ruptures and missile impacts. The reserve ships worked to form a wedge with *Cape Fear* in the centre, where the others ships' missile defense capabilities would be heightened.

***

Clarke pushed the throttle open on *Eagle 302* and banked twenty degrees to starboard and then twenty degrees to port in an effort to dodge an incoming missile. He had passed the standby warning on to the squad and was now about to break through to the moon's thin atmosphere and come in for a hot landing on top of the target.

Anti-missile cruisers were sent forward to clear the way through the heavy flak from both the moon and orbiting shields. The shields were small weapon platforms that started out life as third-world satellite killers. Now they guarded against people like Heather and the TAF. Several fragments of flak did ping off the drop ship hull, but none penetrated deep enough to have any effect.

The TAF anti-missile cruisers fired on the platforms, creating a path for the drop ships straight to the moon's surface. Heather did not know if any of the other shuttles got caught in the flak.

Clarke got on the intercom again. "Stand by. Fifteen minutes to ground."

Everyone in the cramped drop ship hit their harness release and swung it out of the way. Holding

258

on to the grab bars on the ceiling of the cabin, they checked each other out and verified their own statuses.

Taylor contacted Fitzpatrick in *Eagle 300* on the platoon net to confirm the target and download any final orders or updates. Second squad would land with the first wave to take point, while the third and fourth sections would take a flanking position. Taylor had the command and support squad while Fitzpatrick would take up a position just inside the wedge.

Power armour would move forward to drive out any hard targets. The company was to use third platoon to form part of the vanguard with first and fourth platoons. The TLAG armour squadron, the Horse Guards, would provide heavy cover while the seventh artillery group, would set up at a distance of thirty kilometers from the target drop zone and provide long-distance artillery support.

Part of the JTF unit had already landed and surveyed the artillery pads for the seventh. Others in the JTF made their way forward and prepared to paint high-priority targets for the ground support fighters and bombers. The other companies would help form a ring around the pirates and take on the main garrison stationed on the moon.

Taylor updated the squad on final orders and made sure that everyone had updated contour maps from CIC. The troopers did a final weapons and comm check and stood ready, the white lights replaced with red blackout lighting. Heather lowered her face shield, her emotions masked as the shield locked on her helmet and her internal systems came online.

***

"General Wadas is on the comm, sir."

Hobbin sat back in his command chair and wiped his face and forehead with the towel an aide handed him. He threw it over the back of his chair and drank water from a small bottle before cutting in the comm feed to the general.

His throat was dry and felt as though scales of skin were flaking off and going into his lungs. The smoke from burning and melting wiring and fiber had been thick on the bridge, and although it was being evacuated through the ventilation system, it would still be a problem for some of the pirates. Two of them were wearing breathing masks in an effort to prevent choking.

"General, you're about to get company, and it looks like a full regiment headed your way. Can you hold them?" asked Hobbin. His tone was as dry as his throat. Although he wanted to hold the TAF at bay, and even push them back, he was more pragmatic than that. He knew that even if Wadas could hold the regiment, they would not have the resources to make a cohesive counter push.

He was beginning to wonder why he was trying to hold anything at this point and not just making a run for it. The officers and crew of the *Cape Fear* would not complain if he gave the order to skip off into deep space to lick their wounds and fend for themselves, keeping any profit. At least that's what he hoped they would say.

The reply from Wadas did not take long. "Admiral, you're full of shit and you know it. I have nothing to keep these assholes from overrunning this garrison. We have no heavy weapons other than a dozen power armour suits and a few tank busters. Everything else was loaded on transports for the

260

assault on the Confederation. I have no clue if the ships are still in one piece or not. Communication is not worth talking about between the base and the garrison, so cut the bull. What do you want? I'll hold as long as I can and take as many of them with me, if that's what you want. Unless you can get some transports down here to get us off this shithole rock!"

Hobbin was taken aback by the general's tone and words, though he could hardly fault him. General Wadas was also ex-military, coming from the Stevenson Planetary Alliance. Originally settled by humans from Finland, Sweden, and East Russia, the Alliance had settled a four-planet system that was ideal by all standards. Wadas had wanted more out of his career, however. The Stevenson Alliance was not at war and their relationship with Earth was pristine, so Wadas had little to do except push paper and take part in parades.

Now he certainly had more to focus on.

Wadas slammed his fist into the pickup and cut the camera feed. The monitor went blank and Hobbin jumped back slightly, as if to avoid a punch.

"Well, fuck you and everyone who looks like you," cursed Hobbin as he cut the feed and turned his attention to the chaos raging around him.

***

Wadas stood and rubbed his hand where he hit the comm pickup. It hurt like hell, but it relieved his frustration and disdain for Hobbin and the situation. His aide, Colonel Bradish, had been standing out of range of the camera and now moved closer. He took the general's hand and looked at it slowly, turning it over to see if there was any outward sign of damage.

"Nothing broken," he said matter-of-factly before releasing Wadas's hand.

"I'm broken," replied Wadas with emphasis. "I can't believe the mess these idiots have dropped us in. I told that fool King that we needed to have the transports on-site for both training and making an escape in case of attack. Then the jerkoff gets himself killed, which we both know was no accident. Hobbin gets pushed upstairs and I tell him the same thing. What do they do? Nothing!"

He kicked the console and sent a portable lamp and field pack flying to the ground.

"What did they think I was going to do with the blasted ships? Bug out and take this bunch of newbies off on some fool crusade for power and riches? Shit, I'd have been lucky if they were up to the task we were training them for."

Bradish picked up the lamp and field pack—it was his, so he put it on. Then he faced Wadas.

"Your orders, sir?"

Wadas knew his bitching and complaining was over and it was now time to take action. "Time to contact and status?" he asked.

"Long-range graviton sensors show the displacement wave fifteen minutes inbound. We have all ground-based defenses warmed up and on standby. All spaceborne defense platforms are already trying to cut down the odds but the TAF moved up anti-missile cruisers to take out the platforms. It's a foregone conclusion that we are about to have the TAF drop in our laps."

"What about our troops and their deployment status?"

"All our men have been issued rifles and all the ammo they can carry. Arcs of fire have been set and everyone has standing orders to wait for the command to open fire—and not before, under penalty of death. Our sub-commanders have their orders, with two platoons at the garrison headquarters and the remainder at the command bunker."

"Under penalty of death" sounded like a joke to Wadas. *We're all dead anyway,* he thought. *What's an hour or two when you're about to come under fire?*

"Pull everyone off the GHQ and move them to a point three kay from the command bunker. We'll give away part of the store to draw them closer to a heavier concentration of fire."

Wadas walked over to the holo-table and moved the curser to show the GHQ and command bunker. He pointed to an area partially hidden behind a small hill.

"Put them here, set up an ambush. As they come around this bend, hit them, slow them down, and get them to redeploy. It will make it easier for us to mount a counter if we can get them to commit early."

Wadas was hopeful, but only slightly. He doubted any commander worth his rank and pay would fall for it, but it was all he had left.

"We need to hold the command compound."

***

Clarke closed the heat shield on the canopy. As *Eagle 302* began to kiss the upper levels of the moon's thin troposphere, the temperature of the outer skin would begin to rise, causing an intense light from the flames like a welder's torch. On Earth, the troposphere started at about six hundred kilometers. Here, the thin upper reaches started at four hundred and fifty kilometers above the dry, windswept surface of the moon.

It would be a fast insurgency as the drop ships from the troop carrier *Athabaskan* screamed to disgorge their payload. *Eagle 302* buffeted as its skin temperature increased and it dove deeper toward the moon. Clarke was counting down the altitude as he used all his experience and skill to control the tiny craft. At three hundred kilometers he rammed the throttle to full power in a dive that threatened to rip the ship apart.

At the same time, the gunner acquired and locked in targets based on the level of threat, overlapping his arcs of fire with the drop ships to either side. Clarke released the commander's hold back and gave the weapons-free signal to the gunner, who let loose the initial salvo of air-to-ground missiles.

The commander had control of the weapons in the initial stages of an attack run, due in part to several devastating incidents during the early part of space warfare. Anxious gunners were so focused on hitting the target that they would fire too early in the descent. The missile would launch into the white-hot plasma that enveloped the ship as it broke through the atmosphere. The missile tubes would allow the hot gases from the descent entry plume to enter before the tube lock engaged, and the ship would exploded as it careened out of control. Hot gas and the accompanying friction entered the tube chamber, and past AIs could not react fast enough to compensate for the resulting spin. It would tear the ship apart. With current AI advancements on the newer NCC class drop ships that the JTF use, premature firing was not a problem. Others did not yet have the updated systems to avoid the problem.

The air-to-ground missiles blasted from their tubes and then kicked into near light speed to slam into their targets. The drop ships were loaded with maximum yield warheads, and the resulting mushroom cloud told a story of devastation on the ground. *Eagle 302* was still two hundred kilometers from target when the first impacts vaporized buildings, vehicles, and bodies.

Taylor gave the standby signaled to the squad. Heather could not see outside nor watch the impacting first salvo. The monitor feed was cut to give her squad time to get ready mentally without distraction.

The tiny ship flared as it neared the surface, coming in for a landing just outside the command bunker compound along with the rest of the regiment. It was a last-minute change of target and a hot landing.

The command compound was spread out over nearly 160 square kilometers and was originally an ore processing and manufacturing facility for the mining company. Prefabricated administration and accommodation buildings were designed in a wide "U" shape; the ore processing, maintenance and assembly buildings were rectangular, with few windows. The landing field was located to the northwest of the main compound, with two large slag waste storage ponds to the south and southeast. The waste ponds created an artificial windbreak to the compound, but unfortunately, contaminated particles blew off the top of the slag and into the living quarters where the miners were once housed—and where the pirate garrison now stood.

The TLAG drop ships with Heather's platoon glided to the southeast of the closest slag pond, near a service road that ran right past the main entrance to the compound. Other companies and platoons landed to the west of the compound to secure the launch area and any shuttles or assault ships on the pad. The armoured squadron landed north of the compound along with supporting ground troops, with orders to push directly for the command building. The command building was actually a series of buildings, none higher than three stories around an open compound.

Heather focused on getting out of the drop ship as soon as the ramp lowered. She could feel the ship flare as the nose rose and the ramp dropped open. They were still twenty meters from the ground, but it did not take more than a second for the rear of the ship to drop the distance. The engine pods rotated and kicked up sand and rock as she ran out the rear with the squad.

"Go! Go! Go!" Taylor barked from the ramp.

Each trooper double-timed down the short ramp, turning either left or right, and headed for cover and a firing position that would give them a good line of sight to the compound.

The distant sun was not quite over the horizon on the small moon, and it reminded Heather of the start of a hot, hazy day on her own home world. It was an odd thought. Thinking about the stark difference between her beautiful home and this barren and desolate place seemed inappropriate somehow.

She hit the ground about thirty meters from the drop ship and took cover behind a small dirt mound. She quickly scanned the distant compound and the main gate area, increasing the magnification on her helmet display, and cut in filters to eliminate the dust and haze. What she saw was a level of confusion that she did not expect. It was as if they were expecting the attack, but still preparing.

The rest of the squad took up positions as the platoon shook itself out. She watched Taylor communicating with someone on another frequency.

Then on the squad net: "We're moving forward as soon as the DS takes off—it'll make a run and swing back for a second pass before going after the force at the garrison area. Number six platoon will take them on and keep them busy for us. CIC confirms that most of the garrison was moved into this compound so we have our hands full. Once we begin, head for the outcrop" —he indicated on their helmet display— "by the gate. Questions?"

Just then, the platoon drop ships rotated its engine pod and began to throttle up for its first run on the compound. Heather could hear the rumble of the other platoon ships taking off and felt the ground shake.

"Incoming!" yelled someone on the platoon net.

The ground exploded around them. Fourth squad's drop ship exploded in a flash as it was hit head-on by two missiles, sending a shower of sparks and fragments into the air. Heather saw parts of the ship headed her way. She rolled to her left and took off running toward the gate alongside the others. She couldn't tell who, but someone was mowed down by the wreckage as they tried to get up.

In the distance she could see the pirates firing in her direction, ranging rounds hitting the dirt in front of her and coming closer. At two meters from the impacting darts, she dove to her right and ducked behind a small mass of dirt. Debris from the explosion was still raining down around her.

"Get the powered armour up here," said Taylor, breathing heavily. The wind had been knocked from him when he was thrown from his feet by the exploding drop ship.

Heather raised her rifle and zoomed in on several pirates kneeling behind a barricade. She couldn't be sure, but it looked like four or five of them. She took aim, fired a burst, and cut down two, one sagging over the top of the makeshift fortification.

Peter bounded up in the power armour and just short of her position, fired his plasma rifle. She felt the heat as she stood to move forward again.

"Sarge, we have movement—armoured car coming up the main road by the gate," reported a trooper.

"I'm on it," Peter cut in. He took off toward the main road.

"Miller and Brassard, go with him. Carmichael, take your section and make your way up this ditch to the other side of the slag. Set up covering fire for the squad as they swing to the west."

Carmichael acknowledged, already running for the ditch, his section following closely.

Whomp! Whomp! Two mortar rounds exploded behind the squad. Taylor called up artillery to take out the tubes. "Golf two-two, this is India three-zero-two. Fire mission over."

"Golf two-two fire mission, send over."

Taylor verified the grid where he thought the mortars dug in and sent it through his comm-link.

"Fire for effect!" He just stopped himself from shouting as a mortar hit fifteen meters ahead. They were ranging in on his squad, and that did not sit well with him.

"Golf two-two, shot."

Taylor was not sure how long it took for the artillery missiles to impact. It could not have been more than a few seconds, and he could see the explosions in and around a building more than eighty meters from the gate. The sound followed soon after impact. He magnified on the fortified gate area and fired on a few pirates he spotted in the open. He was sure he hit at least one; the others ducked down too low to get the angle on them.

Taylor verified the status on the assault's progress on the platoon, company, and regimental nets. Resistance was heavy all over. The only unit having a better time was sixth platoon, which had overrun a hastily assembled ambush.

I guess the pirates figured we would hit the garrison area first. Too bad for them. Taylor could only smile at the thought.

***

Heather, Miller, and Peter had gone about forty meters and were still a good seventy from the gate. The pirates had redeployed in an effort to stall their advance, but were not coordinated in their defensive position.

"Damn it, Peter, move that gun emplacement off the right-hand building! I can't get a clear shot on the tower," Miller complained from the left side of the road.

Heather took the right side of the road and Peter moved ten meters ahead to what looked like an explosive bunker long since abandoned. It did provide some cover from the rocket-propelled grenades being launched at him. Its thick earthen walls absorbed the concussions and much of the shrapnel.

"Listen, if you can do better, you come up here and wear this thing," Peter retorted.

Heather almost laughed at the chatter between the two, but there were more important things to take care of first.

"Hold one." She could observe the pirate defenses near the building Miller had referred to.

The sun was high in the sky, and with all the dust and rock being kicked up by the explosions and weapon fire, it cast a reddish tint across the landscape. The good thing, from Heather's perspective, was that the sun was directly behind her. She doubted the pirates giving Miller and Peter a hard time had a good bead on her. She narrowed her field of view on the HUD, took careful aim at the head of a pirate crouched on a low roof, and slowly squeezed the trigger.

The dart pierced the right temple and she could see his head fly backward. As his friend looked quickly over at his dead comrade, Heather pulled off another round. The dart went though the pirate's ear and almost took his head off as he spun and fell off the roof.

"Now, Peter!"

Peter did not waste any time as he swung his body around to face the gun emplacement. He stood and moved forward, his helmet targeting systems acquiring his victim just as he pulled the trigger. A blast of plasma tore through the corner of the building near the roof, melting human flesh.

Peter released a volley of twenty-millimeter darts on three soft-skin vehicles moving past his field of view. The drive section of the front vehicle blasted apart, causing it to halt. On the right, flames billowed. The second truck stopped quickly and the driver managed to open the door, but Peter acquired him as the next target. He caught sight of the driver turning to look in his direction, his eyes wide open in horror, just before another volley of rounds reduced him to a splatter of bone and blood.

The driver of the third truck was not able to react in time and drove into the back of the second. Both vehicles exploded as munitions and power packs passed their heat safety tolerance.

Miller took the opportunity to swing around his cover and pepper the gate with darts, hitting three pirates. As he began to move forward however, his luck ran out. As he released the trigger, a burst of rounds fired from a sniper hit his right leg and knee. He screamed in pain and fell forward, his legs were kicked out from under him.

Heather saw him go down, and was on her way over before he hit the ground.

"We need a medic over here. Miller's hit in the knee." She grabbed his harness in the upper back armour plate, pulling him to the relative safety of a defilade a couple of meters away.

Taylor was on top of it. He had set his AI to monitor any hits on his squad members as soon as it happened. A medic was already en route.

Heather pulled open Miller's combat suit controls on the left side and activated the medical protocols. Nanobots and pain suppressants were pumped into Miller's bloodstream. They would flow to the site of the wound and try to seal it to stop the bleeding, while the drugs interrupted the pain sensors in the brain, not quite eliminating pain, but making it manageable.

Others from the squad had already run past to join Peter in taking the gate. As soon as the medic arrived, Heather stood and tore after them, not wanting to miss the party.

The gate area was fortified with makeshift building materials and seemed to be designed to keep people in instead of out. Two guard bunkers were obviously placed there as an afterthought. Neither allowed for a good line of sight to anyone approaching, but several holes were cut for firing, similar to those on old seventeenth-century castles back on Earth. They proved just as ineffective as the old Earth equivalent.

"Carmichael, take your section and move further west, toward the clearing. Meet up with fourth squad and secure a line for us," said Taylor. "We don't want anyone slipping through. The rest of you, start clearing the area and secure it up to these two buildings." Taylor highlighted the area on everyone's HUD.

***

On board the super dreadnought *York*, Affleck sat motionless as damage and casualty reports scrolled across one of his monitors. The flotilla had lost eight battle cruisers, four battleships, and an SD in the engagement. One-third of the fighter component was also destroyed by flak on the first pass in his battle group, and a slightly smaller fighter component was lost in Martin's group.

Part of the burden of command was signing orders that resulted in loss of life. His dreams foreshadowed the eternal struggle of a military commander. Some commanders softened that guilt by blaming the pirates and their actions; Affleck kept it close to his heart.

"Comm, send to all ships, begin blocking and containment."

"Incoming missiles! We're being painted! Time to impact, twenty seconds!" The tactical officer was almost frantic. "Sir, they just showed up. Nothing and then—"

"Steady, ensign. Helm, evasive. Sensors, where did they come from? Find me that ship."

Affleck's voice was calm but concerned. Missiles did not just appear from out of nowhere. They had to be fired from a ship or weapon's platform. At this distance and with such a short flight, it had to be close.

"Scanning now." The sensor officer and two of his subordinates began a narrow scan while the other kept a wide field open on the major battle in the system.

"Contact—nothing in visible light range, but there is a gravity displacement at zero-zero-two by five-five-five point four three. Range, one thousand kilometers. Displacement suggests cruiser-sized target."

The shipwide intercom sounded the collision alert. "Missile impact in ten seconds."

Missile defense guns and lasers targeted as much of the incoming menace as they could. The only saving grace was the missiles were older and slower than the current generation of ship killers.

Still, some of them got through the defensive wall and impacted on the shields. Two made it to the armoured hull. The explosions vibrated throughout the entire ship as hot gas, shrapnel, and fire ripped into the hull and superstructure on the starboard mid-keel area. From the outside, the effect appeared to happen in slow motion. Inside, it moved at the speed of light. The ship lurched, throwing anyone not secured up in the air and slamming them back on the deck.

"Damage status."

There was a momentary delay in the response as damage control teams were still reporting in from the affected areas. In some cases, crews could not get to injured or trapped personnel until bulkheads and debris were moved or cut away.

Finally: "Primary and secondary hull breaches from decks fifty-eight through to fifty-two. Aft corridors affected on those decks between sections four-six-two and six-three-zero. We're bleeding air but blast doors are in place and holding. Casualty report not available yet. No major systems affected. Damaged sub-systems being rerouted now. Close in weapons turrets non-functional in that area. We are compensating for the loss."

Affleck knew that as bad as it sounded, it could have been worse. At least that's what he told himself. He was also keenly aware that his responsibility was the war raging around him and not this ship. That was the responsibility of the captain.

Even so, he still had to know. "Keep me up to date on casualties as soon as they become available."

"Aye, sir."

"Range to new target, lock and load tubes six through twelve—fire when ready."

"Target is moving now. Range is increasing, two thousand five hundred." The weapons officer monitored his staff closely but did not interfere.

He pointed to an area on the screen that the tech had not noticed. Range numbers cycled on the screen as the targeting AI compensated for interference and the clutter of the numerous asteroids in the field. Once the AI locked on, it flashed the icon from red to yellow and put a circle around it, confirming lock.

"Target is headed for cover in the belt. Target is locked—firing now!"

Six ship killers with multiple warheads blasted from their launch tubes, using shipboard targeting to align themselves. The self-contained AI took over and the missiles became autonomous just as they kicked into near light speed. Nothing short of impacting with the target, flak, or exhausting its fuel would stop it.

Time ticked by slowly. Then: "Time to impact, two seconds."

The telemetry on the holo table told Affleck the only detail he needed: the ship killers impacted with the target, and the computers removed the icon from the three-dimensional image. He quickly turned his focus on the ongoing battle on the moon and planet.

Chapter Twenty-Three

Heather dove for cover behind the main gate's swing arm mechanism as a grenade exploded, throwing shrapnel in the air. The sun was in full bloom now, high overhead. Without her uniform, she would have baked, evident from the overheating ground around her. The naked eye could confuse heat shimmers in the distance with targets, but her helmet display picked them up clearly.

She squeezed the trigger slowly and sent darts flying toward another pirate, then watched him drop before she moved on.

On the squad frequency: "Brassard! Take the right tower."

I think the sergeant is getting pissed at the lack of progress, she thought. *I'm getting just a little pissed, too.*

She checked her arc and jumped up, tripping on her first step. She regained her balance and ran for the guard tower on the right of the gate. She could hear the tanks and artillery in the distance, but her immediate concern was the heavy concentration of fire coming from the building closest to her and the platoon.

She reached the tower only to come under fire again. This time, it was Peter who took out the pirates targeting her, releasing a bolt of plasma that burned the two pirates before they could get up and run.

As Heather looked for new threats, she could see the main road split to the left. There was a clearing on the right, just in front of some smaller buildings.

They looked like homes for the miners, with walking paths snaking around the front and sides of each.

Twenty meters in front of that was another compound and another road that forked off the main. She magnified the view to read the sign. The right-hand road led to the landing strip.

In front were two of the larger U-shaped buildings and three smaller ones on the opposite side. A parade square was paved in the center section only, the outer edge torn away by years of heavy vehicular traffic. Just beyond that she could make out the command structures, most on the right side of the main road that ran through the middle of the base.

"Sarge, I can just make out the command buildings from my vantage, about two point five kay north and on the right of the main road. I can't see the other platoons breaking through, but I do see a lot of activity."

"These guys had a lot of anti-armour and it's proven a slow slog for the tanks. Air support is on its way. Command confirms that we're to make our way up the main drag and hit the command buildings from the south side. The other companies will advance from the east and west to act as blocking."

The platoon began to move as pirates died. Third platoon had already gone one and a half kilometers, but still had to fight for every centimeter.

Heather heard the caution signal, meaning the drop ships were on their way in with a close support strike. The platoon hit the ground as a flight of seven ships rocketed just above the buildings on a steep angle.

At less than one hundred meters from the ground, they cut loose salvos of missiles and twenty-millimeter darts. The intended targets were located in the command square, and although Heather could no

277

longer see directly into the area, she could hear the explosions and see the mushroom clouds rising, only to be blown away quickly by the wind. As the clouds parted, a black, pasty material began to rain down—bits and pieces too large to float off with the smoke.

The drop ships did another pass and then blasted off to rearm in orbit, passing over third platoon on their way.

Heather reached an intersection where a small building once stood. Its roof was split in two, with one wall missing and all the windows blown out. It seemed that the explosion came from inside. Second squad fell in to her right, as the remainder of the platoon took cover along the intersecting road.

She read the sign showing the name of the intersecting boulevard: "New Hope." *Not the best name for a road in this colony,* she thought.

Peter was beginning to round a makeshift barricade when he stopped and shouted on the platoon net, "Mine—incoming!"

Heather's heart stopped as she turned her head. She could see Peter start to back away and then saw the puff of smoke from the ground.

Directing her gaze above the ground, she saw the small black object still rising. It was like watching in slow motion, her instincts telling her to run to Peter to try and save him from the impending explosion. At the same time her flight response kicked into high gear and begged her to take whatever cover she could find.

Her mind registered every detail as it was happening, the scene slowly playing out in front of her as she held back the urge to scream. In the end, her survival response won and she dove into a blast hole, getting as low as she could.

The mine was triggered when Peter's armour broke the laser contact as he rounded the barricade. It was designed to explode in a shower of darts on an angle with a killing range of seven to ten meters. It was more of an antipersonnel mine but could do enough damage to power armour to kill its user if it was close enough.

Peter noticed the mine just a second after its initial blast out of the ground, and his quick reflexes and newfound dexterity in the power armour allowed him to back away and perform a not-so-graceful dive out of the danger radius. He landed eight meters from the explosion and could feel darts bounce off his back and legs.

As soon as the mine went off, Heather was up and running toward Peter. As she approached, she could see him moving, and breathed a sigh of relief as she quickly took control of her emotions.

She bent and helped Peter stand, his leg and arm servos doing most of the work. Another trooper arrived to help to steady him and provide cover.

Heather switched to her private frequency with Peter. "You ever do that to me again, I'll kill you myself." Her tone was not reproachful, but relieved.

"If I ever do that again, I'll be sure you're not around to see the aftermath. That was way too close."

The platoon swept forward to the north and east, allowing their sister platoon on their west flank to move into a supporting position. Fighting moved building to building as the pirates dug in.

***

Heather took cover behind a large stone planter near the main entrance to a building. A long sign was posted on the outside of the building. Although it was silted over with dirt and grime, she could still read "Family Relocation Office." The large horseshoe-shaped building had seen better days.

Switching to her thermal imaging system, she scanned the windows overlooking the narrow street as the squad readied itself to cross. Taylor was getting sit-reps from the rest of third platoon in preparation to rush the three-story building.

Many of the windows were broken, and blast holes overlapped the walls and window casings in some places. Heather noticed three or four holes made by a plasma discharge. *Peter's been busy providing cover,* she thought.

Taylor gave his signal and they crossed the street en masse, no one receiving fire.

Heather was just reaching the steps of the main doorway when she caught a glimpse of movement in the entrance. It was further back, maybe a dozen or more steps from the door, in the darker recess of the entrance.

Quickly, she increased the magnification on her helmet and switched to the platoon frequency. "Incoming! Take cover!"

As she spoke, a blast of plasma ripped what was left of the doors from its frame, vaporizing a trooper not quick enough to get under cover. Every other window on the lower level erupted with salvos of darts fired from squad-sized automatic weapons.

The pirates are getting smarter, Heather thought as she hit the ground hard, taking away some of her wind.

It was a thought that meant nothing as automatic weapons fire was directed toward her, but at moments like this, her mind found the smallest fact to grip and elaborate on. The direct fear of dying was replaced with a piece of humor or trivia that had nothing to do with her current predicament.

Somehow, it worked to focus her thoughts, and she rolled on her back, charging her grenade launcher and firing two quick rounds through the entrance. Both exploded as soon as they hit something solid— the first with the pirates' plasma launcher and the second with one of the pirates trying to run for cover.

The subsequent detonations blasted from the entrance in a funnel effect. Heather bent over, experience telling her to protect her head from everything that came flying through the doorway.

Peter boosted the servos on his legs and bounded through one of the windows while other troopers tossed grenades or launched a volley of automatic fire in response to the ambush. As he reached the window, he activated his thrusters, normally used only in near-vacuum conditions, and blasted through the opening, crushing a startled pirate in the process.

He aimed the automatic rifle in his left arm toward his left field of fire and his plasma gun to the right, and fired. Twenty-millimeter darts tore through flesh and bone along the hallway. At the same time, the bolt of plasma burned everything in its path down the opposite side.

The hall was littered with debris from the grenades, plasma, and rifle fire. Building materials and glass, along with remnants of window coverings, some still burning, lined the floor along with the bodies. The corridor ran the full length of the building, with windows facing the street and office doors opposite. Some doors were open, others hung on their hinges. Every thirty meters was a fire door, all of which were open, many twisted right out of the frame.

Peter signaled the platoon. "First level hall clear."

"Second and third sections, secure the building. One and four sections, cover the north end of the street."

Fitzpatrick monitored the regimental net. He was concerned that his platoon might get cut off if the pirates were left to hold any strong points as he moved south of the command buildings. It was going to be a slower process, but keeping two of the squads in the platoon for cover and blocking was the only way he could keep the platoon out of harm's way. Taking risks was part of this job, but taking stupid risks was not going to be his call.

He brought his command squad forward with the special weapons detachments and ordered cave rats to assist the securing of the buildings. Cave rats were autonomous AIs, oval and only fifteen centimeters tall. They were loaded for bear with an automatic rifle, stunner, and a sensor package that would detect heat, movement, and sound, and do it all in very hostile conditions. They were normally used in tight confines, from caves to thick jungle and underbrush to house-clearing operations. They maneuvered on two tracks or as an air cushion vehicle using built-in lift fans. They could also be fitted with laser cutters and sampling tools.

The cave rats allowed troopers to stay out of the danger zone. They also gave the two sections clearing the large administration building a measure of speed, as rats would be released to search the upper and lower floors while the troopers would take on any serious resistance without delay.

Eight cave rats were brought up from transports to the platoon, placed on the landing in the now secured entrance, programmed with a schematic of the building, and assigned routes. The rats then floated away on cushions of air as their AIs took over, charging their weapons and sensors as they left.

"Rats are loose, stand by," said the programmer as she sent the last one away.

Two were programmed per floor, beginning at the south stairwell. Two were also assigned to monitor the north stair exits for escaping pirates.

Almost immediately, the rats picked up movement or heat sources on each of the three floors. Some turned out to be office equipment or power boxes, but others were pirates. The rats took care of them with a quick burst of weapons fire.

Near the end of the hall, on the second floor, was a closed fire door. As the lead rat neared, the second rat detected movement. A lone pirate reached out from one of the side offices just behind the lead rat and fired into the rear of the rat's protective skin.

The AI on a cave rat was fast, and the second rat had locked on the pirate as soon as he was detected. A quick burst in the back and the pirate was split open before he even hit the ground.

Heather watched the progress on the inset in her helmet visor, and ordered one of the backup rats watching the north stars to gain access to the end of the second-floor hall.

As the rat passed through the first fire door, it became evident that someone or something was held up in the closed-off section. A check on her schematic showed at least three inner offices behind the two closed and presumably locked fire doors.

The rats could easily burn their way through the door, but something in the back of Heather's mind said otherwise. She called up one of the snipers in fourth section, stationed across the street in the adjacent building.

"Simm, check the windows of the second floor, north section. Do you see any movement?"

"Wait one."

Simm shifted position and tied in his rifle's scope to his helmet display. The scope was designed to show greater contrast than the combat helmet, separating light and shadow in better detail.

"In three of four windows, I can see into the hall, and nothing. The fourth window is covered with something. It's the one farthest north and it's not regular window coverings—looks almost like armour plating, but I can't be sure. I'm not picking up any movement, but I can see what looks like mounted weapons through the second window. It's too low for me to get a good look from here at this angle."

"Any odd heat sources? Any heat at all?"

"Nothing that...wait one."

Simm was scanning the section of building with his weapon, moving past the second window to the third and then the fourth, where it was blocked.

"I'm getting a heat source but it's not steady. The signature is rising—I can't get any signal through the barricaded window, but I am getting a residual signal from window number three and now number two. It could be a fire."

Heather and the tech controlling the cave rats looked at the monitor of the rat at the far end of the hall, closest to the fire door by the barricaded window. They watched the heat sensor increase on the door. The other two rats at the south fire door did not indicate the same heat signature.

Simm would have seen smoke or flames flicker if it was a fire, Heather contemplated. *What else would increase the heat signature?*

She was about to call Taylor on the squad net when it hit her—something that she had only seen and experienced in training.

"Shit!"

Instead of the squad net, she jumped up to the platoon frequency. "Third platoon, bug out—we have a cascading loop IED and it's about to blow. Second floor north end. Bug out! Bug out!"

She was referring to an improvised explosive device—a sophisticated time bomb made from components found almost anyplace on a battlefield. All it needed was a power source with a capacitor, computer, and explosives, like missiles or entry charges. The power source would feedback on itself, with the computer timed to increase the amount of the power in the feedback loop.

At a certain point, the capacitors could not hold any more power. After that, it was like a mini-meltdown, with a tremendous amount of heat stored in the feedback.

That was what she and Simm were detecting now. This type of bomb would only be used if nothing else was available. It was crude, detectable, and easy to disarm, but you only had a finite amount of time to do it in. Heather could not tell how much explosive was being used or how long they had.

Troopers in second and third squads filed quickly out of the building from every exit, while first and fourth squads moved even further north up the road. They took up positions behind cover from the cascading bomb behind them and the pirates in front.

Heather met up with Peter as they both reached the entrance. Taylor was just behind, making sure no one else was left. The three were the last to leave.

They had just made it around a rubble pile when the north end of the building exploded in a mushroom cloud of fire, smoke, and building material.

It was as if a low yield nuke had exploded, taking three-quarters of the building with it. The remaining sections soon fell in. The explosion also destroyed or severely damaged nearby smaller buildings and started fires in others.

The ground shook violently and troopers in the blast wave were blown back with tremendous force. There were numerous injuries, though most were minor. The majority of troopers had been under cover but five received serious injuries as parts of buildings fell in on them or shrapnel penetrated their body armour.

Fitzpatrick dusted himself off as he sat up, his back against a building wall. "Squad leaders, damage and weapons check."

He quickly switched to the company frequency and called for the evacuation of the five seriously wounded troopers. They would have to be transported by ground effect vehicles until they reached a safe landing zone for the medical shuttles.

Fitzgerald addressed Heather directly on the platoon net. "Brassard, good call and well done. You just saved our hides." On Heather's personal frequency, he said, "Trooper, see me when this op is over. Your talents are being wasted as a trooper."

"Aye, sir," said Heather, exhausted and covered in dust.

***

"The *Shipwreck* is losing containment, sir. Captain Armstrong is giving the abandon ship order and is—" The communications office did not have time to finish as the *Shipwreck* exploded in a blinding flash. The external sensors on the *Cape Fear* compensated for the intensity of the explosion.

"Damn," whispered Hobbin as he quietly squeezed the armrest of his command chair. "Move the *Minto* into a guarding position and take the place of the *Shipwreck*."

He was playing a tightly scripted chess match with ships and their crews and he knew it. There was very little wiggle room for him to effect an escape without someone on his own side getting wise too early and putting a missile up his tail. He was less worried about the TAF ships and more concerned about his own at this point.

Pirates had long memories, and loyalties tended to erode very quickly in a crunch. He had to get the smaller cruisers to blocking in order to get himself and the large dreadnoughts out of harm's way. To do that, he needed to be outside of the system limit to make the slide safely, and the other captains may not like that idea.

***

"Damage to the *Viper* and *Collingwood*—there're still at action stations and engaging on the run. The *Topaz* is withdrawing with extensive damage and casualties. The *Goth* is abandoning ship, life pods are programmed to RV at..." The tactical office giving the briefing paused to highlight the area in yellow before continuing.

Affleck did not speak. He had not been looking forward to this briefing, but he had to know what was still available to continue the fight. The executive officer and his senior staff from all divisions, including intelligence, were either standing around the holo-table or attending via monitor.

Affleck interjected. "Let the *Perth* pick up the survivors and have *Iron Duke* give cover. What's our status on the combat ready ships?"

"Battle group Alpha has supremacy in the air over the planet, but ground troops are having a tough go of it. The pirates are dug in so it's building to building for the most part. Their armour is beginning to have an effect, but not without losses. On the plus side, they are getting the upper hand and have captured several hundred. They've also rescued a dozen engineer miners. The prisoners are being interned at a deep pit mine on the southern settlement. Admiral Martin has confirmed the majority of the pirate fleet was confronted at our end of the operation."

The plot table changed views to show Affleck's battle group and the continuing battle.

"We have a running battle with the pirates making a run for the outer system. CIC's estimate is they are getting ready to slide once they have enough room."

Affleck interrupted again. "This may be a running battle, gentlemen, but I want an end run on the pirates. They are throwing their cruisers and battle cruisers at us to slow down the chase while the dreadnoughts and battle ships make their escape. The cruiser captains cannot be too pleased, considering we keep knocking them down. I want this ended ASAP. Options?"

Affleck valued the input from his officers and crew, regardless of rank. His command approach was to take knowledge from everyone and use the best to the advantage of the whole.

A junior lieutenant spoke, tentatively at first. "Sir? Lieutenant Goldsmith—"

"I know who you are, lieutenant. Speak up."

"Well, we have our carriers and transports along with covering frigates just out of range on the far side of the belt. Why not use their missiles to slow down the retreating dreadnoughts? We could swing around, starting from the rearmost ships, and hit them from this angle."

Goldsmith used the portable pointer and marked the attack vector on the plot. He highlighted the carriers, transports, and covering ships and pulled up the total weapons load for comparison.

Affleck was impressed with the idea and the boldness of the young, relatively inexperienced lieutenant. Others in the gathered group also seemed to feel that this was the best option right now. Surely, running in chase was not working. The pirates had the jump on the lead elements of battle group Bravo and there was not enough acceleration curve for them to catch up before the pirates slid to freedom.

Affleck knew that the carriers and transports had, along with their Kingston class frigates, enough missiles in reserve to do some serious damage to the retreating ships, giving him time to move into a more effective position.

"I like it, Goldsmith. Almost as good as what I was going to suggest." Affleck smiled, as did others. Goldsmith almost blushed with pride.

"Thank you, sir."

"Right, ladies and gentlemen. Comm, relay to all ships a change in attack vector. Tactical and navigation, I want a workup of the new course headings and intercept vectors. Transmit to the battle group. Execute in ten minutes. Let's get this job done, people. CIC, relay to ground force the change."

Chapter Twenty-Four

Hobbin watched the battle play out on the screen as his dreadnoughts took flight, while his smaller ships acted as decoys and blockers for the onslaught of missiles directed at him.

"Updated damage report coming in—"

"Belay that. I don't want to hear it." Hobbin shot the comm officer a look that had the junior wanting to run and hide.

Hobbin did not care. His emotions were churning his stomach and the bile was beginning to rise. He cursed Lebakie over and over and vowed to exact revenge on him. He was running with sixteen dreadnoughts left intact.

Lebakie knew this would happen. He had to have known. But why? What purpose did Lebakie have to do this to me?

The lift door opened quietly and the XO walked in. Hobbin turned his attention away from the plot and faced Westbour. "What are you doing on the bridge?"

Westbour leaned close. "May I see you in private, sir?" he whispered, not wanting the rest of the bridge to hear the concern in his voice.

"What? Now?" Hobbin was surprised. He realized that he did think of Westbour as a friend, the only one he had at the moment, and relented.

"You have five minutes." He regretted the annoyance in his voice. If Westbour had something to say, it must be important.

The two men walked to the ready room attached to the bridge. The door closed and Hobbin turned,

"Okay, out with it." There was that tone of annoyance again!

"I won't keep you, sir, but I have some concerns about..." Hesitation crept into his voice. "About getting away on the backs of the cruiser captains and their crews."

"I haven't heard any complaints from the captains on the capital ships." An attempt at humor, and it wasn't working. "Okay, bad joke, but we need the capital ships for our next move and I need your support on this."

"What next move? We're dead with no place to go! Even assuming we escape, where are we to hide? The TAF will hunt us down!"

Hobbin's expression softened as he heard the defeat in Westbour's voice, but his mood shifted to anger quickly with his reply. "I never said anything about hiding—I want that two-faced bastard Lebakie. He dropped us in this mess and I want him dead."

Westbour flinched. "You're as nuts as Lebakie if that's your plan."

Hobbin's expression did not change. "Report back to your station, Mr. Westbour—before I relieve you of your duties."

Westbour stood to attention, turned, and walked to the door. He stopped and looked back at Hobbin. "Lebakie is not worth this. Not now."

He hit the door switch on the wall panel and walked out.

Hobbin stood watching the door, the conversation erased by ongoing battle playing itself out in his mind.

He recovered himself and reentered the bridge. "Helm control, increase speed to ten percent past safety. Change course to bring us to one hundred kilometers from the belt. Comm, tell the others to follow if they want to get out. Tactical, give me a running count on TAF pursue ships. Put up the latest plot on the big screen."

Everyone on the bridge turned, if only briefly. One hundred kilometers from the churning and unpredictable asteroid belt was too close. It crossed the safety limit by several hundred percent. An asteroid could be as small as a grain of sand or as large as a dreadnought. Some were the size of small moons. An object that size could do a lot of damage to a dreadnought, no matter what type of shielding arrangement it had.

***

Heather reached up and grabbed Peter's offered hand to help her stand.

"Nice," he said on their private net, raising his visor just enough to let her see him smile ear to ear.

"Keep your grin in your pants, you," she replied playfully, and then got serious. "Let's end this crap. I'm tired of playing with these assholes."

She stood and replaced her rifle's power pack, changing her grenade load and magazine with a full one. Taylor was up and moving toward her with the rest of the squad.

On the platoon frequency she heard Fitzpatrick. "Let's get moving, third platoon—the tanks are on the edge of the command building's perimeter with two platoons in tow, but we have to be in place to block. The pirates may be getting ready to break out."

The platoon sorted itself out double time, everyone changing power and ammunition packs. Peter and Ritchie had their power armour reloaded and were moved to the front left flank of the advance.

The sporadic fire in their direction was ineffective. Heather could hear the artillery and armour in the distance with squad automatic and anti-tank guns on both sides blasting away.

The street was now even more littered with debris, and the advance was slow but methodical. The sun was past the midway point in its arc across the moon's sky, but the heat and wind was still strong. Blowing dust reduced visibility for the unaided eye, part of the reason why the pirates' fire was not well aimed.

As they advanced, the platoon drifted in and out of sight, going through and around some smaller buildings, making sure that none of the pirates slipped through. Heather knew that there was another platoon to their left, and the hammer was closing on the command buildings, now within view.

Whomp! Whomp! Whomp! Three mortar rounds exploded to the east and south. *Overshot,* she thought. *They'll range on that, but that means there's a spotter close by to see through this haze.*

She scanned her arc or fire, overlapping with the trooper to her left and right. Not seeing anyone, she called up Taylor and passed on her thoughts.

"I know, I was just thinking the same thing," he said.

Whomp! The round went off twenty meters ahead, blowing some kind of monument apart.

Heather and the troopers on either side dove for cover as sharp rocks flew overhead. Taylor got on the squad net. "Watch for a spotter. He has to be close, and the fire for effect will be next."

Heather stood and cautiously advanced. She took three, then four steps and almost tripped on a culvert that ran along the road. It was not very big and partially covered.

She was about to step over it when she spotted a shadow in the distance, near the end of the culvert just before it snaked around a corner. Visibility was poor with twisting shadows, dust, and smoke.

Too far forward to be anyone in the platoon, JTF isn't operating here, although it could be some part of a structure. If it is a live body, the location would give whoever it was a decent vantage point to watch the advance.

"Sarge, Brassard. One-five-oh meters along the culvert running northwest. I'm going to check it out." Heather signaled the trooper to her right, a newbie, to follow her and cover.

"Watch the building to your front, Brassard. If it is our spotter, he may have friends."

***

Wadas and his aide Colonel Bradish watched the building explode in a mushroom cloud. Bradish winced. He wasn't sure how many men went up with the building, but he knew any loss of manpower was going to hurt.

Wadas had the rangefinders up to his eyes. Slowly he moved them down and focused on the ledge of the building's roof.

"What the hell was that?" he asked.

Bradish could only guess. "That was not TAF. Too much collateral damage. They aren't that careless."

Wadas picked up the portable comm and switched to the all-stations network. "I do not want any more fuck-ups. No one is to set off any booby traps without the express orders of your commanders, and only I can give that order to your commanders."

He turned to face Bradish. "That cost us too much in resources and manpower than what it was almost certainly worth. We have to get the field commanders to think before acting. Get on the net and tell the more experienced ones to get control of the others. I want to pull back all remaining forces into this area."

He showed Bradish a portable reader with a local map of the area, pointing to the smaller grouping of buildings in the southwest corner.

"The TAF haven't reached this area yet. It's our breakout point if we can't hold the tanks until we regroup."

Bradish left Wadas on the roof with another aide and three bodyguards. Wadas could now only think in terms of survival. Any concept of victory had vanished. He chuckled, admitting to himself that he was surprised he wasn't dead as yet.

Wadas also knew something else: if he were doing the attacking, he would have vaporized the surface with planet busters.

"It would have been faster and less messy," he said out loud. One of the guards overheard the comment and raised an eyebrow.

*****

"Right, captain, we're in place with second platoon on the southwest, just on the opposite side of the junction and road." Fitzpatrick raised his visor and looked in the dust-covered sky. The sun was waning now but there was still enough light to see. He noted how little there was to see as he scanned the distance. The air was stale and hot, humid with a faint metallic odor.

"Platoon sergeant, make sure everyone has enough power packs and ammo. Bring up another supply truck if you need to. It's open on the other side of this clearing and you can use that building as cover."

Fitzpatrick pointed out an area west of the platoons' position, near what may have been a sports field of some sort. There, a road led directly to the landing pads northwest and would allow a supply hauler to quickly approach under protection.

***

Heather was listening to the tanks push through in the distance. She could also hear artillery over the horizon as other platoons made short work of remaining pirate forces in the garrison area.

She had heard on the radio in a previous sit-rep that the pirates' ambush had failed due to poor leadership and lack of fire control. Some pirates had apparently fired prematurely and alerted the advancing platoon.

She could not help laughing. *Typical pirate macho male—always shooting his load off before he's ready.*

Laughing felt good. Things had been tense, and it would get worse as daylight turned to night and the pirates tried to break out in the dark.

***

Wadas ran and grabbed a downed pirate's rifle and power pack. He struck the wall with his shoulder and took aim at the troopers climbing over some rubble, downing two of them before changing position.

As he moved by one of the windows, he spotted a tank hung up on debris, the crew commander trying to get a better view of the rocks and building supports his tank was beached on. Wadas stopped, took a quick aim and fired a controlled burst. Darts flew into the upper body of the crew commander and he slumped over.

Wadas could see the gunner slam the hatch and without waiting, began to traverse the barrel in his direction. He fired blind and the wrong part of the building blew apart, throwing more rubble into the street and square below.

Wadas shouted over to Bradish, just coming up the stairs. "Where's my power armour and anti-tank missiles? We could use either one right about now."

"Thurston is pulling out the power pack from the last serviceable PA and jury-rigging it to the missile launchers. It should be ready to launch in a second."

As he spoke, a missile blasted from one of the buildings and hit the base of the tank Wadas had fired on. It punctured a hole in the lower section and then ignited, sending the turret into the sky along with parts of the crew. The lifting fan stopped and the tank body slammed into the ground, the front section still hung up on the mound.

"Everyone is ready to break out," Bradish reported. "I have two sections set up to keep the area clear."

Wadas only nodded. His face was beginning to show some strain, but anyone looking at him would only see a man in control of his world.

On the opposite side of the square, in one of the larger buildings, heavy weapons fire opened up on the TAF trying to gain a foothold on the outer buildings. From his vantage point, Wadas could see TAF troopers go down with little or no returning fire. Then something caught his eye.

"Thurston, get that launcher over to the northeast side. A troop of tanks and support are swinging eastward toward you and your men."

Wadas heard a dull rumble in the distance. "Now what?"

Bradish looked up but could not hear anything. He shrugged, then said, "I'm going to take the two squads and begin to push south. We'll need to start making that hole for us to leave this party, and it's starting to get dark."

Wadas nodded, picking up his weapon and a grenade launcher. He took one last look out the window; he still could hear the rumble. *Maybe it was the tanks,* he thought as he ran to his next position.

Bradish reached the main entrance and with guards in tow, checked to see if it was clear to leave. The wind was beginning to die down but the dust still choked the sky, making it difficult to breathe. He dispatched one of his men to pull the two squads and make their way toward the corner of the building where it was clear, out of the line of sight of TAF snipers and lucky shots.

Wadas was just inserting a power pack on his rifle when the building shook with such force that parts of the ceiling fell in, knocking him to the ground. *Hindsight is 20/20*, he thought as he crawled over to two of his men, neither moving. He undid their helmets to check for a pulse. Nothing on the first. On the second, he didn't even need to check— part of a pipe protruded from the man's neck and ran down his back.

The drop ships that had unleashed the salvo were turning to make a second pass. Wadas could just see them in the distance and did not want to wait for a replay of the last thirty seconds. He stood and gathered the other men with him while he ordered a withdrawal of the area. He was hoping that the TAF would also be hampered by their own ships as they went to ground in an attempt to avoid the air-to-ground barrage.

On his comm he heard Bradish and rifle fire in the background. "We're...off...don't make your...north if you can..." Then nothing but static.

Wadas reached the side entrance to the building and ran for cover behind a short wall. With his back turned to the fire, he took a quick look over the wall to get a better vantage. What he saw was not encouraging.

***

Heather felt the heat of that last round as it buzzed over her head. She had tried to change position but was pinned down.

"I count one, maybe two sections trying to break out," she said to Taylor on the comm.

"Stay low for now, air cover is less than a minute out and it will be danger close."

Staying low is not the problem—getting shot is, she thought. Looking up she could just make out the silhouette of the drop ships on final approach to unload their burden. *That's a wonderful sight right now.*

Chapter Twenty-Five

Dialing up the magnification on her helmet, Heather watched as the ships began to open the missile launch doors. She could see the pods coming out, and as they did, discharging their lethal payload. A smile crept onto her face, knowing what was to come next.

What looked like a thin white cloud was attaching to each missile as they left the pods. She was not able to follow them for too long; the launch rockets only fired for a short time before their main motors kicked in, and the human brain and eyes could not follow them at that speed. She quickly peeked over the wall in time to see the first impacts.

One building's roof collapsed while the rear of blew out. It seemed to take the pirates firing at Heather by surprise, because they stopped their assault, silenced in stunned disbelief.

Taking advantage of the opportunity, she quickly propelled herself up and over the wall, running for a debris mound and shooting several of the pirates who were distracted by the explosions.

Taylor's voice came on the comm. "The tanks and their support are making their move now and pushing the pirates in our direction. We're calling in arty to soften any resistance, so take cover."

She had just managed to drop to the ground when the first ranging round landed in the centre of the command square. The fire for effect followed and destroyed the square and several facades, taking more pirates with it. Less fire came from the square and surrounding area now as the drop ships made their second pass, overlapping their first and getting very close to Heather's position.

She covered her head in a reflex move just as one of the missiles exploded fifty meters from her position. The hard kill radius of an air-to-ground missile was fifty meters, so Heather had to make sure that she was well out of the line of the shrapnel expelled by the blast.

She winced and closed her eyes as darts, rocks, and other debris flew over her head and body, some landing close by. She felt the concussion from the explosion throughout her body and it hurt as the pressure wave blew past her. After the drop ships made their pass and the artillery moved on, she checked to make certain that she still had her original body parts.

The only resistance right now was a small group making a run toward the landing pads. She wasn't sure what they thought they would find there, as it would be one of the first sites secured by the TAF. There would be no getting out for these pirates.

She got the all-clear signal from Taylor and was ordered to head over for an "O," or orders, group in a secure area. Calling it a secured area was somewhat subjective. While it was not taking any current fire, it was still within the hot zone and snipers were always a concern. Still, it was far from their current centre of operation for the platoon.

**

Wadas was about to call Bradish back when the first ranging round hit the square. It did not seem like any time had passed between the first salvos from the attacking ships and the artillery.

Wadas knew that it would end here, and he experienced a certain peace about the whole thing. He was a little bitter about not making his mark in the universe. *The original premise had been brilliant*, he thought. Striking at the heart of the Confederation and taking what should have been theirs in the first place seemed to him, at the time, to be the ultimate challenge, and he welcomed it.

The first artillery rounds landed and he felt the impact and blast heat the air around him. Choking dust swirled around, making it harder to breathe. He coughed and bit his lower lip as he readied himself for what was to come.

He looked around, his back still to the wall. Part of him wished for an exit. Maybe he could make his escape later, when things quieted down.

But no escape route opened up, and it didn't matter any way. The next explosion knocked him off the wall and tossed him forward onto this stomach.

His rifle flew from his hands as he stopped his face from hitting the ground first. He tasted blood and had a difficult time breathing as his chest tightened. He took one more breath before the next series of rounds hit.

***

"Damage to main engineering sections, main motors are offline, helm and navigation controls are off line." The young officer at the helm section showed a remarkable ability to remain calm. The situation that the *Cape Fear* was in would bring most people to a breaking point. Hobbin was impressed, thinking sarcastically that he should promote him. *Too bad he won't live.*

But that thought was quickly replaced by one of determination. His desire to survive and chase down his former employer was still strong.

"Tactical, what's happening with the other capital ships?"

"We're five minutes from our turn—escorts are scattered throughout the outer system as they try to regroup. I count eight that have bugged out. Nine capital ships remain with us as the others have been crippled or destroyed and two ran."

"Give me a countdown on the turn, starting at two minutes. Use chemical thrusters to assist."

"Aye, sir." The tactical officer was about to execute the order when: "Stand by! New targets— range ten thousand kilometers on intercept course!"

Any calm was now gone. The young officer at helm control swung his head, his jaw dropping and his eyes wide open.

Hobbin rushed to the plot table and watched as several more red icons blinked into existence. It felt like he had been tied to a post and rammed by a super dreadnought.

"Missile launch detected. Multiple inbound."

"Move the escorts up to intercept."

"Sir!" The officer's mouth had gone dry, and he tried to swallow. "Escorts are dropping back and say that they are not staying. It's all of them, sir. The only ones left are five older *Graften* class frigates, and they aren't going to be able to do much."

That wasn't really news to Hobbin. He knew it was only a matter of time before the other captains would try to get out while the getting was good. And the getting was not going to get any better.

"Time to impact."

"One minute forty-two seconds."

"Less than two minutes till…shit."

Hobbin hung his head for a moment then straightened and walked back to his command chair.

"Helm, plot a course into the asteroid field. We may lose their target lock inside."

No one argued. It was the only option left. They had a better chance of escaping an asteroid than several dozen ship killer missiles heading in their direction.

Hobbin quickly realized, however, that nothing ever goes as planned.

"Sir! Secondary multiple launches, new group of targets. Time to impact, thirty seconds!"

More than a dozen missiles hit the already crippled ship. With most of their self-defenses out of commission, it was inevitable that the majority would impact.

Hobbin died as the *Cape Fear* exploded in a blinding flash of light, along with any dreams he may have had about getting rich and getting revenge.

Someone once said that revenge is a dish best served cold. Hobbin, just before the *Cape Fear* became a short-lived sun, realized that revenge is a dish best not served at all. At the very least, it should be warm and fresh, lest you not survive to see it cool down.

***

Affleck wanted to shield his eyes from the flash but let the computer screen do that for him. He knew it was almost over, and the cleanup would bring other challenges to this task force, his flotilla, and his men and women.

"Launch search and rescue with fighter cover. Make sure armed guards accompany the SAR techs."

Affleck checked the plot to see how Martin's battle group was doing. "Signal to all remaining pirate ships: surrender and prepare to be boarded."

Martin was in the middle of mopping up stragglers and holdouts on New Gloucester and the inner system. Resistance on the planet was lessening. The majority of the pirate ground forces seemed to have been on the moon—and therefore his problem.

Martin's battle group had also lost ships in the engagement. Three dreadnoughts, six frigates, and four battle cruisers were not coming home. There was no estimate yet of the number of lives lost. Search and rescue was still finding life pods, with and without survivors. Affleck knew the numbers would be high no matter what.

Of Affleck's battle group, eight frigates were lost, destroyed, or damaged beyond salvage this far on the fringe. He had also lost six battle cruisers and five dreadnoughts, two due to collisions with asteroids. The losses to the ground forces were not yet known, but the names would be downloaded soon.

The largest losses were to the fighter squadrons: over a third lost in the initial engagement, another fifteen percent lost during the running battle.

Affleck turned away from the screen and stood. He straightened his tunic and stepped off his command platform.

"Comm, relay to all ships and regiments, orders group in ten hours via comm." *That should give us enough time to finish cleaning up*, he estimated.

"Signal to carrier group. Launch recon under heavy cloak. Set up system pickets, maximum range."

***

Heather rolled over the pirate's body and took a sample of DNA. She never liked this duty but knew that they had to identify everyone.

All humans had their DNA recorded at birth and stored in several linked databases on a number of settled worlds. When the human DNA banks were first proposed in the early twenty-first century, there was an outcry from civil liberties groups, who called it an invasion of privacy. But in the end, it was the only way to identify the millions who died due to war and famine on Earth. By the late twenty-second century, even the staunchest civil liberties groups were calling for the DNA, not just from the newborn, but from everyone.

After taking the sample, she saved the data for upload when she reached the *Athabaskan*. Something she was eagerly looking forward to.

After the close support drop ships finished, it was the artillery's turn. The bombardment had left very little of the buildings and the square. It became a difficult task to find all the bodies in the mess. Only about three dozen pirates had managed to surrender—a tiny percentage of those involved in the fight.

Heather came upon another body, its arms twisted and part of its head gone, exposing brain matter and bone. She looked at the face and realized it was a young man, maybe in his early thirties. It was hard to believe that he was part of this group bent on inflecting so much destruction and death on the Confederation.

The lower remains were still buried in rubble, but Heather did not need much of a body to take the sample. She bent, placing the probe on a clear patch of skin near the neck, then pressed the sample button.

It only took a few seconds. When she removed it, a small white patch appeared. The upper layer of the dermis had been collected, burned off as the analyzer stored the DNA sample.

"Second squad, prepare for retrieval. Those cataloging bodies, continue and we'll get you transport on the next round," Taylor said as Heather stood and moved to the next body.

Oh, well, a few more hours on this rock isn't going to make much of a difference, she thought.

Peter was being retrieved in the first round. It was difficult for someone inside power armour to take DNA samples. He made his pleasure known by teasing her about it.

"I wish I could stick around and help but, well, gotta go. Have fun, sweets."

That ended quickly when she showed him a little surprise—a remote training unit happily supplied by Ritchie. His eyes went wide as the memory of his first training in power armour came flooding back to him.

"What are you doing with that horrific device?" he demanded. "If you really loved me, you'd put that away." Heather, laughing, reminded Peter that any displeasure he caused her could be sent right back to him.

Peter quickly apologized and promised her a very large and well-prepared meal in her quarters when she arrived on board.

Chapter Twenty-Six

Thomas Veale sat behind his desk and read the initial report he had just received from Affleck's flotilla. The message packet had arrived an hour ago, but it was only delivered once it was decoded and removed from the remainder of the personal and administrative messages. It had been sent three weeks ago. Messages from the fringe were quick, considering the distance in thousands of light years traveled. But the sender and the receiver still had to take the time delay into account.

Veale was impressed at the amount of data recovered and at Affleck's success in foiling the pirates' plans to attack the Confederation. He was, of course, disappointed that the capture of Joseph Lebakie could not be expedited—indeed, that even his location was still a mystery.

That part was most disturbing. Lebakie was still on the loose and would no doubt resurface. *On the bright side, he won't do it with this group of cutthroats*, he thought.

Sitting across from Veale was Vice Admiral Cunningham and Francis Leyton, both of whom had read the report when it first arrived.

Leyton spoke first. "I trust we are all in agreement that Affleck and his people did very well to bring this to a successful conclusion."

The other men nodded as he continued. "I also believe that we are of the same opinion about the lack of information on Mr. Lebakie."

"Gentlemen," said Veale, putting down the reader and looking at both men. "I have to report to the Prime Minister this afternoon and I need to know we have a plan for following up on this operation. It hasn't ended here, and the Confederation has to be prepared to meet the challenge when it arises."

He did not want to sound desperate, but he knew that politicos had a different take on reality. For them, it came down to public perception and reaction.

"The PM should be pleased with the outcome if you just leave off the bit about Lebakie. Maybe he won't ask," said Cunningham. The three men began to laugh.

"That's what I love about you, Cunningham," chuckled Veale. "You can always see the bright side." He wiped away a tear.

Cunningham responded with less humor in his voice. "You may think I'm joking, but think about it: Lebakie was not captured, but attacks on shipping will be down. If you want to calculate a percentage, consider that in the past eighteen months the majority of pirate attacks on shipping were attributed to those pirates. We have eliminated the New Gloucester system. There will be an immediate ninety percent reduction in attacks on our merchant fleet. The PM does not need to know, at least not now, that this was only phase one. He, and the rest of the New Confederation, believe that the immediate threat is over—and isn't that what they have been clamoring for?"

Leyton looked skeptical. "You are verging on becoming a bureaucrat, my friend, and we just purged a number of those vile people not that long ago. What you are suggesting—stop me if I'm wrong—is to mislead the Prime Minister and public in believing that Lebakie, or his capture, does not matter in the grand scheme of things. We should look at the immediate value of the current completion of the operation and later on, when we have more intelligence, we can take out this…super pirate."

He paused, his gaze distant, then said, "I think that I must agree—for now. Having the political administration on our backs to push things to a level we are not prepared for is asking for trouble. We need more intel, and it will take time if we are to get credible information to launch another mission."

Veale mulled over the discussion before speaking. "I also have to agree with the logic—but only for the time being. I do not want to see this pushed on the back burner for the sake of political expedience or in a misguided effort to remove political pressure on mounting another operation."

He picked up his reader and scrolled through several documents before finding the one he was looking for.

"This is a preliminary plan for mounting an operation against Lebakie—an outline, really."

He beamed it to both men, who took out their own portable readers.

"Take a look at it. I want feedback by the end of the calendar month. That should give you and your staff enough time to formulate a response."

***

Heather released the harness and stood at the shuttle docked with *Athabaskan*. She had spent the last two days with other members of the platoon, cataloging the dead and recovering any data left intact on the moon. She was tired. Her eyes were heavy and her legs felt numb as she gathered her kit and weapon.

"Now comes the fun part: the cleaning," someone said sarcastically in the next row over as they began to ready their equipment.

She felt the same way, but why complain about it? She, like everyone else, knew that it was part of the military life they'd signed up for.

The hatch lock cycled and the ramp lowered to reveal a very busy boat bay. Both navy ratings and troopers were busy with after-action tasks: cleaning equipment, removing and stowing ammunition and missiles, and removing power packs from the plasma guns.

She noticed JTF troopers loading an assault shuttle, but for the life of her could not think about or care about their upcoming mission. She was too tired and more concerned about getting her own gear cleaned and stowed.

She found Taylor checking over one of the drop ships and reported to him. He took the DNA scanner and signed it in on her reader before giving her the okay to get cleaned up. She still had to pass muster with the RQM before being released from duty, but at this point, she was too exhausted to worry about it.

The first appointment she had was to get debriefed with regimental command and navy intelligence. She dropped her kit and headed to the debriefing area just off the company ready room.

The door slid back as she approached and she was met by a navy spook. He was a petty officer second class, but looked old enough to be a chief petty officer. The service strips showed that he had served forty-eight years in the navy.

A lifer, she thought.

***

As the canopy raised and her crew chief climbed the steps, Saunders removed her helmet and rested her head on the back of the seat. Her hair was sweat-soaked and her face glistened in the fighter bay lighting.

"Glad to see you brought my bird back in one piece," said her crew chief.

"Glad to see where your loyalties are," she replied. "I'm delighted to see you too."

He squeezed her arm as she climbed down from her fighter, and she turned to him and nodded. "I'm okay," she said quietly.

"I'm pleased to see you safe and sound." His voice was soft, almost fatherly, and he had a glint in his eye.

"How many made it back?" she asked gently.

"At last count, thirty. Search and rescue is picking up a dozen or more that ejected in the last attack, but no word yet on the rest."

"Damn, that's over half the squadron lost in one engagement. I hope it was worth it," she said quietly. There was a hint of bitterness in that last line, but in the back of her mind, and on an intellectual level, she did know it was worth it. The consequences would have been far worse if they hadn't succeeded.

"When is the memorial?" she asked.

"I haven't heard as yet. I think they want to get final numbers from search and rescue."

Saunders put her helmet into its carryall and walked out of the bay toward the showers without another word.

***

Fitzpatrick squinted and pinched the bridge of his nose. His eyes were dry and heavy and the exhaustion was starting to catch up. He just finished dictating the last letter to the family of a dead trooper.

The last two hours had been spent getting the letters ready for the next message packet. Each letter was different and personal. Fitzpatrick could have used a generic letter and just inserted the name, but he, like all good commanders, took the time to say what really happened, how their loved ones lived and how they died. The truth was the least he could give the families.

The entry chime sounded. "Enter," he said.

The door slid open and Captain Thomas entered, a weary smile on his face. Fitzpatrick stood, only to be waved back down.

"Good evening, captain. I didn't expect to see you," Fitzpatrick said, surprise in his voice. He only hoped this was not a problem call.

"Just thought I'd stop by my platoon commanders and see how things were going." Thomas noticed the letter on the reader's screen. "Oh." He waved at the reader. "I see you, too, are trying to catch up on the letters home. How many do you have left?"

"I just finished the last one, sir."

"Good. I'll see you at the mess dinner, then?"

Fitzpatrick nodded and Thomas left. Fitzpatrick did enjoy the officers' mess dinners. It gave him a chance to socialize—a very important part of career advancement in any military.

For now, however, sleep was the order of the moment.

Chapter Twenty-Seven

The market was busier than normal today. People of all shapes, sizes, colours, and planetary origins buzzed about, buying from stalls selling fruit, vegetables, jewelry, electronic devices, and clothing.

The odor of fresh breads and exotic pastries was mixed with the spicy tang of foods from a hundred planets. To breathe in deeply invited a feast for the olfactory centre.

Children wearing bright, loose clothing played among parents or caregivers. Everyone spoke at once, in many different languages. The mixing of sounds was as inviting to the ears as the smells to the nose.

Small transports skirted around parked air and ground effect vehicles, making their daily deliveries to shops and stalls. The market, composed of a dozen streets and intersected by several more, was a colourful mosaic of stalls, shops, galleries, cafés, and dance clubs.

On one of these streets, two men sat drinking coffee. The café had both indoor and outdoor seating but on a day like this, outdoor seating was preferred. Old iron fences divided the seating area from the road. Flags of the human-settled worlds lined the rooftops of the buildings along the other side of the street.

The men sat across from each other. Soft music played in the background as they spoke quietly.

"I agree, the market district does bring out a myriad group of people," said the first man. "I wonder, however, if we can dispense with our business. This place is a bit too..." He searched for the right word. "Pedestrian for my tastes."

His accent was slight, but had a middle European slant. He wore a plain black suit, the collar on the jacket turned up in the style of the day.

He sipped his coffee and placed the cup down. "I have read the final report from Admiral Affleck, and it does not paint a glowing view of your efforts. My employers are not happy and are clamoring for blood—chiefly yours."

The other man sat relaxed, dressed in a casual and colourful outfit that blended in with the rest of the crowd. "I hope you were able to set the record straight, Mr. Smith?" he asked.

"I was not, sir." Smith shot him a knifelike stare, his face red.

"Don't—*don't* get huffy or threaten me. My organization and my plan are well on target. This may come as a surprise to you, but this so-called setback is not what it seems. This was always part of the overall plan. Call it a planned interruption in order to assess data."

Smith nearly fell off his chair, choking on his coffee. His accent was stronger when he managed to speak. "I would not call this waste of tens of billions of credits 'planned'! And certainly not a wise plan!" He almost shouted and had to stop himself, looking around to check if he was overheard.

The other man sighed and leaned back in his chair. "I must confess, Mr. Smith, that I find your shortsighted vision and attitude disconcerting."

"You know, I never did appreciate these names you insist on using," Smith said, trying to deflect.

"Let's stay on topic, shall we? You and your string-pullers do not control me or my timetable."

"Mr. Lebakie, I must protest!" Smith flinched when he realized what he'd said, fear showing in his eyes.

Joseph Lebakie did not react, either to his name or to the outburst. He knew the market area was too noisy to be overheard unless someone used a whisper mike to eavesdrop, and his men had already cleared the area and set up special devices to create an electronic dead zone. He was a professional. Not something he could say about his companion.

"You can protest all you want, Mr. Smith. The fact remains, this is my operation." He enunciated each word clearly, choosing it carefully. "I am the one taking the risk, I am the one doing the work, and I am the one who will dictate the timetable and sequence of events."

Relaxing, he went on. "Don't worry, you'll live long enough to see profits on your investment. You're only, what, a hundred and ten?"

"I am ninety-six, sir! And that investment and the information we provide is what allows you to mount this operation." Smith was insulted. He stood, indicating, at least as he was concerned, that the meeting was concluded.

Before turning to leave, he looked Lebakie in the eye and said through clenched teeth, "I, too, am not a man to be toyed with, Mr. Lebakie, and my employers have powerful friends who do not take lightly to failure. Good day to you, sir."

He walked away quickly, almost mowing down a family with their two children.

Lebakie watched him leave, shaking his head.

"I really hate that man and his cocksure self-important attitude. Ah, well, better the devil you know than the one you don't," he said to himself.

After a second he added, "I can always have him killed later on."

Lebakie finished his drink slowly, in no hurry to leave. Although he'd put on a self-assured face for his meeting, he was tired, exhausted from hours of evaluating data from New Gloucester and the defeat of the pirate force.

He only had one regret from that project—the loss of his friend King. He did not regret having him eliminated, but was sorry King had forced his hand. He had been the only person Lebakie could take into confidence.

He stood and paid the bill, leaving a small gratuity for his server in order not to draw too much attention to himself, and walked into the crowd. His next steps were already going through his head, ready for execution.

About the author:

Author of the romance novella Jamaican Heat, the sci-fi opera Death's Door: Where Right and Glory Lead, and several short stories, I spent ten years in the Canadian Armed Forces where I had the experience of a lifetime in the artillery and armored corps. After retiring from the military in 1990, I studied social work and began a new phase that expanded my world. Fast forwarded to 1996 when I moved to Ottawa and began to write Death's Door: Where Right and Glory Lead. This is when I realized how my life was about to take another turn, opening up a new chapter and a new adventure. Death's Door: Where Right and Glory Lead is book one in the Death's Door saga. I have several other sci-fi projects on the go including book two, Beyond Death's Door: Fortune Favours The Brave. Visit me at:

http://wdesouza3.wix.com/williamdesouza

Printed in Great Britain
by Amazon